What people are saying about *In Plain Sight*, book 2 of the Ivy Malone Mysteries

"Ivy Malone is destined to become a classic sleuth, right up there with Jessica Fletcher and Miss Marple."

Patricia H. Rushford, author,
the Angel Delaney Mysteries

"*In Plain Sight* portrays a lovable, sassy LOL who solves murder mysteries and breezes down banisters. Lorena McCourtney provides plucky-paced entertainment full of heart and laugh-out-loud wit."

Janet Chester Bly, author, *Hope Lives Here*

"I'm hooked on Ivy Malone. *In Plain Sight* is like my favorite mocha milkshake—sweet, dark, rich, and refreshing! I love how Ivy slips around nasty-people radar and ends up solving the case once again. Go, Ivy, go!"

Lyn Cote, author, The Women of Ivy Manor series

"Ivy Malone is such a realistic character she could be your next door neighbor. Wonderfully written."

Lois Gladys Leppard, author, the Mandie books

"This is one to read and savor!"

www.myshelf.com

"McCourtney's writing goes down like an icy lemonade on a hot summer day. It's smooth, finished, and delightfully unpredictable. *In Plain Sight* is the perfect summer read."

The Northwest Book Reviewer

"I am a devoted mystery reader and, in particular, a devoted fan of Ivy Malone. This self-proclaimed LOL (Little Old Lady) will bring you LOL (Lots of Laughs)!"

Lauren Winner, author, *Girl Meets God*

Other books by Lorena McCourtney

The Ivy Malone Mysteries
Invisible (winner of the 2005 Daphne du Maurier Award for
      Inspirational Romantic Mystery/Suspense)
In Plain Sight

The Julesburg Mysteries
Whirlpool
Riptide
Undertow

Watch for the next Ivy Malone mystery coming soon!

Book 3

An
Ivy Malone
Mystery

O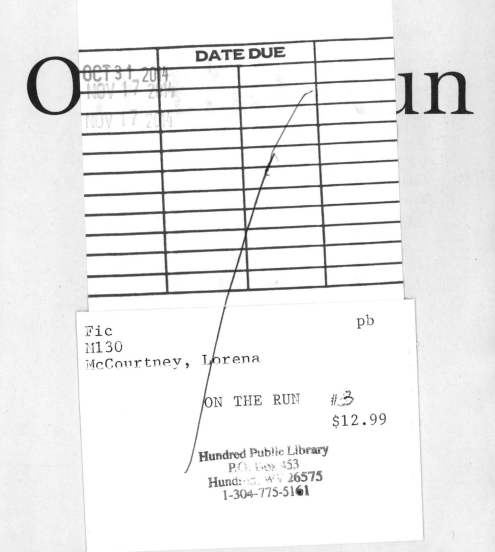un

© 2006 by Lorena McCourtney

Published by Fleming H. Revell
a division of Baker Publishing Group
P.O. Box 6287, Grand Rapids, MI 49516-6287

Printed in the United States of America

Library of Congress Cataloging-in-Publication Data
McCourtney, Lorena.
    On the run / Lorena McCourtney.
        p.   cm. — (An Ivy Malone mystery ; bk. 3)
    ISBN 0-8007-5956-7 (pbk.)
    1. Women detectives—Fiction. 2. Organized crime—Fiction. 3. Older women—Fiction. 4. Oklahoma—Fiction. I. Title.
PS3563.C3449O5 2006
813'.54—dc22   2005016515

I will say of the Lord, "He is my
refuge and my fortress,
my God, in whom I trust."

Psalm 91:2

The pickup had been tailing me for at least the last thirty miles. I slowed. It slowed. I speeded up. It speeded up. We were as synchronized as the wiper blades swishing back and forth on my windshield.

Not good.

In the same jittery brain wave, I scoffed at my reaction. No reason to think this was a malevolent Braxton honing in on me like a heat-seeking missile programmed to the temperature of a little old lady in polyester slacks. Probably just a cautious driver who didn't want to take chances passing on a curvy, rain-slicked highway.

"No need to get all sweaty handed and jelly kneed, right?"

Koop, who never gets sweaty handed or jelly kneed, opened his one good eye and regarded me with mild interest. Koop is a stubby-tailed, one-eyed Manx with orange fur and a laid-back disposition. Except for an aversion to cigarette smokers, in whose presence he turns into Psycho Cat. We'd adopted each other at a rest area in Georgia.

Now he surprised me by suddenly jerking alert. He hopped down from his usual spot on the passenger's seat and prowled the length of the motor home, even jumping up on the sofa and peering out the window, stub of tail twitching. Do cats get vibes, like my old friend Magnolia from back home claims she does? Maybe hostile vibes from that pickup back there behind us?

I peered into the motor home's oversized mirror, trying to get a better look at the vehicle. It was a light-colored pickup, not new, not ancient, nothing threatening about it. But wasn't that exactly the generic vehicle the Braxtons would choose if they were closing in on me? I couldn't tell if the driver was man or woman, or even how many people were in the pickup. Neither could I make out the license plate.

"Okay, we'll give them an invitation to pass, one they can't refuse," I told Koop.

Ahead was a straight, tree-lined stretch of highway with a nice dotted line down the center. No other vehicles were in sight. I slowed to a crawl. An arthritic centipede could have passed us. But the pickup didn't. It stayed behind, maintaining what was beginning to look like a calculated distance.

My hands turned sweaty on the steering wheel. What did the driver have in mind? Forcing the motor home into a fatal crash on a hill or curve? Picking just the right spot for putting a bullet through a tire or window?

Oh, c'mon. Wasn't that a bit melodramatic? How could the Braxtons have found me? I hadn't stayed more than a few days in any one place in the last couple of months. I'd contacted my niece DeeAnn and my friend Magnolia only by prepaid phone card. I never told anyone where I was heading next.

I glanced at Koop again. Next thing I'd be suspecting he was wired for espionage, sending cat-o-grams to the Braxtons with a high-tech tracking system implanted behind that scruffy orange ear.

No matter how I tried to pooh-pooh my way out of my fears, however, the hard fact was that the Braxtons were out to get me. I'd been instrumental in convicting one of the brothers for murder. Drake Braxton, the leader of the clan, had vowed to turn me into roadkill. They'd already tried to burn my house back in Missouri, with me in it. When I hid out at my niece's place in Arkansas, they'd tracked me down and planted dynamite in my old Thunderbird. Which was when I'd decided that hitting the road would be a prudent plan, both for my safety and the safety of my niece and her family. Surely, I'd thought, they couldn't find me if I kept on the move. A rolling motor home gathers no Braxtons.

And I'd rolled steadily during the last couple of months. From Arkansas to Florida, up the eastern coast, now back inland to this wooded valley somewhere in Tennessee. I'd met wonderful people. I'd met strange people. I'd visited an eclectic variety of churches. I'd been encouraged by the love of the Lord I'd found in most of them. I'd been discouraged by internal squabbles in others. In some congregations I'd been no more visible than an organ note hanging in the air; in others I'd been welcomed like a wonderful new friend. From other travelers I'd accumulated invitations to visit people all over the country. Never had I encountered anyone I even remotely suspected of stalking me.

Which didn't mean the Braxtons *weren't* stalking me. And had found me. Because, at the moment, this isolated road seemed an ideal spot to commit exactly what they'd threatened: roadkill.

What now, Lord?

An immediate answer. A sign! No, not a lightning bolt from heaven. A road sign. Stanley, Population 42.

"Hang on, Koop," I muttered. Just beyond the sign I whipped the motor home hard to the right. At which time I was reminded that motor homes, even smaller ones like my twenty-one-footer, do not take kindly to abrupt changes of direction. It tilted like a vehicular Leaning Tower of Pisa and wobbled for a precarious moment before settling back on solid ground.

My attention was elsewhere. I held my breath as I peered out the window. Would the pickup slither in behind me? Two guys with machine guns get out and close in on me? No. Without even slowing down, the pickup zoomed right on by.

Oh, happy day! I let out my breath and wiped my sweaty hands on Koop's fur when he jumped into my lap.

Okay, I'd imagined hostile intentions where none existed. Making the proverbial mountain out of a molehill. Or perhaps, in these days of computer speak, making a gigabyte out of a kilobyte would be more appropriate. But isn't it better to be on guard than sneaked up on?

Now I had time to inspect Stanley, Tennessee, which appeared to consist of a lone gas-and-grocery and a few shabby houses on the far side of a field. Muddy water puddled the potholes around the gas pumps, a wet flag drooped overhead, and a gray mule peered over a nearby wooden fence. Posters advertising chewing tobacco, Campbell's soups, and, incongruously, a cruise to the Bahamas covered most of the windows on the weather-beaten building. A man in old black work pants, khaki jacket, and a faded red cap ambled out the door.

Given the price of gas and my limited finances, I'd intended to wait until I reached a discount station before gassing up, but the place looked as if it could use some business. I eased the motor home up to the pumps. The man peered up at me through heavy bifocals. Tufts of gray hair stuck out from under the cap that read "Voorhee's Heavy Equipment—We'll Dig for You!" I slid the window open.

"Fill 'er up?"

I was pleasantly surprised that I didn't have to do the fill-up myself. "Yes, please. Regular. I'll have to unlock the gas cap." I slipped on a jacket and opened the door. The rain had let up, and the air smelled fresh and woodsy, with just a hint of wet mule. I unlocked the gas cap, and he stuck the nozzle in. The gas gurgled. The motor home guzzles gas like Koop gleefully downing his favorite treat, a half can of tuna.

"Nice rain," I offered conversationally. I hadn't talked to anyone except Koop for two days. He's sweet but not a big conversationalist.

The man nodded.

"Planning a cruise to the Bahamas?" I motioned toward the poster.

He gave me a "what planet are you from?" look, and I felt properly chastised for my frivolousness. When the tank was full, he surprised me by climbing up to clean my bug-speckled windshield, an action I appreciated more than small talk anyway. I told him I'd go inside to pay.

A gray-haired woman with a perm tight enough to offer the bonus of an eyebrow lift took my money and rang it up on an old-fashioned cash register.

"You folks travelin'?" she inquired as she peered between the posters at the motor home. Unlike the man outside, she sounded hungry for small talk.

"Just seeing the countryside." To divert attention from myself, which is what I usually try to do, I asked, "Is your town named for some special Stanley?"

"Zeke Stanley. Story goes he was the slickest thief and card

11

shark in three states. Could steal yer horse out from under you right while you was settin' on it."

An impressive though questionable talent, but possibly one that would interest my friend Mac MacPherson, who wanders the country looking for little-known places and events to write about in his travel articles. I'd been thinking our paths might cross somewhere on the road, but so far that hadn't happened.

"'Course, ol' Zeke eventually got hung for his troubles. Used the same rope he'd just stole from a guy he was playin' cards with to hang 'im, they did. Called poker justice, ain't it?"

I thought she probably meant poetic justice, but perhaps, in Zeke's case, poker justice was appropriate.

The door opened, and the man stuck his head inside. "Left front tire's runnin' low. I knocked on yer door, but I cain't rouse nobody. Want me to air 'er up?"

Even the woman looked surprised. Three whole sentences in a row.

"Yes, I'd appreciate that. Thank you."

The woman inspected me again after the door closed. "You ain't travelin' alone, aire you?"

"Well, uh, yes, I am."

I expected disapproval and dire warnings, but instead she just tilted her permed head in curiosity. "Don't you git lonely?"

It was a question I'd heard before, and I answered it as I always did. "No, I'm fine. Traveling alone can be a wonderful adventure." I thought about adding, as I'd heard another woman traveling alone say, "My cat's better company than most husbands. Never argues and doesn't snore."

However, dearly as I love Koop, I can't say he's better company than a husband. I also have to admit that, even though I'm enjoying my traveling adventures, and the Lord is always with me, sometimes I do get a bit lonely.

"You headed anywhere particular?" the woman asked.

"Not really." The words unexpectedly struck me as more dismal than adventurous.

"What're you doin' in Stanley?"

"Just passing through."

She nodded sagely. "That's what most people do in Stanley. Kids, they pick up'n leave soon as they can figure a way to get outta town." She paused, and her old blue eyes went dreamy. "That's what I'd like to do someday. Me'n Tom, git us a motor home like your'n, put pedal to the metal, and just *go*."

"It's the kind of thing you should do while you still have each other," I advised impulsively. Harley and I had always intended to travel together, but we never got around to it before he was gone.

I put my hand to the back of my neck and rubbed at muscles that were beginning to feel stiff as dried jerky. The incident with the pickup, even if it had turned out to be a non-incident, had left me feeling kind of strung out. I didn't want to drive any farther today. "Is there an RV park around here somewhere?"

"Old Man Feister rents out a few trailer spaces. Mostly permanent locals, but he takes in an RVer now'n then. You go to the left at the Y down the road. Little farther on, gravel road turns off to the right. Miser Lane." She giggled, as if the name were an inside joke. "But you gotta watch close. It's easy to miss. Feister's place ain't much, but it's cheap. And there's a nice creek. Tell 'im Annie sent you."

Cheap sounded good. Even with an occasional free night in a rest area or Wal-Mart parking lot, living on the road was costing more than was comfortable on my limited Social Security and CD income. "Okay, Annie, thank you. I might do that." Then, to get off the subject of my plans, and because, as always, I was curious about the people I met, I asked, "Were you born around here?"

"No. Come from Iowa. Not much to do 'round here," she

13

added, "but we got a nice little church with a potluck every Wednesday night."

"Sounds great." It truly did. Old Man Feister's place, just outside Stanley, Tennessee, was surely the middle-of-nowhere kind of spot the Braxtons would never think to look for me. With a creek and a potluck as a bonus.

"You take care now, hear?" she said as I opened the door.

"You too." I gave her a thumbs-up sign. We little old ladies of the world have to stick together.

Outside, Taciturn Tom was running water in a tank for the mule. I waved and got a jerk of his head in response. I started the engine and threaded my way around the potholes. Three miles down the road I took the left fork at the Y. It would be good to stop and relax for a few days.

But a half mile farther on I saw it. My heart shimmied. My toes cramped. My teeth tingled. Bad vibes. Very bad vibes.

It was the pickup, closer now. Dirty white color. A dented fender. Silhouettes of two people in the cab. No coincidence here. They'd hidden and waited to see which fork I took. The orange fur on Koop's back popped up like porcupine quills.

I started looking frantically for Miser Lane. If I could get off the main road, into the safety of people and trailers . . .

Too late. I saw the leaning sign for Miser Lane just as the motor home sailed past it.

It wouldn't have meant safety anyway, I realized regretfully. Because the Braxtons would have my location pinned down, and they'd figure a way to get me.

My only chance was to lose them.

I tightened my hands on the steering wheel, swallowed hard, and did what Annie back in Stanley wanted to do. I put pedal to the metal and *went*.

2

The pickup speeded up right with me. We raced down the two-lane highway in excellent movie-chase form, screeching around curves, barreling around slower traffic, tearing across railroad tracks just before the gates came down to block traffic from an oncoming train. All we needed was the usual dénouement of the movie chase scene, the flaming crash. Which, I hoped, would be them, not Koop and me.

No crash. No flames. Just an ominous whine in the motor home's engine echoed by an ominous jab in my left temple. One of us was going to blow.

Fortunately, what blasted through first was a realization that the persons most likely to get hurt here were some innocent bystanders. I guiltily slowed down. So did the pickup. When we met a state police car a few minutes later, we were both moving as sedately as if we were in a Fourth of July parade.

I didn't know whether to be relieved or even more uneasy. Apparently the two men did not have in mind pulling some spectacular road stunt. But they obviously had *something* in mind. Following until I had to stop, then whopping me over the head with a hubcap? Sneaking up and committing some deadly vandalism in the night? Or something more sophisticated with propane lines and barred doors and "accidental" asphyxiation? ("Out-of-state woman and cat found dead of fumes in untidy motor home. Elder carelessness suspected.")

I decided this lightly traveled road was not the place to be with killers stalking me. At the next crossroads I turned south, and an hour later hit busy Interstate 40 headed toward Memphis. But by the time I reached the city, the pickup was still with me.

Okay, maybe I could lose them in Memphis. I took an exit. So did the pickup. We plowed into an area of motels, gas stations, and fast food outlets. I drove sedately into a gas station as if I intended to fill up, but at the last minute I gunned the engine and zipped out the far side. I went a few blocks and turned. Again and again.

A line plotting my movements would look like the path of a hyperactive worm with a fixation on geometric turns.

I couldn't tell if I'd lost them, but eventually I lost *me*, wandering through everything from an area of industrial warehouses to another of gated estates. Finally, in a residential neighborhood of modest homes, I pulled under the branches of an overhanging tree and parked. It was almost dark now. I waited apprehensively.

As a card-carrying member of the Aged into Invisibility generation of women, I can count on being invisible in any number of situations. Store clerks often can't see me. Young men, especially in the presence of a young woman, never know I exist. In any given crowd, I am as unnoticed as the birds pecking at crumbs on the ground. But, encased in a few thousand pounds of motor home, my visibility quotient rises.

Still, after half an hour, no dirty pickup with dented fender had pulled in behind or cruised past. A good sign, but I knew it was too early to count my escape a success. I figured my stalkers would assume I had to stop for the night and perhaps start checking parking lots or RV parks. A gray-haired little old lady couldn't just keep on truckin' down the interstate, right? I was tired, but truckin' on was exactly what this LOL intended to do.

I rolled from Memphis to Little Rock, grabbed a few hours sleep in a mall parking lot, and later filled up with gas in Ft. Smith. By midafternoon I was in Oklahoma City. I was hopeful I'd ditched my hawk-eyed friends in the pickup, but I still felt about as safe as a possum crossing the road in traffic.

Why? Because now the two men were familiar with both the appearance of my motor home and the license plate number. Although they may well have had that information before they began tailing me. So even if they weren't right behind me at the moment, they might still pick up my trail.

On sudden impulse I didn't head west out of Oklahoma City as I'd originally planned and as I hoped the guys in the pickup assumed I'd do. Instead I made a sudden switchback to the southeast, heading out through Norman and then on through ever smaller towns. Wherever there was a choice of roads, I chose what looked like the least traveled.

And the farther southeast I went, the more surprised I was. I'd always thought of Oklahoma (whatever little thought I'd ever given Oklahoma, I must admit) as just one featureless plain, flat and bare enough to make the world's largest bowling alley. Not so. Here was good farmland, rivers and lakes, and by dusk I was into thickly forested hills, with real mountains not far in the distance.

By now I was both physically and mentally frazzled from long hours of driving, my neck stiff from craning it in all directions and keeping watch for a dirty white pickup with a dented fender. I decided that at the next likely looking place, I was stopping for the night.

And just around the next bend, there it was! A sign saying Dulcy, Oklahoma. An optimistic announcement, I decided a moment later, since I saw no evidence of a town. Oh yes, there it was up ahead, a neon lariat endlessly circling a café sign. Closer I spotted a metal building with a dusty parking lot and a sign that said Dulcy Farm Supply. At this hour the store was closed, and I didn't see that bane of all RVers, a No Overnight Parking sign. The lot was also well lit with a couple of big yard lights. Yes! I whipped into the lot, pulled over close to the building, and shut off the engine.

I stretched my tired back and heard a popping sound in my neck. But I was home, at least for the night. "This is what's nice about an RV, isn't it, Koop? Home is wherever your wheels are parked."

I opened the door for a quick inspection, with Koop peering out between my ankles. The air smelled like pine and hay, with a hint of barbecue somewhere, and a stream gurgled in the grassy field on the far side of the road. Nice. But I didn't see any particular reason to linger in Dulcy, and I figured on being up and gone long before the store opened in the morning. Maybe I'd head on down to Texas.

Koop and I had a quick dinner, I read a bit in Romans, and then I climbed up to bed, beat. Outrunning Braxtons is tiring work.

Especially when I couldn't be sure I *had* outrun them. Just because I hadn't spotted them didn't mean they weren't out there.

I heard a few trucks go by in the night, and once a train whistled in the distance, like some lonely creature calling for its mate. But neither those night sounds, nor that nagging worry about the two men in the pickup, kept me from sleeping peacefully.

Maybe too peacefully, because I was not up and away at crack of dawn as I intended. I was still asleep, Koop curled against my backside, when hammering on the door woke us. I lay there, heart also hammering, as the whole motor home shook under the onslaught.

3

"Hey, anyone in there?" a woman's voice called.

A female Braxton? Had they switched teams on me? The bed in my motor home is up over the driver and passenger seats. I leaned over the edge and warily tried to figure out what was going on. A beam of sunlight shafted through a gap in the curtains beside the bed.

"I'm here," I finally called back since it appeared the woman intended to pound until someone answered or the door collapsed, whichever came first.

"I'm sorry to bother you, but I can't get my hay truck up to the loading dock with your rig parked here."

"Oh, I'm sorry. I'll move right away." I hastily climbed down the short ladder and, still in the skimpy pajamas my grandniece Sandy had given me—from Victoria's Secret, of all places—scooted into the driver's seat. I shoved back the curtains across the windshield, pulled across the parking lot, and watched the woman expertly back the big truck up to the loading dock.

A few minutes later she came to the door again. By this time I'd put on jeans and an old sweatshirt and had a pot of coffee going. I opened the door a crack, uncertain if I was about to be threatened, peremptorily ordered off the premises, cited for trespassing, or what.

"You okay?" she asked.

The concern in her voice surprised me. So did the woman herself. Given the strength of hammering on my door, I expected someone young and belligerent, probably with a gold ring hooked into some unlikely portion of her anatomy, but this woman was near my own age, and her smile was friendly. Her elegant white hair and gentle face suggested she belonged in a church choir, but her body was long and lean and competent looking in faded jeans and plaid shirt rolled up to her elbows. Pearl earrings completed the unlikely combination. At her feet a small black and white, bulldoggish-looking animal inspected me with big, inquisitive eyes.

"I'm fine. I just overslept a bit, I guess."

"That's good. I was getting worried somebody might be sick in there. Maybe even dead."

"I was tired, and it looked like a good place to stop for the night."

We peered at each other through the crack. I was curious about her. That looked like a lot of truck for a lone older woman to be driving. Koop inserted himself into the crack and inspected the small dog. The dog put its feet up on the step, and they warily touched noses.

"Would you like a cup of coffee?" I asked impulsively.

"Hey, I sure would! I usually get coffee down at the Lariat, but theirs tastes like it could dissolve brake linings."

"I'll get some chairs, and we can sit out there."

I stepped outside, unlocked the storage compartment, dragged out a couple of webbed lawn chairs, and put the awning down for shade because the day was already getting warm. She dropped into a chair, and I went inside and returned with two mugs of coffee. By then Koop, apparently having made a non-aggression pact with the dog, was using his one good eye to study a white-faced steer on the far side of the fence at the edge of the parking lot. His stub of tail twitched, as if he was undecided as to whether the creature was friend, foe, or food. I think Koop was a city cat, where cow creatures are not part of the landscape, before he took to the road with me.

"I guess I'm curious what you're doing here," the woman said in her straightforward manner. "You don't look like our usual tourists."

"Which are . . . ?"

"Oh, you know. Families camping. Guys fishing. Macho young males looking for the roughest, muddiest places in the mountains to go four-wheelin' or dirt biking. Hunters in the fall." By now she'd apparently figured out there was no man with me because she added, "Not a woman alone."

While I contemplated how to explain myself, she suddenly leaned forward. "Maybe you're here to work for the Northcutts?"

"Are the Northcutts looking for someone?"

"I suppose so, since that guy from California left."

"Why was that?"

She leaned back in the chair. My diversionary technique hadn't fooled her. She knew I didn't know any more about the Northcutts than Koop knew about that steer. "I guess you're not here to work for the Northcutts."

"No, but I could be." Yes, indeed. I looked around. Dulcy had a certain understated appeal. The country scent of hay mingled with the piney scent of woods, and unseen birds trilled from a clump of oak trees beyond the stream dancing in the sunlight. A truck hauling logs went by, trailing another scent of fresh-cut wood, and the driver and the woman sip-ping my coffee exchanged waves. On impulse I waved too, and a second friendly wave came in return.

Maybe it was time to lay low for a while. If I could get a job here, I'd be out of sight, not out on the road where the Braxtons could spot me. I'd also save money on gas if I stayed in one place for a while. *Is this why I'm here in Dulcy, Lord, to work for the Northcutts?*

"What do the Northcutts need someone to do?" I inquired.

"I think that was one of the problems with the guy from California. He was in the Lariat a couple times when I was there. Had a chip on his shoulder the size of a big old pine log. He was griping to Tom Cole that he was hired to be a researcher, not a housekeeper or gofer or caretaker for weird birds."

Researcher/housekeeper/gofer/weird-bird-caretaker. An unlikely job description, true. But not totally out of my realm of expertise. Before retirement, I'd been a librarian for thirty years back in Missouri, and I knew something about book research. Grandniece Sandy had taught me how to find my way around on the Internet. I'd briefly held a housekeeper's job in Arkansas, and I had a lifetime of experience keeping house for Harley. I saw no problem with gofering. And weird birds? How weird can a bird be?

"Perhaps I could apply for the job," I suggested.

"Well . . ."

"Too old?"

She laughed. "Too normal. I don't know the Northcutts personally, but from everything I've heard they're . . . different. That guy from California sure was."

"Different how?"

"Well, not my idea of a 'researcher,' that's for sure. He always wore those baggy camouflage clothes. You know, the kind that look as if they could conceal anything from

23

a machine gun to six months' supply of survival rations? Sunglasses too, day or night. He wouldn't eat a hamburger at the Lariat. He told Tom he preferred to eat only meat he'd killed himself because you never know what's in commercial meat. He had some kind of symbol tattooed behind one ear, and his head was shaved. The only name he'd give anyone was Ute."

"Ute?" I repeated doubtfully.

"Ute."

"And what about the Northcutts? How are they different?"

"Ummm . . ." Here she seemed to waver. "They're Californians too. Not that being from California is a crime or anything," she added hastily. "But they're also movie people." Her tone wasn't derogatory, but it suggested that being "movie people" could explain almost any peculiarity.

"Movie stars?"

"No. Writers or something like that."

"Why in the world would they be here in Dulcy?"

"Good question. Actually, they aren't right here in Dulcy. Their place is about twenty miles out toward the mountains. They bought the old Morris place. Buck Morris used to take guided hunting trips out in the mountains, but they sold out after the lodge burned about five years ago. Well, half burned, and the Northcutts had the part that was still standing remodeled to use as a house."

Perhaps my look said none of that sounded terribly "different," because she added, "They never come to any local doings. Never shop at Gus's. They drive a Hummer. Which a lot of us might like to have," she admitted, "but none of us can afford. They have an unlisted phone number, which no one else around here has. About as friendly as a pair of rattlesnakes, from all I've heard. A friend at a bookstore—"

I peered down the road, empty except for that circling

neon lariat in front of a nondescript brown building with a tall false front. "Dulcy has a bookstore?"

She laughed and made room for the little dog wanting to jump into her lap. "No. Except for a rack of old romances and westerns over at the secondhand store. The real bookstore is down in Hugo. It's about sixty miles. Anyway, this friend says they're always ordering books. Everything from Civil War and Old West history to books on soap making, edible insects, time and space travel, and how to avoid shark attacks. I guess no one ever told them we don't have a big shark-attack problem here in Dulcy."

"Maybe the Chamber of Commerce should advertise that fact. Who knows? You might have a big influx of rich tourists once they realize it's a shark-free zone."

Her blue eyes twinkled. "It's also a Chamber-of-Commerce-free zone."

"So you think it would be a waste of time for me to go see the Northcutts about the job?"

"Not necessarily. If you want something, my theory is, go for it. Just be prepared to get run off, if they're in that kind of mood. That's what they did to Link Otterly when he went out there to see if they wanted to sell some timber off their place."

"Run off how?"

"Mrs. Northcutt came out with a bow and arrow. One of those high-powered kind that looks half medieval, half science fiction. A crossbow, I think they're called. I guess she didn't actually let fly with an arrow, but Link said he skedaddled because it sure looked like that's what she had in mind."

The Northcutts did sound a bit eccentric, but, when you get right down to it, aren't we all? Maybe the residents of Dulcy just didn't take to outsiders. Perhaps the man who thought he'd been threatened had misinterpreted the woman's actions. I tend to feel kindly toward anyone who invests in books, for whatever reason.

"Can you tell me how to get out there?"

"I'd better draw you a map. Most of the roads around here aren't marked, and they're really out in the boonies. But the road dead-ends at their driveway, so you can't miss it. And you sure can't miss their sign."

I got paper and pen, and she sketched a map, with directions about various landmarks. We also exchanged names. She gave hers as Margaret Rau and said she was driving the hay truck for her husband because he was recuperating from hip replacement surgery. "And this is Lucy," she added, giving the dog snuggled in her lap an affectionate pet on her slick black hair. "She's a Boston terrier."

I thought, even as I was telling her that I was Ivy Malone, that perhaps I should have given a phony name, just in case someone came inquiring. But being up-front and honest is a hard habit to abandon.

"Here, I'll add my cell phone number," Margaret said, scribbling a number at the bottom of the page. "Call me if you get lost."

"Actually, I don't have a cell phone."

"You don't?" She straightened in the chair, her expression alarmed. "A woman on the road alone should never be without a cell phone. You do carry a gun, don't you?" she added, as if she assumed everyone did.

I'd thought about getting a gun, but I figured I'd probably shoot my own foot or disable the motor home in some disastrous way before I managed to hit any bad guys.

"I have Koop the Attack Cat here." I gestured to where he was now atop a fence post looking down on the steer. I smiled. "But mostly I put my trust in the Lord."

She nodded. "I believe in trusting the Lord too. But I figure it doesn't hurt to have a gun, in case someone needs convincing the Lord is looking out for me."

An interesting concept, I decided.

"Well, time to get back to work. Ben is taking care of the grandkids while I'm driving the truck, and they're a handful." She laughed, and I had the impression from the tanned lines on her face that she laughed a lot, no matter what the adversity. "I think he's counting the days until school starts."

I was curious about why they were raising the grandchildren, but she set her coffee cup on the dusty ground and stood up to leave.

"It's been nice meeting you, Margaret," I said.

"You too, Ivy. I hope you get the job. Maybe I'll see you around again. There's a little community church you'd like down there past the Lariat." She hesitated. "But you really should have both a cell phone and a gun. Get a nice little .38." She sounded knowledgeable on the subject.

"Dulcy doesn't look like a center of crime."

"No, but we had something terrible happen just a few days ago." Her voice turned somber. "A young guy was shot out by the lake. Bullet to the back of the head, just like some gangland execution. It's got everybody shook up."

"They don't know who did it?"

"No, but he was the sheriff's nephew, and the sheriff has every man on the force running around with a fine-toothed comb looking for clues." She smiled wryly. "Not that our local sheriff's department *has* all that many deputies or fine-toothed combs."

"No motive?"

"Rumors, of course. Mostly about Eddie being mixed up in drugs. You wouldn't think kids would turn to drugs way out here in the middle of God's green earth, would you? But they do."

A hint of sadness in her voice made me wonder if she

had personal knowledge of kids and drugs, but she didn't elaborate.

"Anyway, be careful," she added.

The news about a local killing was worrisome, but logic said that whoever targeted a young guy involved with drugs wouldn't be concerned about a gray-haired LOL and a one-eyed cat in a motor home.

Margaret started back to the truck, then turned to call in a more cheerful tone, "Don't let the Northcutts weird you out. That's the kind of advice my grandkids give, whatever it means."

I put the chairs away, rolled up the awning, gathered up my cat, changed to tan slacks and white blouse—this was, after all, a possible job interview—and headed for the Northcutts' place out on Dead Mule Road.

I kept Margaret's map on my lap, turning at the cross-roads where I saw the dinosaur made of welded pieces of junk, and turning again at the pond with birdhouses on an island. Out here the road was washboard gravel, and some of the potholes looked large enough to bury a small dinosaur, but the wooded hills sloped green and beautiful to bubbling creeks. The mountains made hazy blue silhouettes basking in the sunshine. Here and there land had been cleared for pastures, although none of the places looked overly prosperous.

I saw rural mailboxes occasionally, but there was none at the Northcutt driveway. I knew I was at the right place anyway because the road ended here. There was also the sign, the one Margaret had said I couldn't miss. She was right.

**Keep Out
No Trespassing
This Means You!
Violators Will Be Prosecuted**

All in red letters big enough to warn off low-flying airplanes. I paused, second thoughts rampant. The Northcutts were making no bones about a hostility toward visitors. Perhaps I should have called ahead. . . . No, couldn't do that. Unlisted phone number. Which, in combination with the sign, now suggested something more deep-rooted than a mere preference for privacy.

There was a gate, metal. I got out to look and wasn't surprised to find a padlocked chain linking gate to solid iron post. No buildings were visible from here. Dense trees tangled with underbrush crowded the barbed wire fences leading away from the gate on both sides. A canopy of overhanging branches turned the driveway into a green tunnel leading into mysterious depths.

I listened, straining my ears for any sound of activity beyond the gate. Nothing at first, and then something soft and faint, not quite identifiable. An odd thrumming sound.

Drumming? No. The noise was too irregular, and it wasn't deep enough for a big drum, not *rat-a-tat-tat* enough for a smaller one. Definitely not a foot-tapping musical beat. Some peculiar "movie people" thing?

Whatever the activity was, in spite of a well-developed "mutant curiosity gene," as a friend calls it, I was not inclined to wander in and interrupt. The place felt . . . what? Not exactly scary. But if this were a movie, now is when the sinister music would start.

Not everything that first looks like opportunity comes from the Lord, I reminded myself.

Yet I was disappointed. Parking the motor home here at the Northcutts' while working for them would mean not having to pay rent at an RV park, which would be a big help financially. And in spite of the slightly creepy ambiance, which was probably the product of my own imagination, the place was nicely secluded. Not a spot where the Braxtons could likely sneak up on me.

Then the indistinct thrumming stopped, but, oddly, the silence was suddenly more disconcerting than the peculiar sound. A hush hung in the air, poised, as if waiting for something to happen. The whish of an arrow, perhaps? I found myself fingering the whistle that always hangs on a cord around my neck. Although I had the feeling that out here I could blow my lungs out and only whatever creatures lurk in deep, dark woods would hear.

Enough. I turned back from the gate. I was heading back to Dulcy.

Yet Margaret Rau's words echoed back at me: *"Don't let them weird you out."* The phrase had meaning now, because I was definitely getting weirded out, and that annoyed me. I don't like quitting without making a better try than this. That stubborn curiosity gene wasn't totally inactivated yet.

Okay, the situation was a little offbeat, I granted. Locked gate, hostile sign, strange thrumming sound, woods dense enough to conceal an army of guys with shaved heads and strange tattoos, uneasy silence. But it surely wasn't *weird*, and no one had leaped out with crossbow or any other weapon to run me off.

There might be a job waiting here, a job that could put me in an ideal spot to evade the Braxtons.

Determinedly I headed for the fence. I was going in.

4

I crawled through the fence and walked down the gravel driveway, briskly deleting the headlines trying to banner across my mind: "Deserted Motor Home Found on Isolated Road. Owner Vanished. Foul Play Suspected." ("If only the cat could talk," mourns neighbor.)

Except there didn't appear to be any neighbors available for mourning or anything else.

I kept to the center of the narrow gravel road, arms hugging my sides, trying to stay as far as possible from the walls of dense trees and brush crowding in on either side. I bolstered my nerves by humming a cheerful old cowboy song about "those Oklahoma hills." Although I doubted the cowboy had the Northcutts' darkly forested hills in mind.

I saw the house as soon as I rounded a bend in the green tunnel. It stood in a good-sized clearing, its size and rustic log construction impressive even though the building was probably only half the size it had once been as a hunting lodge. It was stubby on one end, where the burned portion had been hacked off and replaced with a two-story wall. A tall, many-armed TV antenna and a massive stone chimney topped a sloping, dark green metal roof, and a railed deck ran all the way along the front of the building. A huge bell hung from a high metal arch over the sidewalk leading to the front door.

The old place should have felt warm and welcoming. All those wonderful old logs silvered by age and weather, the railing inviting the propped feet of family and friends relaxing on the deck. That huge chimney hinting at a winter fire roaring companionably within.

Yet instead of having welcoming warmth, the house felt cold and forbidding, brooding even in bright sunlight. A low wall of stone and weathered concrete extended from the hacked-off end of the building, apparently the foundation of the portion that had been burned. The enclosed area might have been made into a lovely garden of grass and flowers, but it held only weedy mounds of dirt and a stack of debris left over from the burn.

Windows in the two-story section of the house next to the burned area were aluminum framed, no doubt a practical modernization, but the bare metal made a jarring contrast to the rustic logs. An open shed divided into three parking slots stood to one side, one of the spaces occupied by a squat, flat-topped Hummer painted in camouflage colors.

I saw nothing in particular to raise the hackles on the back of my neck, but rise they did. I clutched the whistle.

Then, with embarrassment, I realized I'd been standing there staring for several minutes. If the Northcutts were watching, my actions were probably not working in favor of employment. I gave my hair a quick finger pat and strode briskly toward the oversized front door. Although, as I approached it, I realized that unless the Northcutts were peering out an upstairs window, they couldn't have seen me. Heavy drapes shielded the windows all along the one-story, front section of the house.

A knocker made from a horseshoe hung in the middle of the door, a doorbell beside the door. I chose the doorbell and heard a no-nonsense buzzing inside when I pushed it.

No one came to the door. So maybe they were in a part of the house where they couldn't hear the bell. I used the metal knocker, taking an example from Margaret Rau and pounding energetically. Still no answer.

That faint, soft thrumming started again, this time punctuated by a few short, odd grunts. Now I could tell that the curious sounds were coming from around back of the house. I considered going out there, but I didn't want to walk in on something odd. Who knew what the Northcutts were doing? Maybe some bizarre ritual to ward off shark attack?

I dug a scratch pad out of my purse and wrote a message saying I had come about the job and would be back tomorrow. Or, if they came into Dulcy, I'd be in the motor home with Arkansas license plates parked there somewhere. I figured, given what I'd seen of Dulcy, they'd have no trouble finding me. I tucked the note under the horseshoe knocker.

I didn't mean to try the doorknob. Honestly I didn't. I just kind of stumbled as I was putting the note in place and grabbed the knob for support. The door was locked, of course. But at the same time I heard something inside. Not an identifiable sound, just . . . something.

Which seemed odd. If whoever was inside could react to the sound of my hand on the doorknob, surely they could have heard the doorbell and my pounding. Or perhaps they simply chose not to respond?

Then I heard another noise, and this one was definitely identifiable: the ringing of a telephone. It went on and on, at least a dozen rings. Apparently the Northcutts did not believe in answering machines.

The ringing phone definitely proved it, I decided. Even if I'd heard something inside the house, the Northcutts were not at home.

I was back in Dulcy shortly after noon. Around a bend from the Lariat, I found the main part of town. What there was of it. More out of curiosity than need I went into the one grocery store, Gus's Groceries, and bought cottage cheese, cat food, and a couple of oranges. The store was no supermarket, but it had adequate meat, dairy, and produce sections. Next door was a tiny beauty salon.

Dulcy had no sidewalks, but I wandered dusty paths along the road to the post office, a gas station, and a combination pizza parlor and video rental place. Jerry's Parts and Repairs had a sign announcing their expertise in off-road vehicles, and an antique shop exhibited dusty-looking dolls in one window and secondhand rakes and pitchforks in another. One long, fairly new-looking building held a tax-preparer/accountant's office and a real estate office. Two empty sections were optimistically labeled "Available Now!" A modest motel had four cars in the parking lot and a lit Vacancy sign. Another sign identified an old-fashioned school building with a bell tower as Dulcy Elementary. There didn't appear to be a high school. A fence separated the small, white church Margaret had mentioned from the pasture surrounding it.

I drove back to the Dulcy Farm Supply intending to park there again for the night, but at the last minute I circled through the parking lot and didn't stay. The store had several customers, but I was aware now that it was isolated from the rest of town. I'd been fine there last night, but I couldn't ignore the fact that a murder had recently been committed in the area. I'd also felt a little edgy ever since my visit to the

Northcutt place, so now I drove on to a big truck-parking area across from the Lariat.

In fact, by evening I was strongly considering *not* driving out to the Northcutts' again the following day, maybe just heading on to Texas.

"Well, we'll decide in the morning, okay?" I said to Koop.

Koop, a most congenial traveling companion, offered no comments.

I watched a half hour of fuzzy TV on the small set that operated off the motor home's battery and was getting ready for bed, brushing my teeth but not yet in pajamas, when someone knocked on the door. Both Koop and I jumped. Who would knock at this hour? The weird Northcutts? Prowling Braxtons? Local killer?

I was tempted not to answer, but the thought occurred to me that it could be an annoyed property owner warning me that RVs were not allowed to park here overnight, maybe threatening to send the sheriff or somebody if I didn't move. I cautiously nudged the curtain at the window beside the door so I could see out. The tall, jeans-clad female figure standing there reassured me. Margaret Rau, no doubt checking to see if I'd gotten the job.

I quickly unlocked the door.

I stared at the woman standing in the oblong of light cast by the open door. Tall and lean, yes. Also clad in jeans. But all similarity to Margaret ended there.

My first shocked impression was "punk rocker." Young. Short hair standing in rough blond spikes all over her head. Garish black and blue makeup around her eyes and a blotch of purplish blush on one cheek. One lurid red earring. But what in the world would a punk rocker be doing here in—

I blinked, and my perspective jumped.

Not garish eye makeup. Not purple blush. Two black eyes

35

and bruises! Plus a swollen nose, a raw scrape on her cheek, and others on her forehead and jaw. And that was no red earring; it was a scab of dried blood. She was also standing with most of her weight on one long leg, as if there might be other bruises and injuries, maybe worse ones, that couldn't be seen.

"I'm sorry to bother you but. . . ." She glanced around as if thinking something might rise up out of the shadows and grab her. A truck had stopped at the edge of the road.

"Child, what happened to you?" I gasped.

"I'm okay. Just a little accident."

Little accident? Her face looked as if she'd tangled with a concrete wall and a meat grinder. But there was a defiance in her tone, as if daring me to make something of the claim of a "little" accident.

"You're hurt! We'll get you to a doctor—"

"I don't need a doctor. Just . . . Could you pretend you know me, please?"

I had an instant flash about crimes that started this way. The supposedly injured person on the roadway who rises up and robs or murders the Good Samaritan who stops to help. The innocent-looking young woman in cahoots with a gun-toting cohort hiding in wait to strike.

I hesitated. *Lord?*

The young woman's tall figure swayed and her eyes rolled, and she reached out to the motor home to steady herself. I didn't hesitate any longer. I grabbed her hand and pulled her up the single step to the doorway. Inside the small motor home, she towered over me, at least five foot ten, maybe more, to my five foot one. I pushed her to the sofa and locked the door again. Then I went to the refrigerator and poured a Styrofoam cup of water from the jug I keep in there. She looked as if she needed something.

She drained the cup thirstily, then sat there with cup and

36

hands tucked between her knees. I had the feeling she was embarrassed at having asked for help. Koop jumped up to check her out. She stroked his back in an absentminded way, and I could tell she had a nice familiarity with cats.

"Do you live around here? Can I take you to family or someone?"

She shook her head, then winced as if the movement hurt.

"Do you have other injuries?"

"I'm okay."

"I'll get some ointment for the scrapes." I'd spotted another raw place on the back of her hand. "Where was this accident?"

She made a vague gesture in the direction of Texas, which took in a lot of territory. I squeezed a dab of ointment on her cheek. I didn't think it stung, but she jerked back as if just the touch alarmed her.

"A car accident?" I prodded when she didn't seem inclined to elaborate.

"Yeah."

"How did you get here?"

"Walked some." She sounded wary, on guard in spite of an obvious physical exhaustion. "Hitchhiked some."

I refrained from offering a sermon on the dangers of a young woman hitchhiking or walking the roads. "Was anyone else hurt?"

"No."

"You were alone in the car?"

"Yeah."

"You're not very informative," I muttered. She shrugged. "What about the car that was wrecked?"

"What about it?"

"Did you just walk off and leave it? What became of it?"

"I called someone. They'll take care of it." Another hint

37

of that what's-it-to-you-lady defiance. She turned and lifted the curtain a few inches so she could peer outside.

"Are you looking for someone?"

A hesitation. "The last guy I rode with acted a little odd. I told him I wanted out because I recognized the motor home and knew you. He was still watching when I got to your door. That's why I asked you to pretend you knew me." I believed that, but somehow I suspected it might be short of the whole truth.

"What's your name?"

"Abilene." Her mouth twisted in a humorless smile. "What was my mother thinking, right?"

"Abilene what?"

Another of those brief hesitations before she said, "Tyler."

Now I wondered if she was reluctant to tell me her full name, or if the delay gave her time to make up a phony one.

"Abilene seems a bit formal. Do people call you Abby, perhaps?"

"No." She sounded as if anyone tried Abby on her, she'd clobber 'em. She also looked, in spite of her current physical condition, as if she could probably do it.

I slowly put the cap back on the ointment. We studied each other. The bruises around one eye, I now saw, were turning color, taking on a yellow and greenish tint, which suggested they were older than a car accident within the last day or two. Though the scrapes and other black eye looked recent enough. Odd. A rotation of her shoulder under her lightweight denim jacket suggested it was also hurting.

"Have you done something criminal?" I asked bluntly.

Her blue eyes flared in surprise. "No!" Then another of those hesitations. This time I suspected it was because a reluctant honesty made her say, "At least I . . . I don't think so."

"Drugs?"

"Not unless you consider an occasional aspirin a big deal."

"Would you like a couple of aspirin now?"

"Yes. Please."

I got the aspirin and more water. A sharp noise banged outside as I handed the cup to her, the backfire of a car leaving the Lariat. Abilene jumped, spilling half the water, and I realized she was even more jittery than I'd been at the Northcutts. I got a handful of paper towels. I started to get down on my hands and knees to sop up the spilled water, but she grabbed the towels and did it herself.

"Sorry," she muttered as she stood up. I opened the door to the cabinet below the sink, and she stuffed the wet towels in the trash container I keep there.

I could tell my questions were making her edgy. I didn't want to do that. She looked as if she'd been through enough already. But there were a couple more things I had to know.

"How old are you?"

"Twenty-two."

I squinted at her. Was that true, or was she upping the number a few years to give herself legal, of-age status? At first glance I'd guess her to be younger than twenty-two, maybe a lot younger, but on closer examination she looked possibly even older than that. Especially in the eyes, as if something had aged her inside. I decided that, for now anyway, I'd just accept her number.

"Where are you headed?"

"I . . . haven't decided yet."

That made two of us, so I could hardly criticize her for that.

We regarded each other for a thoughtful minute. Finally I said, "If you don't mind being kind of scrunched up, you can sleep on the sofa here tonight."

I had instant second thoughts about the impulsive offer, but in her hesitant "Yeah?" I detected some doubts of her own.

"I won't knock you in the head and sell you into white slavery, or whatever the term is these days, if you promise not to knock me in the head and steal my motor home and cat."

The smile was slow but genuine this time. "Deal," she said.

That settled, I asked, "Do you have luggage . . . or anything?"

I couldn't see anything, of course, but I figured she might have stashed something before knocking on my door.

"I had some, but I couldn't get it out of the car." She shrugged. "There wasn't anything important in it anyway."

"You don't have *anything*?"

"I'm not naked," she pointed out a bit tartly. She wore jeans, sneakers, and a faded blue blouse under the denim jacket. She put a hand to a cord around her neck and yanked a leather pouch out from under the blouse. "And I have money. I can pay for sleeping on your sofa." The hint of defiance was back.

"No, no, child. Of course not." Hastily, before she decided to change her mind and walk out into the dark night, I added, "I'll fix you something to eat." I didn't make it a question because I didn't want to give her a chance to say she wasn't hungry when I was certain she was.

I scrambled three eggs, opened a can of peaches, warmed milk for hot chocolate, and made toast on my little thingama-jig that works on the gas stove. She ate everything the way Koop ate his first meal at that rest stop in Georgia. Afterward I told her she could take a shower if she'd like, but in the motor home, with water in short supply, she'd have to do it like I did: you wet yourself down, turn off the water while you lather up and wash, then do a quick rinse.

She nodded, and I could hear her following my instructions in the tiny bathroom a few minutes later. She came out wearing the same clothes, of course; she had no others. The leather pouch still dangled from the cord around her neck. It looked wet, as if she hadn't taken it off even in the shower. I had nothing that would even come close to fitting her, including pajamas, so she wound up sleeping in her underthings.

This parking place was either more noisy than the Dulcy Farm Supply lot or I wasn't sleeping as soundly. Trucks came and went. One parked beside us and left its refrigerated unit running noisily. Also, I now realized, the Lariat was as much beer joint as restaurant, and it didn't close until well after midnight. Late departers seemed to feel obliged to do a *vroom-vroom* of pickup engine, a raucous good night to friends, and a squeal of tires.

Neither the awkwardness of the pouch, the noise, or the cramped sofa kept Abilene from sleeping soundly, however. Which wasn't surprising, considering how exhausted she looked.

In the morning, with the kind of resiliency I could vaguely remember from my younger years, the exhaustion was gone from her face and shoulders, and her blue eyes were less murky looking. Although the bruises were still there, and she still seemed wary and nervous. And it would take more than a good night's sleep to do anything for that hair. It was no more than an inch in the longest spots and angled almost to her scalp in others. It looked as if it had been cut with a WeedEater. By an operator with a short attention span. It had one asset, however: no combing necessary. She just ran damp fingers through it, and it spiked up like blond exclamation points.

I fixed a big breakfast of hotcakes and eggs, and we sat down at the tiny dinette together. She was ready to stab a hotcake as soon as I set the plate down, but she jerked her fork back when I said I'd offer the blessing. She was looking at me curiously when I lifted my head a minute later, as if this was as foreign to her as finger bowls would be to me.

"I appreciate everything the Lord gives me, including this meal," I said.

"Oh. Well . . . uh, amen, I guess," she said awkwardly. She glanced around as if thinking she might spot God sitting on top of the refrigerator, and then dug into the hotcakes. Each time I asked if she'd like another one, she said yes.

We ate on Styrofoam plates, because I didn't want to use up water washing dishes, and after the fifth hotcake she finally crumpled her plate and put it in the trash.

"That was good, really good. Thank you."

"I'm glad to have the company. Usually it's just Koop and me."

"Well, time for me to hit the road," she said briskly. She picked up her jacket and peered out the window, automatically putting a hand to her chest to check on the leather pouch. She gave Koop a long, swooping good-bye caress. I sensed a certain regret in it. She liked cats. Koop had spent half the night at her feet. "I really do appreciate the food and your letting me stay here and everything."

I started to protest. *You can't hit the road. You have no place to go. No way to get anywhere but by hitchhiking. No clothes, nothing!* And if there were more than a few bucks in that pouch, I'd be much surprised. I was also certain that saying any of that to her would have as much effect as talking Kantian philosophy to Koop. I hastily took a different approach.

"I have to drive out in the country this morning. Why don't you come along?"

Until that moment I hadn't made up my mind to go back to the Northcutts, but if it would keep Abilene from hopping in some stranger's truck and taking off, I'd do it.

"Why?"

Why come along? "Well, uh, why not?"

She apparently found no fault in that logic, but then she asked warily, "You going to see family or friends or something?"

"No. I'm going to apply for a job."

"What kind of job?"

"I'm not sure. Maybe research or secretarial, maybe house-work or caretaking. I was out there yesterday, but no one was home."

"Is there more than one job opening?"

"I don't know that, either. Would you like to get a job?"

"Maybe."

"Then let's go see."

She hesitated a moment, then nodded. I put things away so nothing would fly around while the motor home was moving, working fast before Abilene changed her mind about coming along. Koop settled into Abilene's lap in the passenger's seat as if he'd always ridden there.

While I drove, I tried to find out more without being rudely inquisitive. It's a fine line, not one someone as curious as I am walks easily. "What part of Texas are you from?"

"I'm not from Texas." She was staring out the window as she spoke, and a sudden straightening of her back suggested she'd blurted that information without thinking.

"But wasn't the car accident down there?"

44

A considered delay while she apparently decided how much to explain. "I've been living there for a few years, but I'm not from there."

"Oh, I see. You've been working or going to school?"

"Working. Oh yeah, definitely working." Her tone wasn't exactly sarcastic, but a certain wryness suggested some masked meaning in the words.

"So, what do you do?"

"Cooking. Housework. Taking care of kids. Farm work. Whatever."

Cutting hair with a WeedEater, perhaps?

Unexpectedly, she volunteered a small bit of information. "I'm from Kansas originally."

"That explains why you don't sound Texan, then. What took you to—"

"I guess you're from Arkansas," she cut in before I could get another question out. "According to your license plate anyway."

And just like that, Abilene turned the small talk on me, and I found myself answering her questions and telling her about living on Madison Street in Missouri with Harley for years and years, being a librarian, losing my best friend, Thea, to a heart attack, and deciding to see the world in this motor home I'd bought in Arkansas. Although I have to admit I omitted some minor details about a couple of murders and the fire-setting, car-bombing Braxtons.

We reached the Northcutts' driveway and their hostile sign. The gate was still padlocked. "We have to walk from here."

If Abilene thought this an odd approach to job hunting, she didn't say so. I cracked a window for Koop and locked the door. But at the gate I stopped short.

Yesterday the chain had been arranged so the padlock was on the inside . . . hadn't it? Today it was on the outside.

45

Was my memory at fault, or did this mean someone had been in or out?

Nothing unusual about that, I decided. I hadn't been able to raise the Northcutts at the house yesterday, probably for the simple reason that they weren't home. Now they'd come home. Good. We'd get to see them today, then.

We walked down the driveway. Today I didn't hear the odd thrumming noise until we were in the clearing around the house. This time I could also see a faint cloud of dust rising from behind the house.

I went directly to the front door. My note was still there under the horseshoe knocker. I rang the bell anyway. Maybe the Northcutts didn't use their front door and hadn't seen the note. The Hummer hadn't been moved, and I didn't see any other vehicle. The drapes on the windows hadn't been opened. After punching the doorbell several times I went back to where Abilene was waiting by the arch and bell.

"I guess this was a wild goose chase. Apparently no one's home again." Or maybe they were out back doing who-knew-what again. A little awkwardly I asked, "Does the place feel kind of . . . creepy to you?"

I expected her to look at me as if I'd just suggested I thought the house was haunted by little green elves. Instead she muttered, "Yeah, it does feel kind of creepy." But instead of backing off, she added, "Let's go around back. Maybe someone's working back there."

With Abilene saying it, investigating behind the house sounded quite reasonable. I followed her long strides in that direction. The soft, irregular thrumming noise got a little louder. We rounded the corner of the house, and then I saw where the noise was coming from.

"Ostriches!"

"Emus," Abilene corrected as the whole mob—herd? flock?—spotted us and dashed on long, spindly legs to the fence. They had a large, grassy pasture, wooded at one end, in which to roam, but it was worn to bare dirt here at the corner closest to the house. More dust rose to join the hovering cloud. "I knew some people back in Texas who raised them."

Were these the "weird birds" the Ute guy from California had objected to? Shaggy, brownish-black feathers drooped around their heavy bodies. They had long necks, some with blue throats, fuzzy heads, big, inquisitive eyes, and wide, flattish beaks. Their height was variable, depending on whether they stretched those long necks up high to look down on us or curved them down low to peer up at us. But some were at least five or six feet tall when they did the stretch thing.

The birds milled around at the fence, some making that odd, thrumming-drumming sound, others contributing the grunts. I thought there were twelve of them, although it was difficult to count when they bounced around like popping popcorn. Considering that we were total strangers, they seemed inordinately glad to see us. Or maybe from an emu point of view, people all look alike.

"The females make the drumming sound. Males do the grunts." Abilene studied them a moment longer. "I think they're hungry." She strode toward the fence before I could say more than, "I don't think we should—"

"And thirsty too. They don't have any water."

She turned on a faucet, and the birds crowded around to get drinks from the shallow trough.

"These people ought to be thrown in jail for running off and leaving these birds to get hungry and thirsty!" she declared indignantly, and she sounded as if she'd gladly help round up the errant owners herself.

A big shed stood at one end of the fenced-in area, one side of it open to provide shelter for the birds. Abilene opened the door on a small room at the end of the shed. Several metal

47

barrels stood inside. She grabbed a bucket and scooped feed into a trough that could be filled from inside and accessed by the birds outside. I stayed outside the shed, watching. A noisy squabble started at the trough, with much flapping of ridiculously small wings.

I admired Abilene's initiative and concern for the birds, but I kept expecting angry Northcutts to come running out with shotgun—or crossbow—yelling at us to get away from their emus. Were they valuable creatures? I had no idea. I suspected, however, that not even a shotgun would keep Abilene from giving the Northcutts an earful about neglecting their animals.

However, no armed Northcutts appeared, just more dust from the milling crowd of emus. I waved a hand in front of my nose.

"I guess there isn't any point in our hanging around," I finally said.

Abilene turned, slowly surveying the whole layout. A large old barn with shingles missing from the steep roof stood at the far end of the clearing. It had an abandoned, unused look. Closer were several newer metal outbuildings, purposes not readily discernible. Two huge tanks on metal stands stood off by themselves, one marked with a red, hand-painted G, the other with a D. Over near the woods, a big target of red and white circles was fastened to a protective backdrop of hay bales. For crossbow target practice, perhaps?

"Will you come back later about the job?" Abilene asked.

"I don't think so. I've been here twice now. I think I'll just move on."

Abilene stuck her thumbs in the front pockets of her jeans and stretched her shoulders. "I'll just hang around here for a while, then."

"Hang around? Why?"

"I wouldn't mind working here. Taking care of emus and stuff. Maybe when the people come back they'll give me a job. If I leave, who knows when the emus will get fed again?"

I appreciated her concern for the big birds, but remaining here by herself was surely out of the question. "You can't just stay here, with no one around—"

"I don't see anyone to stop me."

True, but . . . "You don't know how long they may be gone, and you haven't any clothes, or food, or place to sleep—"

"I'll manage."

It occurred to me that she'd probably spent a night, or perhaps several nights, hiding and sleeping along the road before she'd knocked on my door.

"But if no one comes, or if they come home and won't give you a job, how will you get back to Dulcy?"

"Hitchhike. Walk."

I couldn't approve of that plan, but I could see that Abilene was a most self-sufficient, resourceful—and stubborn—young woman. I still didn't like the idea of leaving her here. "Okay, I'll stay too. For a while."

The day was getting warm. A big oak shaded the deck on this back side of the house. A set of modern, sliding glass doors had been added to the house, the aluminum framework again looking out of place against the old logs. The drapes on this side of the house were also closed, although those covering the sliding glass doors showed a gap at the top where they weren't quite pulled together. I was tempted to climb up and peek inside. I squashed the temptation. What kind of person visits someone's home and starts climbing around to peer in the windows? We sat in a couple of wooden lawn chairs on the back deck. There were only two, as if the Northcutts didn't invite guests to sit with them.

The emus, satisfied now, squished those long legs under them and settled down on the ground, looking rather like

49

long-necked feather dusters. Insects droned in the quiet air. Within a few minutes my eyes drooped. Between the beer drinkers at the Lariat and the truck with the refrigerated unit, I hadn't slept much last night.

Abilene sat for a while, but within a few minutes she started prowling restlessly. I heard her, but my eyes stayed shut anyway. Next thing I knew, when I opened them, I saw that she'd carried her lawn chair over by the sliding glass doors and was standing on it so she could peer through that gap at the top of the drapes. Her nose was pressed to the glass, hands shielding her eyes.

I started to chide her, but curiosity got in the way. "Can you see anything?"

"I'm not sure," she said slowly. "But I think you'd better come look."

Something in her tone made me discard my "nice ladies don't
peek" reluctance. She stepped off the chair, and I climbed
up on it.

It took my eyes a moment to adjust to the drape-dimmed
rooms. The one I was peering into looked as if it had once
been the dining room for lodge guests. A heavy, oblong table
big enough to seat at least twenty people stood in the center
of the room, but there were only two high-backed chairs
next to it now. And apparently only a small section at one
end of the table was now used for dining. Piles of books,
magazines, and manila folders covered every other inch of
the surface. A heavy, old-fashioned manual typewriter sat
on a metal typing table nearby, and another larger wooden
desk held a computer and printer. Shelves filled with books
covered an entire wall, and two four-drawer filing cabinets
crowded one corner. But I didn't see anything to put that
odd tone in Abilene's voice.

"In the other room," she said. "Look in there."

Not much of the other room was visible through the arched doorway. As I looked down on it through the high-up gap in the drapes, all I could see was one end of a dark sofa, and only the lower half of that was visible. An oversized table lamp blocked the top. Then I spotted them.

Feet. Legs.

Two people were sitting on the sofa.

My first reaction was a panicked and embarrassed, *They're going to stand up and catch me looking in their window!* I stumbled backward. Abilene caught me before I tumbled off the lawn chair.

"What do you think?" she asked.

I hadn't seen anything about the feet and legs to indicate anything unusual, but it did seem odd that the people hadn't come out to investigate our presence. We hadn't been particularly quiet. And there was a peculiar immobility, almost a mannequin-like lifelessness about the legs, as if . . .

I hastily detoured that warped train of thought.

"Perhaps they're napping," I said.

"Maybe the doorbell isn't working, and that's why they didn't answer it," Abilene suggested.

I could see we both wanted to come up with mundane explanations for the unmoving feet and legs, but I had to reject the possibility of a non-working doorbell. "I could hear it buzzing, so they surely could too."

"Two people napping sitting up seems . . . peculiar," Abilene said.

True. We looked at each other uneasily.

"I'm going to knock." Abilene ran down the deck to another door and pounded. I climbed on the chair again. The feet and legs on the sofa didn't move even though Abilene hammered hard enough to rattle the door. I knuckle-rapped the sliding glass door. Still no movement from the legs.

"Maybe we should go back to town and call the authorities," I said. The creepy feeling now was strong enough to add crashing cymbals to yesterday's sinister mood music. "This doesn't look right."

Abilene didn't answer, and I turned to look at her. I couldn't see much of her complexion under the bruises, but I thought she'd paled. At mention of authorities?

I remembered that last night when I asked if she'd done anything criminal she'd hesitated momentarily before saying she didn't think so. But she hadn't sounded positive. Perhaps we should get down to specifics on a definition of criminal activity?

Not right now, because another thought occurred to me. "Maybe they're ill! A heart attack or stroke or—"

"Both at the same time?"

Unlikely, but who knew? Margaret Rau hadn't mentioned how old the Northcutts were. Maybe something had happened to one of them, and when the other tried to help, that person had collapsed too. Such things happen.

If that were the case, driving all the way back to town to tell someone about this would take much too long. If they were ill, so ill they couldn't come to the door, they needed help *now*. Oh, for that cell phone Margaret had recommended! But I didn't have it, so I trotted along the side of the house looking for a way in. All the curtains were pulled, sliding windows tightly shut. Around the corner, on the stubby back side of the house where there was no deck, a frosted-glass window, smaller and higher up than the others, probably a bathroom window, was open an inch or two. Abilene saw me eying it.

"I don't think I can crawl through that," she said doubtfully.

"I can." I was reminded of a flying leap I'd once taken through a bathroom window to escape a guy with a gun. This would be a piece of cake next to that. "But I don't think the lawn chair will put me up high enough to do it. Can you lift me?"

Abilene inspected my petite-cum-scrawny frame. "I've lifted bales of hay that weigh more than you. I grew a *squash* that was as big as you."

I suspected that, size aside, she was doubtful about my being limber enough to climb through the window, but she politely didn't voice her doubts. She knelt below the window. I climbed on her shoulders and draped my legs around her neck. She stood up, hands gripping my ankles, and together we edged closer to the wall. I yanked the screen off first, then got my hands on the edge of the sliding window and pushed and pulled until it was open as far as it would go. I braced a hand on the window ledge and scrambled to a standing position on Abilene's shoulders. She didn't wobble under my weight, didn't even complain when I accidentally jammed a finger in her ear.

"We're pretty good at this. Maybe we should try out for one of those cheerleading squads where they do that pyramid stuff." Abilene's voice was muffled, maybe because I now had a foot blocking her mouth.

I scrunched and squeezed through the opening. The bathroom was a simple oblong shape, with the window over the toilet stool. I clambered down to the stool, wishing the lid had been left down because the curved seat was slippery—

I crashed, glasses flying, one foot plunging into the toilet bowl, hands spinning the toilet paper dispenser as I frantically grabbed for anything to keep my face from smashing into the counter.

"Are you okay?" Abilene called.

"More or less." What looked like acres of toilet paper now covered the bathroom. Coils of it spread on the floor. Banners of it draped the sink. I yanked a streamer of it out of my hair. "But forget trying out for that cheerleading squad."

I hauled my foot out of the toilet, grabbed a towel, and dried off my pants leg and shoe as best I could. I fumbled around until I found my glasses, blessedly unbroken, and washed my hands. I followed a hallway to the kitchen, squishing wet blobs in the carpet along the way, and opened the outside door. Abilene wrinkled her nose when she stepped inside. Yes, there was a smell, I realized now. An extremely unpleasant smell. I'd been too involved in my tangle with the toilet bowl to notice it before.

Abilene tiptoed warily from the kitchen through the dining room to the room where we'd spotted the legs. Something about the ambiance seemed to call for a tiptoe. I followed. A few feet from the sofa, we both stopped short.

Two people sat on the sofa.

They were holding hands.

They were both quite dead.

And the smell . . .

I couldn't tell what kind of wound the woman had, something ghastly in the throat or chest area, and what I guessed was coagulated blood covered her body in dark, unmoving streams and clots and blobs from the neck down. It had soaked into her clothing, into the sofa, into the clothing of the man beside her.

The man's wound was more precise. A neat hole punctuated his temple. I didn't look at the exit wound beyond a quick glance to see that most of the side of his head had been blown off.

Flies buzzed everywhere. On the bodies, on the bloody furniture, on *me*. I swatted at them frantically.

Then I couldn't see to swat because my eyes started watering and spinning in dizzy circles, and nausea rose like something live clawing its way up my throat. Death. The smell, the blood, the flies . . . the sickening *awfulness* of it all. I circled around behind the sofa to get away from seeing it all. The sofa was at the rear of the big room, but there was a wide space to walk behind it going from front door to dining room.

"I-I've seen dead people at funerals," Abilene said in a strangled-sounding voice. She put a hand over her nose and mouth. "But never like this."

"Don't touch anything." Although it was an unnecessary warning, since neither of us were making a move toward the bodies. It was well beyond time to check for a pulse.

I moved around to the front side of the sofa again when my eyes—and stomach—finally stopped spinning. Now I saw that a handgun lay on the sofa next to the man's fingers.

This time it was Abilene who croaked, "We'd better call someone."

I appreciated that whatever her personal apprehension about the authorities, this was more important. "Right."

What I wanted to do was plop down somewhere until my knees gained some stability, but I forced myself to look for a phone. It was on an end table beside another sofa set at right angles to the one the bodies were on. I brushed away more flies as I staggered unsteadily to the end table and reached for the phone to dial.

We both jumped when the phone rang under my hand, then stared as if it were a snake rattling, ready to strike. I hesitated, uncertain what to do. Had I any right to take a phone call for people who were sitting here *dead*?

But my inability to let any ringing phone simply keep ringing won out.

7

I picked up the receiver and cautiously said, "Hello?"

Moment of silence, and then a male voice, obviously surprised by my voice instead of one he was expecting, said, "I must have dialed the wrong number."

"Are you trying to call the Northcutts?"

"Yes, I am. Who is this?"

"Who are you?" I shot back. I had no intention of blurting the news about the dead Northcutts to the local Hummer repairman or emu salesman. For a moment I thought he was going to demand that I tell him who I was first, and we'd be ping-ponging back and forth in some argument totally inappropriate to the grisly situation.

Instead he said in a dignified tone, "This is Frank Northcutt. And I repeat, who are you and what are you doing in my parents' house?"

"Your parents," I echoed. "Oh dear . . ." Their son. And I had to break the news to him.

"What's going on? Is something wrong?"

"My name is Ivy Malone. I heard there might be a job opening here—"

"Ute quit?" the man broke in. "Or did they fire him?"

"I'm not sure . . ."

"Whatever, good riddance. I told them he was bad news. The guy should have had 'psycho' tattooed behind his ear, instead of whatever it was he had there. But they wouldn't listen, of course." He sounded exasperated.

"I came out from Dulcy yesterday. I rang the doorbell and knocked, and no one answered. Then I heard the phone ringing inside the house, and no one answered that, either, so I decided no one was home . . ."

Wrong, I realized now. I'm no expert on determining time of death, but it now looked as if the Northcutts had indeed been "home" then. Right where they were now. On the sofa. Holding hands. Dead.

A puzzling thought: if they were dead then, what was that noise I'd heard here inside the house?

"Maybe it was me you heard when the phone was ringing. I tried to call at about 5:30."

No, I'd come to the house considerably earlier than that, so the ringing I'd heard must have been someone else calling. But I didn't bother to explain. I was stalling, dreading breaking this news. But I had to get on with it. "Anyway, a friend and I came back today, and we still couldn't rouse anyone. The emus acted hungry, as if they hadn't been fed—"

"Those stupid birds," he muttered.

"We became concerned, so we . . . let ourselves into the house." I didn't give him time to ask how we accomplished that. "And we found . . . Oh, I'm so sorry to have to tell you this, Mr. Northcutt, but we found your parents here, and they're . . . dead."

"Dead?" He said the word in a perplexed way, as if the fact didn't really register with him. He repeated it a moment

58

later when it did register, his voice jumping an octave in shock. *"Dead?"*

"I was just going to dial 911 when the phone rang."

"You're telling me my mother and father . . . both of them . . . are *dead*?" He sounded incredulous, and I couldn't blame him. To make an ordinary phone call to parents and then have *this* come down on you. "I don't understand. Are you sure? How . . . ?"

"They're here on the sofa, and they appear to have been . . . shot."

"Shot? You mean someone broke in and *murdered* them?"

I gave the bodies and gun a sideways glance, uncertain what to say. Murder? Maybe. But with the gun right there by the man's hand . . . "I'm sorry. I'm not handling this very well. I-I think I should get hold of the authorities and let them figure out what happened here. There is a 911 system in this part of Oklahoma, I hope?"

"I think so. I remember Jock saying something about calling it a couple of times. Look, I'm coming, of course, and I'll get there as soon as possible. But it's a long drive, and I have to make arrangements about the kids and work. I'm the postmaster here, and Mikki is in Austin at a cosmetologist convention. I'll have to get hold of her. This is just so hard to believe. You're sure they're dead?"

He still sounded shocked and distressed and distraught as he rambled, but at the same time oddly fretful and fussy. As if all this might be an annoying mistake, and he didn't want to make the trip unless he was positive there was no uncertainty about his parents being dead.

"I'm afraid there's no doubt about it. They're dead." An unexpected possibility surfaced. "Unless, of course, these two people *aren't* your parents."

"I can't imagine who else would be in their house. My folks don't often have guests. They aren't the hospitable type."

"It was just a thought."

"But maybe . . . I mean, they had a couple of new deals going, so it's possible someone else was there . . ." I heard a glimmer of hope in his voice. "Okay, Jessie—"

"Jessie?"

"Jessie, my mother. I always called my parents by their first names."

"Oh." *Movie people*, I found myself thinking, then chastised myself for being judgmental just because this was something I couldn't imagine ever doing with my own parents long ago.

"Jessie is 61. She's 5'8", about 135 pounds. Short gray hair, blue eyes. She always wears a pair of gold earrings shaped like the Oscar awards. Jock had them made for her after they won their Oscar."

I would've liked to know more about that, but this was hardly the time to ask.

"Jock is 64, maybe 160 pounds . . . he's lost weight recently. He's also gray-haired, what's left of it anyway, and blue eyes."

I forced myself to study the bodies more closely. For a moment I thought, *Hey, maybe this isn't them!* These people both looked heavier than the weights the son had just given. Then, with sick realization, I saw that the excess weight was an illusion. The bodies, after being closed up for some unknown amount of time in a house in warm weather, had started to bloat as well as smell.

It was also difficult to tell ages, but sixties looked about right. I couldn't distinguish eye color, but both the man and woman had gray hair. And small gold earrings hung at the woman's ears.

"The descriptions fit." I swallowed. "They're both wearing blue jeans and jogging-type shoes."

"Yeah, that's what they usually wear." The hope fizzled out of his voice. He sounded baffled but resigned now.

"I'm so sorry . . ."

"I don't suppose you have any idea how long they've been dead?"

"No, I'm afraid not. It's . . . quite warm in here."

"So they were probably already dead when I tried to call yesterday?"

He sounded unnerved by that, and I understood. I felt unnerved too, knowing two people had been dead on the sofa when I was so impatiently ringing the doorbell and banging the horseshoe knocker. Was it possible, if I'd barged in then, I could have called for help and saved them?

I reluctantly studied the bodies more closely. Her wound was definitely in the throat, gaping and messy, probably a direct hit to an artery, from the way the wound had bled. A dark shadow surrounded the bullet wound in his temple. I remembered from various mysteries I'd read that this probably meant a powder burn, the result of the gun held close to the skin when fired. He'd undoubtedly died instantly when the bullet hit his brain.

"I-I'm fairly certain they were already dead when you tried to call."

He pulled himself together. "You'll contact the authorities, then?"

"Yes, and we'll stay here at the house until they arrive. If you want us to, that is. I realize you don't know us—"

"I'd appreciate your staying. A deputy or someone will probably need to talk to you anyway. Although if there's a chance the murderer is still hanging around . . ."

"We'll be careful, but we haven't seen any sign of anyone else around. I almost forgot. The gate is chained and

61

padlocked. Do you know anything about a key? We had to park out there by the gate, and I think the police will need to drive up to the house."

"Look in the kitchen, in one of those drawers to the left of the stove. If you don't find it there, try a nightstand in the bedroom. Theirs is the downstairs one. My folks were real fanatics about keeping that gate locked all the time. I always thought it was a big waste-of-time nuisance." Again that twinge of exasperation, but after a moment's pause he added somberly, "But, considering what's happened, I guess they had a right to be concerned."

"I don't know that they were killed by an outsider . . ." I was afraid the son might be getting a wrong impression about the deaths, but neither was I comfortable jumping in with speculations about the situation. It certainly looked as if the man had killed the woman, then took his own life. But there was also the thought that things were not always as they seemed on the surface. Not my place to speculate, I decided firmly.

"We'll try to have the gate unlocked by the time the authorities get here, then," I said.

"Thank you. I just can't believe this. I knew they had some problems, maybe even some enemies, but I always thought . . . Well, never mind. It was probably a burglary gone bad. I don't suppose you can tell if anything is missing?"

"No, I'm afraid not."

"How about the Hummer?"

"It's here."

"The first person the police better check on is Ute. Though it won't surprise me if he's a hard man to find. I heard him telling once about how he went out in the mountains in Idaho with nothing but a pocketknife and some matches and lived off the land for six weeks." Another pause, as if he were

62

pulling himself together again. "I'm sorry, I'm rambling. This is just so unbelievable . . . What was your name again?"

"Ivy Malone. The friend here with me is Abilene Tyler. She fed the emus," I added.

"Those stupid birds," he repeated and abruptly hung up without saying good-bye.

I told Abilene what he'd said about a key, and she went to look for it while I dialed 911. I told the woman who answered that the Northcutts had been shot, and the gun was here. "But it isn't an emergency situation requiring an ambulance. They're definitely dead. And have been dead for some time, I think."

"No pulse? No vital signs?"

"No. Bloating has started, I think, and there's . . . considerable scent."

She asked for the address, the 911 system in this area apparently not outfitted with the equipment that automatically shows address information when a call comes in. I couldn't give her an address, of course, beyond Dead Mule Road. But when I added the information I'd acquired from Margaret Rau, that the Northcutts were the movie people who'd bought the old Morris hunting lodge, she immediately said, "Oh, okay, sure, I know where that is. The movie people. I just didn't recognize the name. Things have been so hectic around here."

I had the impression, not that she didn't *care* that the Northcutts were dead by gunshots, but that she wasn't terribly surprised. Outsiders, you know. *Movie people*.

She asked a few more questions, warned us not to touch anything, and then said she'd get someone out here as soon as possible.

"Have you any idea how long it will be? It's a little . . . unnerving being here alone with the bodies."

"I can't say for sure. A report about an off-road accident

with a body just came in, and two officers are headed out there now. And what with people calling in with all kinds of tips and information about the murder that have to be checked out . . ." She sounded distracted, even a little rattled.

"Murder?" I repeated, though I thought I knew what she was talking about, from what Margaret had said.

"The sheriff's nephew, Eddie Howell. Someone killed him out by the lake. But an officer will be out to see you as soon as possible."

"Thank you." I put the phone down and turned to find Abilene holding a key but staring at a sheet of paper leaning against a book on the coffee table.

8

I hadn't noticed it before. Perhaps because a sheet of plain white paper, even a blood-spattered one, does not tend to catch your attention when you're confronted with two gunshot bodies and an army of flies.

I had to step closer to the bodies so I could read the lines of typing, and closer was not where I wanted to be. What I *wanted* was a can of Raid so I could blast those buzzing flies, but even without the 911 woman's warning I knew that wasn't proper procedure. Bug and larval evidence can help fix time of death, so blasting any of the local fauna was surely a no-no. We'd just have to keep swatting. And trying not to breathe too deeply.

The typed message had no salutation, not even a to-whom-it-may-concern.

> We believe the world is beyond hope or help. We no longer want to live in or be a part of it, and we choose to leave it in loving togetherness.

At the bottom were the typed names, Jock and Jessie Northcutt, with the signature of each above a printed line. His was one of those illegible scrawls, but hers was blocky and precise, the dot over the *i* in her name in the shape of an angular triangle.

I irrelevantly noted that the book the paper had been leaning against was titled *Emus: The Bird for Survival*.

Unfortunately, the emus obviously hadn't helped the Northcutts survive.

Abilene's gaze skittered from note to bodies to gun. "They . . . they're saying they committed suicide together?"

"That's what it sounds like."

That's what it had looked like even before I'd seen the note, and the note seemed to leave no doubt. I suspected a comparison would show that it had been written on that old typewriter in the living room. The type was irregular, the *e* a little off kilter.

The sequence of events appeared obvious now. They'd composed and signed the note together. He'd then shot her from several feet away as she calmly awaited the bullet. Then, while she was bleeding to death, he'd sat down beside her on the sofa, taken her hand in his, lifted the gun with his other hand, and put a bullet through his own temple.

A death pact between them. Leaving this world "in loving togetherness." I shuddered.

Why? Why would these two people take this tragic, irreversible action? What despair could have been so overwhelming that they saw *this* as the only solution? Now I also had to wonder, what would their son think? Would death by suicide pact be more or less horrendous for him than murder by some outsider?

But another thought slithered in behind that obvious conclusion. What if this wasn't what it looked like? What if it was a staged scene, a phony note, murder set up to look like a suicide pact?

I quickly discarded the thought. Maybe I did read too many mystery novels.

"I'm going to go out and unlock the gate." Abilene sounded as if she was suddenly frantic to get out of the house, away from the bodies and flies and smell.

I dug in a pocket and brought out my own keys. "You can drive the motor home back."

She eyed the keys but didn't reach for them. "We can get it later."

"There's no point in your walking all the way back here in the heat."

"That's okay. I don't mind." She said it politely and waved her hand dismissively, but I heard an underlying stubbornness that puzzled me. Why be stubborn about something so trivial?

She went through the dining room and kitchen to the back door, which was still standing open, but stopped short. I could see her through the wide arched doorway to the dining room.

"Is something wrong?" I called.

"No, I guess not. For a minute I thought I saw something moving back there in the woods. But it was probably just a bird or squirrel or something. I'll be back in a few minutes."

After Abilene left, I found a row of switches on a nearby wall and used my elbow to snap them on. I jumped when the lights flared on overhead, startled by the source. Three chandeliers made of intricately entwined antlers hung there like a row of barbaric crowns for a trio of medieval kings. *How many wild creatures have given their heads for these monstrosities?* I wondered, appalled. Above the chandeliers, the sloping ceiling disappeared in shadows laced with dark beams. A huge, rock-embedded fireplace, with another slab of rock for a mantel, stood at the far end of the room. A horseshoe grouping of sofas and chairs faced it, with other groups of furniture scattered around the room. An upright piano draped with a Navajo blanket stood off to one side, a television on the other. A huge antlered deer head on a wooden plaque hung over the fireplace. It was slightly askew, making the deer look as if it were watching the big room with the cynical expression of one who has seen it all before. More Navajo rugs and blankets hung on the walls, along with several oversized paintings of generic-looking mountains and lakes.

This must have been a general gathering place for guests when it was a hunting lodge, and probably used by the Northcutts as an oversized living room.

Stairs led up to a railed balcony overlooking the room below. The upstairs probably held a number of bedrooms for lodge guests at one time, but it looked as if there was space for only a couple of bedrooms now. A tawny skin hung over the railing. I couldn't identify it, but a glitter of claws told me I wouldn't have wanted to encounter it when the skin was occupied.

Carpeting covered the hallway floor, but the floor in this huge room was hardwood, with area rugs, mostly of the colorful Navajo variety, scattered here and there.

The general effect was rustic, pleasing but impersonal, the kind of thing that would look good in a lodge brochure. The dining room, with all those books and folders, appeared considerably more lived in. I wondered where the Northcutts kept the Oscar their son said they'd won.

I headed back to the bathroom to make certain I'd cleaned up the tangle of toilet tissue, but along the way I peeked through the open door of what had been, according to Frank Northcutt, his parents' bedroom. The drapes in the bedroom were also closed, and it was too dark to make out more than

68

shadowy shapes of furniture. I felt a moment's apprehension when I flicked the light switch. Would it reveal some bizarre light fixture of entangled hooves or teeth, perhaps?

No, thankfully, it was just an ordinary glass fixture.

The large room held a four-poster bed of dark walnut, with a matching mirrored dresser, two chests of drawers, two nightstands, and a couple of chairs upholstered in dark green. All were massive and impressive, almost as impersonal as the over-antlered room out front. There were no photos or mementos, no dirty socks on the floor or open books on the nightstands, but there was a delicately lovely music box on the dresser plus a collection of antique perfume bottles.

But what most caught my attention was a double-doored, tall, wooden cabinet in one corner of the room. One door stood partly open, a ring of keys dangling from the lock. Craning my neck I could almost . . . but not quite . . . see inside the cabinet. Was this where the Northcutts kept that Oscar? Or what *was* in there?

I hesitated, but curiosity overrode guilt for my nosiness, and I walked over and nudged the door open, again using my elbow. Elbows leave no prints. At least I've never encountered elbow prints in my reading. I stared at what the open door revealed. Not a Hollywood award.

Guns.

At least a dozen of them were leaned neatly against the green felt that lined the big cabinet, some narrow and long barreled, some short and squatty. Handguns hanging from hooks covered a side wall of the cabinet, some large enough to intimidate a terrorist, others small enough to be concealed in a purse. Or garter, perhaps, if you were the Mata Hari type.

I'm familiar with gun names and numbers from mysteries I've read. Winchesters and Remingtons, Glocks and Sigs, Berettas and Rugers. And 30-06s and 10 gauges, .45s and 9mms. But my ability to actually identify such guns is close to nonexistent, and I had no idea if the long-barreled guns were rifles or shotguns, legitimate hunting guns or subversive guerilla weaponry. Why would anyone need so *many* guns?

One space on the handgun wall was empty. It didn't take an expert to suspect where that weapon was now.

Another point on which I was reasonably certain was that this was no elite collection of fancy guns kept only for display. These were working weapons, unadorned and deadly looking. Several were equipped with what I guessed were telescopic sights. Maybe even night-vision sights.

On the floor of the cabinet were several more items that totally mystified me. But which I strongly suspected would give me shivers if I knew what they were. Now I also noticed that leaning against the outside of the cabinet was a strange and vicious-looking instrument, probably the thing Margaret had called a crossbow.

Margaret Rau had said the Northcutts were "different." I had to agree. Not your garden-variety suburban neighbors.

I started back toward the door to the hallway, but curiosity got to me again. I detoured to peer in the bathroom, which was considerably larger and more elegant than the smaller one I'd fallen into. Another twitch with my elbow on the light switch revealed double sinks, an octagonal tub, a huge, separate shower, and enough mirrors to make me feel as if I was watching myself over my own shoulder.

The mirrored door on an oversized medicine cabinet stood open. I tiptoed closer. Why tiptoe? I don't know. Perhaps it just comes with the territory when you're prowling where you probably have no business being, and there are two bodies just down the hallway.

The cabinet held a mundane assortment of items: laxatives, antihistamine pills, Band-Aids, Ben-Gay, Advil and Tylenol, plus some herbal concoctions I'd never heard of. A plastic bottle of Tums spilling multicolored pills lay on its side on the marble counter below.

Nothing unusual, and yet . . .

Wasn't the sequence of events suggested by bath and bedroom just a little odd?

Open bathroom cabinet door.

Take antacid pills.

Get gun from cabinet.

Shoot mate and self.

Although it was conceivable that Jock or Jessie may have been looking for a pain killer or tranquilizer to make the suicide process easier. A second glance at the medicine cabinet suggested all the items in it had been marginally disarranged, as if someone had poked through everything. Which meant . . . what?

Not my place to speculate, I once more told myself firmly. The authorities were on their way.

In the dining room the books and thick manila folders pulled me, but I bypassed them. More a reaction to the pervasive scent coming from the other room than determined control of my curiosity, I had to admit. Outside in the sunshine I breathed deeply of fresh air. Even the dust raised by the emus had a good, earthy, natural scent, unlike the tainted air inside the house.

I felt too edgy to sit, so I wandered around, eying the big tanks and outbuildings. Frogs croaked somewhere out of sight, suggesting water back there in the woods somewhere. Several of the curious emus came to the fence to watch me. One had the peculiar habit of blinking just one eye. Probably just the emu version of a tic, but it came across as a conspiratorial wink. I couldn't agree with Frank Northcutt's derogatory judgment of the emus as "stupid birds." There seemed an inquisitive intelligence in their bright eyes following my every move. They hadn't been making any of those odd noises since we'd arrived and Abilene had fed them. They struck me as sociable birds who liked to be around people.

After a few minutes I had the peculiar feeling that more than emus were watching. And Abilene thought she'd seen something out in the woods . . . Which reminded me of the son's comment that we shouldn't hang around if a murderer was still in the vicinity.

I then reminded myself that, from all indications, there *was* no murderer, just a sadly misguided couple who'd given up on life. Which didn't keep me from whirling a couple of times, trying to catch whoever or whatever might be slyly spying from cover of the dense woods.

I saw nothing, but the being-watched feeling was strong enough to send me back to a lawn chair on the deck. I may be curious, but I'm not without a prudent sense of caution, and the house felt safer than the woods. Although it hadn't provided safety for the Northcutts . . .

Abilene returned a few minutes later, but it was at least an hour and a half before we heard a car approaching. By then, we were sitting on the back deck. I was wishing I had something to drink, but I wasn't about to raid the refrigerator. We circled the house to meet the car.

Two officers, one middle-aged, the other much younger, got out of the dusty white car marked with a county sheriff's department emblem. The older man with steel-gray hair and a generous belly introduced himself as Sgt. Dole, and the younger man, who could surely be a poster boy for clean-cut, handsome police officers everywhere, as Deputy Hamilton.

"Sorry to take so long getting here," Sgt. Dole said. "A report came in about an off-road rollover accident with a death involved, and I was investigating that when the call about this situation came in. Actually, as the crow flies it isn't all that far from here. Although it's a long way around by road."

"I understand there's also been a murder in the area."

"Right." Sgt. Dole checked his watch as if he had something on his mind. "Bad stuff. We're not usually so deep in bodies around here."

Sgt. Dole was also inspecting Abilene as he spoke, as was the younger deputy, both men obviously taking note of the black eyes and bruises. Abilene's toe ground nervous circles in the dust, and her gaze skittered everywhere but directly at them. Once her glance darted toward the woods, and I was afraid she might actually cut and run.

Quickly I identified myself and said I'd made the call to 911. "The front door is still locked, but you can get in the back way." I motioned around the house. "The bodies are on a sofa just beyond the dining room. We're assuming they're Mr. and Mrs. Northcutt, although we don't know that for certain. Their son is on his way and can positively identify them, of course. But I didn't think to ask him where he was coming from, so I don't know how long it will take him to get here."

"You've already notified the son of this?" The older officer's bushy eyebrows did hairy calisthenics of disapproval.

"He happened to call just as I was going to dial 911. So I didn't feel I couldn't *not* tell him, with them sitting right there beside me . . . dead."

"You're . . . what? Relatives? Friends?"

"We just happened to be here looking for jobs," I explained. I thought that might raise the eyebrows again. Possum-gray LOL and nervous, spike-haired blond with bruises. *What kind of jobs did these two hope to find?*

All Sgt. Dole said, however, was, "But you're not from around here."

An observation, not a question, but I couldn't tell if it meant he knew everybody in the county, if he'd noted the Arkansas plates on the motor home, or if we just stood out as not-from-here people. So all I said was, "Margaret Rau told me the Northcutts might be looking for someone."

"And how did you 'happen' to find the bodies inside the house?"

Sgt. Dole had instantly zeroed in on the weak point in our good-citizen involvement here. I hastily explained about peering through the sliding glass doors, being concerned that the people we could only partially see might be ill, not having a way to call, and so finding entrance through a window.

"We didn't touch anything," I assured him. "Except the phone, of course." I didn't feel it was necessary to tell him about my plunge into the toilet bowl. Or my excursion into the master bedroom. I'd been careful not to touch anything there.

Sgt. Dole frowned at my statement about climbing through the window but made no comment other than to warn, "Don't leave. We'll want to ask you some further questions."

9

Sgt. Dole led the way into the house. The younger deputy and I followed. Abilene stayed behind. I suspected she wanted to keep as far away from the officers as possible, though I still didn't know what that was all about. Both men stopped short just inside the arched doorway to the big room. The chandelier lights were still on. I thought the gruesome scene would shock even the most experienced of police officers. The flies were still buzzing, and the smell not improving. But I saw no change of expression on either face when I edged up beside them.

I tried to keep myself as cool and controlled as the two officers. "There's a note," I said, pointing to it. "We hadn't noticed that yet when I talked to their son."

Sgt. Dole stepped forward to read the blood-speckled note. He looked at the bodies again and shook his head. "What would make people do something like this? Nothing's that bad, is it?"

I assumed the questions were rhetorical, although I agreed

with Sgt. Dole's implication. Nothing warranted *this*. I remembered my own despair when our son, Colin, died in an overseas ferry accident while he was in the service, his body never recovered. For a time, life had hardly seemed worth living. But I'd had the Lord to lean on, and he'd carried me through, as he always does if we let him. Which the Northcutts, whatever their troubles, apparently had not.

Sgt. Dole extracted a cell phone from an assortment of police equipment on his belt. He moved toward the fresher air and turned his back to us as he spoke into the phone, but I could still hear most of his end of the conversation.

"Yeah, the Northcutts, those movie people out here at the old Morris lodge . . . What? Yeah, gun's right here, a .38 it looks like . . . right. About like that old couple out on Webley Road four, five years ago. Remember them? Except the wife was the one who pulled the trigger that time . . . What? . . . Yeah, cancer or something that one was, I think. At least this time the note's typed and more readable, with everything spelled right." Sgt. Dole chuckled, as if some inside joke was involved here.

The possibility of illness hadn't occurred to me. Had one of the Northcutts been painfully, perhaps terminally ill?

Sgt. Dole glanced back at the bodies, apparently in response to another question. "I'd guess two or three days. Though it could be less. It's warm in here, and you know what that does to a body. Not pretty."

Still on the cell phone, he looked at his watch again. "I wanted to get out to talk to that Watson kid who was a friend of Eddie's. He's been dodging me for three days. But I guess it'll have to wait if the ME can't get here right away." He rubbed the back of his neck as if frustrated by the delay.

"They're contacting the medical examiner," Sgt. Dole said when he turned back to us. "But he's out at the rollover site now, so it's hard to tell how long it'll take him to get here.

Going to be rough on local folks, losing two fine young men so close together."

"But this second death was an accident, wasn't it, not like the murder of the sheriff's nephew?"

"An accident just waiting to happen. You can't believe where some of these kids try to take their four-wheel drives and dirt bikes. Places I wouldn't tackle with anything but a helicopter. But they think they're invincible at that age." Sgt. Dole shook his head. "This kid's Jeep rolled down an embankment and threw him a good hundred feet. The medical examiner may have to put the poor kid back together before he can autopsy him. But at least we can wrap this one up quick," he said as he nodded toward the bodies on the sofa.

"Will the Northcutts' bodies also be autopsied?"

"Probably, unless the family has some big objections. Although it doesn't take an expert and a bunch of lab tests to figure out what happened here. They obviously didn't die of infected toenails or eating tainted potato salad. Right, Mike?"

Sgt. Dole's answer to my question had been pleasant enough, if a bit morbidly facetious, but I detected a smirk and note of hostility when he addressed his partner.

"I would assume an autopsy would be standard procedure in a situation such as this," the younger deputy said, his manner stiff.

"'Cause that's how they'd do it back in Chicago, right? See, we're not as backward here in Hickville as you thought." Sgt. Dole laughed and spoke an aside to me in mock confidential tones. "Mike was formerly with the Chicago police force. He just recently joined our little department, and he gets frustrated with our slow-movin', backward country ways."

Deputy Hamilton looked as if he'd like to drop one of

those antlered chandeliers on Sgt. Dole's head, but he didn't say anything. Me, I was curious about what had brought a young, big-city police officer to rural Oklahoma.

"And even if we aren't as high-powered as those hotshots on the Chicago force, we get the job done." Sgt. Dole nodded. "You can bet your electropherogram and your mass spectrometry and all your other high-powered techniques that we're gonna nail Eddie's killer. Old-fashioned legwork is still what matters most."

"I'm a strong believer in legwork. And I'm sure we'll get the killer."

I wondered if Sgt. Dole caught Deputy Hamilton's meaningful inflection on *we*, as if the younger man were subtly reminding the older one that he was part of *this* force now.

The whole exchange irked me. This was no time for personal infighting. We had two dead bodies here. Sgt. Dole's conversation with the sheriff's department headquarters indicated he thought what had happened here was exactly what it looked like: Jock Northcutt had killed his wife and then himself, a mutually agreed upon homicide/suicide. But it also seemed to me that there were questions that shouldn't be ignored, just in case.

"Will a comparison be made between the bullets that caused the deaths and the gun there on the sofa?" I asked.

Sgt. Dole's head jerked around as if to ask, *Where else do you think the bullets came from? Serial killer hiding up in the rafters with an Uzi?* "Big city police forces may have the time and money for frivolous investigations—" Here a meaningful glance in Deputy Hamilton's direction. "But we don't. We have our hands full with Eddie Howell's murder where we *don't* know where the bullet came from."

"But maybe *this* is murder. Murder has been made to look like suicide."

My mouth dropped open in surprise. Even though I'd

tried to discard it, that was exactly what had been niggling in the back of my mind. But I wasn't the one who said it. The two officers and I all turned to look at Abilene. I hadn't realized she'd slipped in behind us. I was almost as surprised that she said anything at all as by what she said. I was certain that drawing attention to herself was the last thing she wanted.

And draw attention was exactly what her comment did. Both officers studied her appraisingly, but this time she kept her chin high and met their gazes without faltering. "I know it looks like the man killed the woman and then himself, and probably that's what happened. But maybe not."

I took a step forward. "There are some oddities in the situation," I pointed out in support of her statement.

Sgt. Dole's gaze flicked to me. "Such as?"

"Doesn't it seem odd that a man who loves his wife would shoot her in the throat?"

"You think there's a polite, considerate way to shoot someone?"

"No, but wouldn't a head shot be more appropriate? Something probably quicker than . . . bleeding to death?"

"People in a suicidal state of mind don't necessarily consider the fine details. Or, under the circumstances, his hand may have been too unsteady for an accurate shot. And if he didn't happen to know much about guns—"

"I think he knew a lot about guns. Probably they both did. There's a cabinet full of them in the bedroom."

I could see "How do you know that?" coming as the next question, and I rushed on like one of those high-speed speakers giving details in a radio ad. "Shouldn't an expert be called in to determine if the handwriting on the suicide note is authentic? Shouldn't Mr. Northcutt's hands be checked for gunshot residue? I don't suppose it's *probable*, but it's *possible* he didn't fire the shots and someone just set it up to look as if he did. That someone else murdered both of them."

Sgt. Dole looked at me as if I'd just suggested one of the emus had sneaked in and assassinated the Northcutts, but his voice was patient when he said, "Gunshot residue tests aren't as reliable as many people think. Gunshot residue has been known to show up when a gun was merely fired in the vicinity of someone's hand, but not necessarily fired *by* that hand."

Okay, I'd read that somewhere too. "But two shots were obviously fired, and if Mr. Northcutt's hands show *no* gunshot residue—"

"Residue can also deteriorate in a fairly short time, so that wouldn't necessarily prove anything." Sgt. Dole frowned as if he was annoyed with himself for giving this murder scenario even minimal credibility by arguing with me. But he was still polite and somewhat resigned sounding when he added, "Deputy Hamilton or I will be present at the autopsy, Mrs. Malone. We'll keep your concerns in mind. But at this point I see nothing to suggest anything other than exactly what the note says, a suicide pact."

I felt a little foolish then. Did police officers often have to cope with amateurs who thought they were experts because they'd watched a few too many TV cop shows?

"There is one other thing," I added almost reluctantly. "I'm almost certain when I was here yesterday that I heard a noise inside the house. But the Northcutts were surely already dead then."

"Old houses creak and groan. In heat, they sometimes even snap and pop."

"Also, I think the chain and padlock on the gate may have been different today than yesterday, as if someone had been in or out."

Sgt. Dole didn't sigh out loud, but I suspected he did a mental sigh. "We'll see what Sheriff Howell says."

Now that I was really thinking about it, there were other points that interested me. Why had the Northcutts called 911 a couple of times, as their son said they'd done? Had there been trespassers on the property? Or threats? Why did they own such an impressive arsenal, if not for protection from some danger?

"I could check out the gun cabinet and dust for fingerprints," the younger man, Deputy Hamilton, suggested. "Photos of the scene might also be helpful."

Sgt. Dole's verbal response was cooperative. "Sure. Cover all bases." But something in his attitude said he thought Deputy Hamilton was playing big-time Chicago cop and wasting time with frivolous investigation.

"I'll go get the camera."

Sgt. Dole once more looked at his watch when Deputy Hamilton left. "No need for you two to hang around any longer. But keep yourselves available in case we need to talk to you again."

"Available how?" I said.

"A phone number will do." He pulled a notebook out of a pocket.

"No phone," I said.

"An address then."

"Sorry. No address either."

Sgt. Dole frowned at me as if he thought I was playing games, and he was not in a game-playing mood. "You're telling me you're homeless?"

"No, we're not *homeless*. We live in the motor home, the one parked out there by the gate. We just don't have any . . . fixed place of residence."

I didn't say Abilene and I had always been together, but I used "we" as if we had. Abilene might be nine inches taller and thirty or forty pounds heavier, but I felt protective of her.

Sgt. Dole gave our no-phone-no-address status a frown and then said, "I'll need to see some identification, please."

"I left my purse and driver's license and everything in the motor home. I'll have to go get it."

Sgt. Dole looked pointedly at Abilene. I had the impression that it was her identity more than mine that really interested him anyway. She, with obvious reluctance, extracted the leather pouch and loosened the drawstring. She pulled out a small card and handed it to him.

He glanced at it. "I need something other than a Social Security card. Something with photo identification, please, Ms.—" He looked at the card again. "Ms. Morrison."

I looked at Abilene sharply. Ms. Morrison?

"I don't have a driver's license."

No driver's license?

"The Social Security card is all I have," she added.

"I see. I think you'd both better hang around for a while, then." He wrote the name and number from the Social Security card in his little notebook and handed the card back to Abilene. I had the feeling this would shortly be run through some criminal database.

"Ivy Malone," I put in helpfully. I rattled off my own Social Security number, as if this were some standard system of handling identification, although I knew it wasn't. He wrote both down, though I doubted he had much interest in me or my number. "I'll run on out to the motor home and get my identification."

"You stay here." Sgt. Dole pointed a commanding forefinger at Abilene, as if he suspected that once she got to the motor home she might just keep going.

"I'd appreciate it if Abilene could come with me. The heat and stress and all, you know." I gave a genteel flutter of fingertips that suggested I might go into a swoon at any moment.

I'd asked for Abilene's company partly for her benefit, because I doubted she wanted to be left alone with officers asking nosy questions. Partly for my own benefit, because, who knows? Maybe I would feel swoonish in the heat.

But mostly I'd asked because there were a whole lot of questions I wanted to ask Abilene myself.

10

Sgt. Dole muttered something that didn't sound particularly gracious, but he didn't stop Abilene when I started toward the door and motioned her to follow. Along the way we met Deputy Hamilton coming in with a camera and what I thought might be a kit for dusting for latent fingerprints. He didn't say anything, but he gave us a friendly smile.

I waited until we were around the bend in the green tunnel before jumping into my questions for Abilene. She was walking along with her head down and thumbs jammed in her front pockets, apparently not intending to bring up the subject herself.

"Okay, now, about these names. Tyler and Morrison. What's going on here? Which is it?"

Her chin flew up with that hint of stubbornness I was beginning to recognize. "I was under the impression a person could call herself whatever she wanted. I read that somewhere in a book. That it's okay as long as it isn't for criminal purposes."

"Then perhaps we'd better talk a little more about what's *criminal*. You were in a car accident, right?"

She nodded.

"You were driving?"

Her chin dropped a fraction of an inch. She knew where this conversation was heading. Another nod.

"But you don't have a driver's license."

"No."

"The law says you can't legally drive unless you have a driver's license."

"I know. And I know I shouldn't have been driving. But I . . . I didn't know what else to do. I know when you asked earlier if I'd done something criminal, I said I hadn't. I was thinking of crimes like bank robbery or holding up a gas station. Or murder. And I never did any of those." Another drop of chin. "But, since I was driving without a license, I guess I should have said yes, I did do something criminal."

I figured this needed further discussion, but first things first. "Okay, let's get back to these names. Which is it, Morrison or Tyler?"

"Well, both, sort of. Tyler is on my birth certificate, but I've never used it. I went by my stepfather's name all the time I was growing up."

"And his name is Morrison?"

"No, his name is Grigley. Tom Grigley."

Getting answers out of Abilene felt rather like trying to extract nails with my teeth. "So Morrison is . . . ?"

"My husband's name."

I stopped short right there in the middle of the green tunnel and stared at her. "You're married?"

"That's what having a husband usually means," she muttered.

"And he's . . . where?"

"Back in Texas, I guess. Unless he's . . . around here some-

85

where." She peered toward the underbrush as if afraid he might be peering back.

"You're . . . umm . . . separated, I take it?"

"I guess you could call it that."

"What would *you* call it?"

"I . . . left him."

She met my eyes and said the words defiantly, as if daring me to challenge her, but what I did was look at those black eyes and bruises with an awful truth dawning.

"He did this to you?"

She hesitated, and for a minute I thought she was going to invent some story about falling down steps or running into a door, but instead she warily issued a part-truth. "I got one black eye and twisted my hip in the accident."

"But the other black eye, the earlier one, and all the bruises and sore shoulder, he did all that?"

She hesitated but finally nodded, her gaze focused on the road again. I could see the shame, like a sludge oozing through her, as if this was somehow her fault.

"Don't, Abilene." I grabbed her upper arms—I had to reach up to do it—and yanked her around to face me. "Don't blame yourself. Not ever. Whatever he did to you is not your fault. No man has the right to do something like this to his wife. You must not blame yourself. How long has he been doing this?"

"Since a couple months after we got married."

"I take it you had no idea what kind of man he was before you married him?"

I still didn't blame her. I still felt horrified and appalled at what the man had done. But I was also a bit exasperated. Starry-eyed kids these days, rebelliously rushing into marriage before they know the most basic things about each other . . .

Abilene bluntly pulled the plug on that thought.

"I didn't know anything about him before we got married. I'd never seen him before my folks took me down to Texas and we met him at a courthouse to get a license."

I was still sprinting on my self-righteous agenda of young people's irresponsibility. "You mean it was some kind of Internet thing? You met him on the Internet and decided to marry him without—"

"I never *decided* to marry him at all. He was a friend of my stepfather's, somebody Tom knew when he worked in Texas for a while. Tom and my mother decided I should marry him. Tom always resented me, and I think he figured this was a good way to get rid of me. Usually my mother smoothed things over and didn't let him do anything too awful to me." She stopped and swallowed. "But this time she went along with him. They yanked me out of school in Kansas and took me down there, and a justice of the peace married us."

"But . . . but that's archaic! People don't do things like that these days. At least not in this country. Parents don't decide who their children are going to marry, and then just . . . drag them into it."

"Mine did."

So much for my mistaken scenario of youthful irresponsibility. I felt a big whap of guilt for *my* irresponsible judgment without knowing the facts. "How old were you?"

"Sixteen."

Sixteen when she'd married him. Twenty-two now. Six years the man had been abusing her. She held out her left arm. A ridge bulged just above the wrist.

"He broke it there once. He said I didn't need to go to the doctor, so I just wrapped it as tight as I could in an Ace bandage. I didn't have any way to get to town to a doctor. I-I don't think it healed quite right."

I was so horrified, so appalled that all I could do was look at her. She mistook the look.

"I know. You're going to tell me that I have to go back to him. That I should be a better wife, and then he wouldn't have so many reasons to get mad at me."

"Why in the world would I say that?"

"It's what my stepfather said when I called home and told them after the third time Boone hit me."

I shook my head. "Child, all *I* can say is, what took you so long to leave him?"

We were still standing there in the middle of the gravel driveway. A line of ants marching back and forth across the road had now included my foot in their pathway. An unseen bird chirped with incongruous cheerfulness somewhere in the brush. All very normal, and yet I felt I was peering into a dark world I'd only heard about before. No doubt I've lived a sheltered life, but I'd never before personally known a woman who was physically abused by her husband. Now I knew why Abilene's eyes looked so old. Abuse had aged her on the inside.

She gave me a long, searching look as if she was uncertain whether to trust me. Finally she pulled on the cord around her neck and brought out the leather pouch again. This time she dug out a small photo and handed it to me.

Three children, a boy and two girls, all blond and fair-skinned like Abilene. Their ages appeared to be close together, all under five. Adorable kids but somehow frail and vulnerable looking.

I blinked. "You're a mother? With three children?"

"They called me Mom. I love them like they're my own." She sounded unexpectedly fierce, as if she'd protect them with her life. Which, it dawned on me, she probably had.

"Randy was four when Boone and I got married. Lily was three and Alisha only two. The picture was taken way back then, but it's the only one I have. Randy is ten now, Lily nine, and Alisha eight."

"They're why you couldn't leave even if your husband was abusing you."

"The first time Boone hit me, I was ready to walk out right then. I packed a suitcase and headed for the door. I wasn't about to take what he was dishing out no matter what my folks thought. We were twelve miles from town, but I figured if I had to crawl to the bus station to get away, I'd do it. Then Randy started crying because I was leaving, and Boone hit him and . . . and knocked him clear across the room." Abilene's throat moved in a convulsive swallow. "Then I was . . . afraid to leave."

Afraid for the kids. Afraid of what he'd do to them if she wasn't there to protect them.

"Usually he left them alone when he was on one of his rampages. He'd come after me instead. Which was fine. *Fine*," she repeated with that same fierceness. "Though sometimes, if he was mad enough or drunk enough, he went after them too. That was how I got the broken arm. Because I-I told him he'd have to kill me before I'd let him keep beating on Randy with his belt the way he was doing. He said killing me would be fine and maybe someday he'd do it, but right then he settled for holding my arm over the edge of the table and breaking it. But he stopped beating on Randy," she added with that same protective fierceness.

"Oh, Abilene . . ." My body ached with her pain, physical, mental, and emotional. "Wasn't there something you could do? Go to the authorities?"

"The sheriff down there is Boone's cousin. They hunt jackrabbits and rattlesnakes together. I think he knocks his wife around too. Sometimes I thought about taking the kids and just running with them. But they're Boone's kids, not mine, and I knew I'd never get away with it. So I just stayed and . . . did the best I could for them."

Putting herself between them and their father's brutality.

"But I didn't feel like that at first," she said almost angrily, as if she didn't want me to mistake her for some noble martyr. "At first I just resented the kids. I blamed them for everything. For my having to live in a rundown old trailer with a man I didn't love. Struggling to cook on an old stove with only two burners that worked. Trying to do laundry when the well pump kept breaking down. Coping with all their colds and earaches and Alisha's allergies. Because if it weren't for them I wouldn't have been dragged into marrying Boone." She sounded miserable and ashamed and guilty.

"It was a lot to cope with. And you weren't much more than a child yourself."

"But after a while I knew who was really to blame. Boone. Boone and his bad temper and meanness and stinginess and drinking. And then I just wanted to protect them."

Because she loved them, with a love that was so apparent when she took the photo back from me as if it were the most precious thing she owned. Which it probably was. "What about the children's mother? Where was she? Or was Boone a widower?"

"No. She . . . wasn't around."

"You mean she just walked out and left her children behind?"

"That's what I thought for a long time. Boone talked about her as if she were . . . dirt. But a few months ago I found out differently. Boone beat her too, but she took it worse than I did, I guess. She had a mental breakdown. He divorced her while she was in some institution, and got the kids."

Great guy. Abuse his wife, then take away her kids after he'd driven her into a breakdown. "So then he needed a new mother for them, and you were elected."

She nodded. "I hate Boone. I suppose as a Christian you think that's terrible and I should just forgive him. But I hate him." Her jaw and fists clenched, and the sheen of perspiration on her forehead wasn't just from the heat. "I'm glad I was there for the kids when they needed me. But I'm glad I'm away from him now."

"You finally decided that even for the sake of the kids you couldn't stay?"

Her eyes flashed as she looked at me, as if my assumption bordered on blasphemy. "No, I'd never do that! I'd never leave them at Boone's mercy. *Never.* MaryLou, that's Boone's ex-wife, finally got out of whatever institution she was in. She remarried a year or so ago. A good man. They got a lawyer. A very good lawyer." She smiled with a hint of grim satisfaction. "A few months ago they filed a lawsuit to get the kids. And they got them." Abilene's eyes brimmed with tears, and I knew the tears were for her own loss, losing the kids she loved. But there was no regret or resentment in the words.

I squeezed her hand, not knowing how to comfort her.

"I-I miss them. I miss them so much. But I'm glad she got them. They're better off with her and her husband. Boone can't hurt them now. And MaryLou told me I could visit if I wanted."

"Will you do it?"

"I'd like to sometime. But they're way back in Kentucky."

"What did Boone say about his ex-wife getting the kids?"

"He blamed me. He said if I'd been a better wife and mother, he wouldn't have lost them. He was in a rage after I testified at the court hearing."

"Testified against him?"

"Not exactly against him. But I told the truth. On the way home, he hit me in the face with the can of beer he was drinking." She touched her nose. This hadn't been long ago. Her nose was still a bit swollen. "He said he ought to kill me right then and there. And he would. Soon."

"Did you tell him you were leaving?"

"No."

"How did you manage to get away without his knowing?"

"I'd been saving a little money here and there, trying to get enough to take Randy to a dentist. His teeth were in terrible shape, but Boone said it didn't matter, they were just baby teeth and would fall out anyway."

Still thinking only about the kids, not her own needs.

"So after the kids were gone I packed a few things and took the money and sneaked out in the middle of the night while Boone was asleep." She touched the leather pouch safely hidden beneath her clothes again, as if to reassure herself the money was still there.

Abilene seemed a bit dazed now, and I knew she'd never told all this to anyone before. I put my arm around her waist, and we started walking toward the motor home. It's modest, as motor homes go, certainly no big luxury model, but now it looked like a haven of safety basking in sunshine there at the end of the green tunnel. Abilene didn't really lean on me physically as we walked, but I could feel another kind of leaning. *Lord, help me to help her!*

We reached the motor home, and I started fixing iced tea. Abilene sat on the sofa, absentmindedly fingering a straggly spike of hair behind one ear. I'd been wondering ever since we first met about that strange haircut.

"Boone liked your hair short?" I asked.

She stretched the strand out to what there was of its full length. "He hated it short."

"So that's why you cut it short?"

"No. It was long when we got married, and it got almost down to my waist. It . . . it was the only thing about me he ever seemed proud of. The only thing he ever complimented me on. So I kept it that length even when he grabbed it a couple of times and used it to swing me around and hurt me."

"Oh, child . . ." Desperately needing approval even as she was abused.

"But then he did it again a few weeks ago when he was mad about my saying something 'smart-alecky' to him, and I . . . I vowed he was never going to do it again. I went out to the barn and whacked it off with the electric horse clippers." She touched another ragged strand at her temple. "I guess I got it kind of . . . uneven."

I had to smile in spite of my fresh shock at this new revelation about Boone. A bad clip job on a hedge is *uneven*; Abilene's hair looked like the graph on an earthquake. "Maybe you'll want to let it grow again now."

"Maybe I will."

I handed her the glass of iced tea, and she pressed the cold glass against her forehead for a moment before taking a sip. Her driving without a license didn't seem important now, but I did wonder why she didn't have a license.

"You had a driver's license, but . . . ?" I waited for her to fill in the blanks.

"No, I never had one. Boone wouldn't let me." Koop was already in her lap, purring madly. "He said I didn't need to go anywhere without him, so I didn't need to know how to drive."

"So you didn't even know how to drive when you took off in the middle of the night to get away from him?"

"Well, I kind of know how," she said, her tone defensive. "I drove the old tractor we had for farm work lots of times. But Boone wouldn't let me drive anything else, and driving a car out on the highway turned out to be different than driving the old tractor. A jackrabbit ran across the road, and I lost control trying to miss it. I ran off the road and hit a tree." She smiled ruefully. "I think there was only one tree in that whole county, and I hit it."

"The car?"

"I'm pretty sure it was totaled."

"But you walked away." Not unscathed, but walking. "The Lord must have been looking out for you."

She lifted her head in surprise. "Why would he look out for me?"

"For one thing, he loves and cares about all of us. And maybe he appreciates what you did for three little kids."

"I never took the kids to Sunday school." Abilene shook her head, not one to take credit for something she hadn't done. "I never read them Bible stories or said prayers or told them anything about God." She hesitated a moment. "I don't even know much of anything about God."

"Could you have done any of those things if you'd wanted to?"

"No. Boone was dead set against anything to do with church." But she still looked troubled that she hadn't fulfilled her duties as a mother. Then her blue eyes brightened. "But MaryLou will! She said it was really her faith that got the kids back, and she'll take them to Sunday school. And the dentist too, and give them birthday parties and shoes that fit."

"So they're in good hands and you're free. Maybe it's kind of a happy ending after all."

Abilene managed a wry smile. "Except for Boone's car."

"Does he know it's wrecked?"

"I'd planned to drive it maybe three or four hundred miles, park it at a mall or Wal-Mart parking lot or somewhere like that, and send him a postcard telling him where it was. I knew he'd be boilin' mad, but I figured if he got his car back he wouldn't care much about my leaving."

"But you told him the car was wrecked, and he *was* boiling mad."

"Maybe I should have told him it was wrecked, but I-I didn't. I was afraid it would take too long for a postcard to get there, so I called and told him where the car was. I decided I'd just let the fact that the car was now shaped like a red horseshoe around a tree be a surprise to him." Her smile was grimly humorless.

"You also figured when he got to the car and found it wrecked that he'd send the authorities after you. That's why you're so nervous around the police."

She nodded. "But I was even more afraid if Boone found me there with the car he'd kill me on the spot. That's why I started walking and hitchhiking. I know it isn't safe. But I figured it was safer than being around when Boone got there."

She pushed the curtain aside and peered down the road toward town.

"You think he might be trying to track you down now?"

"Boone gets even with people. Always. I know he slashed tires on the car of a guy he had an argument with. He got fired from a car repair shop one time. It burned down a few weeks later. Nothing ever came of it. But he did it. I heard him and his brother laughing about it. He wouldn't mind killing me. He wouldn't mind killing me at all," she repeated with a tremor in her voice.

In some other situation I might have found such a statement melodramatic and unbelievable, but with what I'd already heard of Boone I had no doubt Abilene's worries were justified. The man sounded capable of almost anything. A brother in kind, if not in blood, with the murderous Braxtons.

But still, the situations were rather different. The Braxtons' brother had gone to prison because of me. "But it is just a car," I pointed out. "Would he really try to track you down because of a car?"

"Not 'just a car.'" Another of those grim smiles. "At least not to Boone. It's a Porsche. And he's had it less than a year."

"A Porsche?"

"A Porsche 911 Carrera, to be exact. He loves that car like . . . like some men love their wife and kids, I guess. He was always polishing it. He had the whole door repainted when it got a nick you could barely see. Lily threw a ball that accidentally hit the car one time, and he grabbed her and shook her so hard her . . . her eyes rolled back in her head. I'd never have taken his precious Porsche if there was any other way, but I couldn't get away from him on the tractor."

"How did he manage to get a Porsche? They aren't exactly cheap."

"His dad died. Each of the sons wound up with quite a lot of money. I never knew exactly how much. But I was hoping we could buy a new mobile home, one of those nice double wides. So the kids could have bedrooms of their own, and we'd have a kitchen stove that worked. I thought we could get Randy's teeth fixed, and take Alisha to an allergy specialist."

"But Boone bought a new Porsche instead."

"With all the options."

My sense of Christian love and charity is sorely tried by someone like Boone Morrison. In spite of the afternoon warmth in the motor home, Abilene suddenly shivered, and I knew she was thinking about Boone coming after her. But a bright thought suddenly occurred to me.

"You said the car was less than a year old. Was it insured?"

"I don't know. Boone took care of things like that. I couldn't even write a check. My name wasn't on the bank account."

"So surely he'd insure his most prized possession. And now he can take the insurance money and buy himself a new Porsche!"

"I never thought of that. Hey, I guess he can!" Abilene's back straightened as if the weight of the Porsche was sliding off her shoulders. Her eyes lit up. "By the time he gets a new Porsche, he won't care enough to come after me. By then he'll be saying 'good riddance,' happy I'm gone!"

Even though it was midafternoon, neither of us had been hungry before, but with this upturn in Abilene's future prospects, I suggested sandwiches. Abilene was no chatterer, but she talked while we ate, about everything from the kids to people she'd gotten rides with while hitchhiking to the emus.

I was pleased that the insurance idea had relieved her worries about Boone coming after her with murder on his mind. But I wasn't so sure everything was hunky-dory just yet.

Had Boone reported the Porsche stolen? What happened when Sgt. Dole ran Abilene's name through official channels? And what about driving without a license and wrecking a car?

After we finished eating, I debated with myself about driving back to the house. I was curious about what Sgt. Dole and Deputy Hamilton were doing there, of course, but I didn't want to expose Abilene to more of Sgt. Dole's probing. I had the impression that the investigation into the murder of the sheriff's nephew had considerably higher priority than Abilene's lack of proper identification or even the Northcutts' deaths, and maybe, if we kept a low profile, running her name through some "wanted" system would slip his mind.

I also considered just picking up and leaving. That had a definite appeal, and maybe it would work. Sgt. Dole might figure looking for us wasn't worth the bother. But my ever-vigilant conscience nixed that. Sgt. Dole, the Law, had told us to stick around. Although I had to admit that another reason for staying was my curiosity about Frank Northcutt. He'd been ready enough to accept the possibility that his parents may have been murdered, with Ute a star suspect. Would he be as ready to accept the suicide-pact assumption?

So what we did was get out the lawn chairs, set them up on the shady side of the motor home, and wait to see what happened. Koop played mighty hunter chasing grasshoppers. A plane too high to see left a graceful jet trail across cloudless blue sky. Abilene and I sipped more iced tea. She seemed considerably more at ease now, probably because she no longer feared Boone might be coming after her. But also, I suspected, because she'd shared her secrets and had nothing more to hide.

It was almost 4:00 when a gray-haired man in a white car, two men in a van, and another police car drove by. I took this to be the medical examiner in the car, with the van for transporting the bodies. No sign of the son yet, which made me wonder just how far he had to travel.

We watched the entourage disappear around the bend in the green tunnel.

"What do you think?" Abilene asked.

The question came out of nowhere, but I didn't have to ask what she was referring to. "I suppose it's what it looks like. The Northcutts made a pact. Jock Northcutt shot his wife, then himself. Sgt. Dole doesn't seem to have any doubts." Although I wasn't so certain about Deputy Hamilton. I gave her a curious glance. "Why do *you* think it might not be a suicide pact?"

She twisted the iced-tea glass on her jeans. "I probably shouldn't have said anything. It's kind of embarrassing."

"Embarrassing?"

"I could never go to the library in town, but twice a month a bookmobile came out to the rural areas. I read some classic stuff that Mrs. Burton—she's the one who drove the bookmobile—said I should. And I like books on interesting places and people. But what I really like best are mysteries." Sounding guilty, she added, "Murder mysteries."

"Me too."

"You?" She turned in the lawn chair to look at me as if I'd just confessed to a secret vice, maybe a hobby of pickpocketing in my spare time. "Really?"

"Really. I've been reading them for years. Cozies. Suspense. Thrillers. Hard-boiled detectives. Lady sleuths. Everything from Nancy Drew, way back when, to Mrs. Pollifax in the seventies to Kinsey Millhone now. And now there are even some great writers doing Christian mysteries and suspense."

"Did you ever read one where murder had been set up to look like suicide?" she asked.

"Oh yes. I remember one called *The Noose Knows*. That was a murder, a hanging, made to look like suicide. Very cleverly done, as I recall."

"Hey, I read that one!" Abilene sounded astonished at this unexpected meeting of the minds. "And it worked too, until the guy's fiancée figured it out. Remember? Something about one of his shoes."

"There was another one, I don't remember the title, but it was a drowning set up to look like suicide. And one had a husband who pushed his wife out a tenth story window and made it look like she'd jumped."

"Oh, I remember that one. He did it at a masquerade party, and she was wearing a Wonder Woman outfit. He tried to claim she was high on something and thought she could fly. It was by, oh, what's her name, the same one who writes those Jetta Diamond mysteries—"

"Samantha Kruger," I said.

We looked at each other in unexpected delight, two people who've just discovered that, in spite of major chasms in age, background, and beliefs, they're sisters under the skin.

Abilene settled back in the lawn chair, frown lines between her eyes. "But those were all made-up stories. Maybe things like that don't happen in real life."

"From what I've heard, fiction writers often use a real

situation as the germ of a story and then build on it. And you know the old saying: truth is stranger than fiction."

"But is it?"

"You see in the news every once in a while how someone has tried to disguise a crime as something else, usually an accident. Some people get quite creative. So who knows how many times disguising a murder as suicide in real life has worked, and the truth was never discovered?"

She nodded slowly. "The authorities decided the fire Boone set was an accident." She gave a snort of humorless laughter. "Of course, since his cousin the sheriff was the one doing the investigating, that wasn't any big surprise."

"Boone didn't mind your reading mysteries?"

"Boone didn't like my reading *anything*. He said it was a big waste of time. Unlike his boxing, football, hockey, car racing, and every other sport on TV, of course. He didn't even like my reading to the kids." Her eyes unexpectedly glinted with mischief. "But I think he objected to mysteries most of all because he was afraid they'd give me ideas about how to kill him."

"Did they?"

"Well, I read one about using rat poison that sounded workable," she admitted. "But there's a big difference between thinking about how something could be done and actually doing it." She was smiling when she mentioned the rat-poison book, but suddenly her jaw hardened. "But if I'd *had* to do something desperate to protect the kids . . ."

Her voice trailed off, and I figured this was a good time to let this subject drop. She hadn't done Boone in, and the kids were safe with their mother now.

We had to move our chairs around the motor home as the shade shifted. Koop gave up on grasshoppers and found a cool spot under a bush to snooze. Finally, after an hour and a half, the vehicles exited. Sgt. Dole and Deputy Hamilton brought up the rear of the parade. Sgt. Dole stopped the car beside the motor home.

"Everything okay?" I inquired.

"We may need to talk to you again after the autopsy, so you'll have to stay in the area. There are several RV parks out around the lake. You can call the office and leave word where we can reach you."

"But the emus need to be fed and watered," Abilene said.

"We were thinking we might park in the yard until the Northcutts' son arrives. We can keep an eye on things and feed the emus," I added.

Sgt. Dole's quick glance suggested that leaving the two of us to guard anything was probably as effective as building a fence out of spider webs, but all he said was, "I can't give you permission to use someone else's property."

"But it isn't as if it's a crime scene," I pointed out. Silent question at the end of that statement: or is it?

Sgt. Dole hesitated a minute longer. "Just don't go near the house. And tell Frank Northcutt to get in touch with us immediately when he arrives. I tried to call his home number but didn't get any answer, so he must be on the road."

It wasn't actually *permission*, and it didn't specifically answer my crime-scene question, but he wasn't kicking us out.

The car zipped off to catch up with the other vehicles. Abilene and I put the lawn chairs away, collected Koop from under the bush, and drove back down to the house. I parked the motor home under a big oak. It would have been nice if we had some place to plug into electricity, but we could manage without it. Though I'd have to find some place soon to dump the holding tanks.

No strips of yellow plastic marked the house as a crime scene, which I assumed meant that the medical examiner agreed the Northcutts' deaths were what they appeared, a suicide pact. Although, technically, there was a crime, of course. Jock Northcutt had killed his wife. Did their complicity in the pact, and his immediately taking his own life, kind of cancel out the crime element?

One of the emus appeared to be walking with a limp, and Abilene, bolder than I, went into the fenced-in area with them and inspected the foot. Toe. Claw. Whatever. All the other emus crowded around to watch. She found a pebble trapped under a toenail and removed it. The bright-eyed emu pecked curiously at her shoelaces. Abilene scratched her/him/it under the chin, and it stretched out its neck in what I took to be emu ecstasy.

I fixed chicken stir-fry for dinner, and we ate outside by the motor home. In spite of the violent deaths, the place seemed peaceful now. Following Sgt. Dole's orders, we didn't go near the house, but Abilene wandered around, checking out the other buildings, all of which, except the somewhat tumbledown old barn, were securely locked. She had a curiosity gene of her own, I realized, plus a youthful boldness that took her places I probably wouldn't venture.

One of which was out in the woods. She disappeared long enough to give me mild alarm, but returned to ask if I had a flashlight.

"Why do you need a flashlight?" The evening was into dusky shadows, along with a few mosquitoes, but it wasn't dark yet. I could still see my watch.

"It's darker out in the woods, and I saw something I want to check out."

"Can't it wait until morning?"

"You don't need to come."

Which meant, of course, that after I located the flashlight, there was no way I was going to be left behind.

We didn't need the flashlight immediately. It was darker in the underbrush and trees, but a trail of sorts wound through the tangle. About every three steps I had to stop and disengage my hair or clothes from some clutching branch or bush. Once Abilene turned the flashlight on to help me get untangled, and I jumped when the beam hit a blob of red on a tree beside me.

"Is that blood?" I gasped, afraid we were about to stumble on more bodies.

"I don't think so. I'm not sure what it is, maybe some kind of paint, but I'm pretty sure it isn't blood. There are some blue and pink blobs too."

"I wonder what it's for?"

"Maybe they were marking the trees for some reason."

Although that seemed unlikely, considering that I also got whapped with a thorny bush blotched with red streaks, and then I started seeing these odd little things on the ground that looked like colorful bits of broken eggshell.

A few hundred feet beyond the clearing around the house, the ground sloped downward, quite steeply in places, and I had to grab bushy branches to keep my feet from sliding out from under me. The air felt cooler and damper, with a faint scent of soggy earth and rotting vegetation. At the bottom of the slope the ground was not quite puddled but definitely squishy. Several times we had to step over trees that had fallen and were in various stages of decay. Once, something unseen crashed through the brush.

"Probably a deer," Abilene said.

Yeah. Probably.

Another dozen feet and Abilene stopped short. She turned on the flashlight. "There."

I peered around her. The beam of light gleamed on patches of dark, swampy water separated by virulent-looking islands of green scum. Unfamiliar, large-leafed plants pushed through the stagnant surface like malignant growths. An enormous spider web hung between two of them. The kind of place where you half expect something of the Jurassic Park variety, with bared claws and too many teeth, to leap out at you.

Nothing toothy rose up, but in the dark mud at the edge of the water I saw what Abilene was targeting with the flashlight.

A footprint.

A *bare* footprint.

A *large*, bare footprint.

"That's the only one?" I asked.

"That's it. One footprint." She tittered uneasily. "I looked around for a large-footed, one-legged skulker, but I haven't spotted anyone yet."

"You thought you saw something moving out in the woods earlier. Maybe it was this same person," I said. "Perhaps we can't see other footprints because they're down in the water."

A reasonable possibility, but the lone footprint here in the mud felt eerily disembodied. It looked as if it may have been made within the last few minutes . . . or been hidden in these shadowy woods since the dawn of time.

"So what was he doing out here? Where did he come from? Where did he go?" Abilene asked.

"Watching us" was the obvious and not reassuring answer to her first question. As for the others . . .

Something rustled, and Abilene arced the beam of light into the branches above us.

Nothing.

Or at least nothing we could see. But I couldn't help remembering that tawny skin with an oversupply of claws draped over the railing in the house. Which had once upon a time undoubtedly prowled out here, live and predatory.

Abilene swiveled the beam of light back to the footprint. "Do you think we should tell anyone?"

"I doubt Sgt. Dole would be interested. It's probably just some nosy neighbor snooping around. Or maybe some kids playing back in here. Wouldn't you have liked to play in a creepy place like this when you were a kid?"

Abilene didn't argue with that practical theory, and it was a fine theory, I thought as we started back to the house. Except for the fact that the gravel road ended at the Northcutts' driveway, and I hadn't seen another house for several miles back. What "neighbor" could have been snooping? And, while this footprint wasn't oversized enough to suggest something of the Bigfoot variety, it was no youngster's footprint.

I ran the generator for a while to build up the battery that operates the lights and TV in the motor home, but the picture was too blurry to watch. Abilene went out to check on the emus again, I read a few more chapters in Romans, and then we went to bed. We really had to get Abilene more clothes, I realized. She couldn't keep wearing what she had on indefinitely.

I worried that the barefoot prowler might come around in the night, but if he did come I didn't hear him. I didn't even hear the sound of a car, but a blue SUV was parked near the house the next morning. I started bacon and pancakes while Abilene was feeding the emus. We'd just finished eating breakfast at the little dinette table when a man appeared at the screen door.

"Hi. I'm Frank Northcutt. You must be the people I talked to yesterday?"

I pushed the screen door open. I guessed midforties at first glance, then decided that worry lines and thinning hair made him appear older than he actually was. He had a short, stocky build, with wire-rimmed glasses over pale blue eyes. His sparse, light brown hair had begun to retreat from a high forehead, and he was already doing a rather awkward comb-over. His light blue shorts revealed sturdy, sandy-haired legs.

"Yes. I'm the one who talked to you, Ivy Malone. And this is Abilene Tyler. She's already fed the emus."

He glanced at the birds but didn't bother to comment on their IQ today.

"You had a long trip?" I asked.

"We live in Pewter, down southwest of Dallas. I'd have been here a lot earlier, but the alternator on the SUV conked out, and I had to stop and get it fixed. So I didn't pull in until about 1:00 a.m., and I didn't see any reason to wake you then." He glanced toward the house. "Apparently someone has already been here to take care of the . . . bodies?"

"Yes. Several officers from the county sheriff's department were here, as well as the medical examiner." I could tell that he was about to start questioning me about details, and I hastily added, "Sgt. Dole asked that you come in to see him as soon as you arrived. I believe they need you to make positive identification."

"I'd better do that, then."

Still, he made no move to go, just stood there looking out over the clearing surrounded by woods. "I guess I'm feeling kind of . . . overwhelmed. The deaths . . . this place . . . those stupid birds." He shot the emus a venomous look, as if they were to blame for everything. "Did the deputies say anything about possible suspects in the shooting?"

"Well, uh, no. But Sgt. Dole wanted to talk to you right away," I repeated.

"I'd better clue him in about ol' Ute then. It wouldn't surprise me if the guy had a record a mile long. I tried to get my folks to run a background check on him, but they wouldn't do it. I always figured he could be into anything from drugs to illegal guns to terrorist activities."

"I wonder why they didn't want to check up on him?"

Frank snorted. "Probably because they distrusted the police even more than they did Ute."

Interesting people, these Northcutts.

"Will your wife be arriving later?"

"I don't know. I told you she was at a cosmetologist convention, didn't I? I wasn't able to get hold of her before I left home. The kids are staying with some neighbors."

"If there's anything we can do to help—"

"The first thing I'm going to do is get that bloody sofa out of the house." He sounded angry and resentful, as if someone should have been more considerate about making such a mess.

I doubted we could help with the sofa. It looked like a job for a couple of muscular moving guys. I also wondered if getting rid of the sofa was a good idea. Maybe it held important clues.

Then I reminded myself that this wasn't a crime that

needed clues or solving. It couldn't have been any more clear who'd done what to whom—Jock had shot Jessie and then himself—than if they'd left a video of the event. Unless someone was very good at making a scene look like something it wasn't . . .

"I still can't believe they're gone." Frank shook his head. "I talked to Jock just a few days ago."

I wanted to ask, "Did he sound depressed? Did he give any hint that he and your mother were about to do something so drastic? Or did he sound nervous and afraid? Did he mention threats? Or perhaps a barefoot skulker in the woods?"

Yet it was not my place to get into any of this before he'd talked to the officers and medical examiner. They were the proper authorities to tell him what had happened here, not me.

So all I said was, "Sgt. Dole is really anxious to talk to you. Although I'm afraid I didn't think to ask where you could locate him. Perhaps the sheriff's department has an office in Dulcy?"

"I'll find out. I appreciate your sticking around. It's very generous of you."

"No problem. We aren't in any big hurry, so we'll be glad to stay longer if we can be of any help."

"That's right, you said you'd come looking for jobs, didn't you?" He gave us both appraising looks but headed for the SUV without further comment.

I expected Frank Northcutt to be back from seeing Sgt. Dole by noon, but by 3:00 he still hadn't showed up. Abilene pooper-scooped around the feeding troughs in the emu's pen. I found a hose and refilled the water tank on the motor home, worried about the gauges showing the holding tanks were almost full, and kept a sharp eye out for barefoot prowlers.

I assumed, when I heard a vehicle coming up the driveway, that it was Frank, but I was mistaken. An old brown pickup with one green fender and the hood anchored down with a wire pulled into the yard. Three large crates filled most of the pickup bed.

An older man got out of the car. He had a surprisingly buff physique under a taut T-shirt emblazoned with the picture of a snarling pit bull and the somewhat contradictory statement "Dogs Are a Man's Best Friend." I was holding the hose and watering some bushes in the backyard, and he walked toward me with an old-cowboy roll of hips. At odds with the imposing physique was a loose-skinned face with sagging jowls and droopy folds around the eyes.

"Missus Northcutt?"

"No . . ." How to explain? Well, I could give the basic facts without details. "No, I'm sorry, but both Mr. and Mrs. Northcutt unexpectedly passed away. I'm just—"

"What d'yuh mean, 'passed away'?" he demanded. "Somebody killed 'em?"

That *murder* was his first assumption startled me. This had never been my first question when I heard someone had passed away. "Why would you think that?"

"They must have had some reason for needin' what I brought to show 'em." He jerked his head toward the pickup. Wrinkled folds of skin armed with the gray stubble of a buzz cut rolled out from under his faded green cap, and a strong aroma of old cigarette smoke hung around him like an invisible fog. Good thing Koop was off taking care of cat business, I thought, because he tends to express his critical opinion of such scents with hisses and snarls. And woe to any smoker who tries to pick him up.

I eyed the crates warily. "You'd have to discuss that with their son. He's in town right now, but he should be back shortly. You're welcome to stay and wait for him." I wasn't particularly eager for him and whatever he had in his crates to hang around, but I motioned vaguely toward the lawn chairs on the deck.

"Does the son live here?"

"No. He came because of his parents' deaths."

"You live here?"

Uncertain whether Frank Northcutt was going to hire us for caretaking, I hedged with, "Ummm, well . . ."

"You better take a look at what I got here. Cleo or Badger could take care of you real good, way out here in the boonies."

111

Curiosity got me, and I followed him to the rear of the pickup. He jumped up beside a crate, opened the door, and grabbed the collar of the creature that lunged out. I should have guessed what was in there, considering the T-shirt.

"This here's Cleo."

Cleo was all white, slick haired, heavy bodied as a tank, her head short and thick, a faint rim of pink around her eyes. I know one shouldn't judge by appearances, which probably goes for dogs as well as people, but Cleo looked as if she could take on anything up to and including the size of the Hummer. And would relish the chance to do so.

"Is she . . . uh . . . trained?" I asked warily, since it seemed to take an iron-armed grip on the heavy leather collar to restrain her.

"Gentle as a kitten till she gits the signal to attack," he said proudly. I shoved my hands behind my back, wary of unintentional signals. "I heard the Northcutts were lookin' for a guard dog, but I couldn't git their phone number. So I decided just to drive on out, since I was up from Hugo delivering a dog to some other folks."

"I don't think we'll be needing—"

"Or if you'd prefer a male, Badger's a humdinger. Bigger too. But a little more money."

"No, don't bother to get him out," I said hastily. "We really don't need a guard dog of any size. You don't know why the Northcutts wanted one, I suppose?"

He looked around at the encircling forest. "Pretty isolated out here. Lot of weirdos on the loose. Though in these times, the biggest dangers ain't lurkin' in the woods, are they? They're sittin' back there in Washington, D of C, pullin' down their fat salaries and takin' away our rights." He nodded knowingly. "Man's got an opinion that don't suit 'em, he's in danger."

"Oh," I said, a bit taken aback by this ominous outlook on civilization. "Well, thanks for coming, Mr. . . . ?"

"Riger. Simon Riger."

"If the Northcutts' son is interested in a dog, I'll tell him to get in touch with you, Mr. Riger."

He reached in a rear pocket for his wallet and handed me a card that revealed only his name and phone number. He shoved Cleo back in the cage and swung over the side of the pickup and into the cab with surprising agility.

"Did you have anyone specific in mind when you asked about someone killing the Northcutts?" I asked. "An enemy or someone with whom they'd had differences you'd heard about?"

"I met a guy they had workin' for them, odd name . . ."

"Ute?"

"Yeah, he was the one said they were thinkin' about a guard dog. Seemed like a nice guy. Maybe he'd know somethin'."

A nice guy. Perhaps "nice," like beauty, is in the eye of the beholder. "Ute doesn't seem to be around anymore."

"That so?" Simon Riger turned the key, and the pickup issued a snort and rumble accompanied by a blast of black smoke. I backed away as he wheeled the battered vehicle around.

"Don't take no Confederate bills," he yelled with un-expected cheerfulness and a departing wave. "At least not yet."

He took off, leaving me mildly perplexed and standing in a cloud of billowing dust. Abilene came out of the emus' shed. I wasn't certain if she'd been deliberately hiding, per-haps because of self-consciousness about the black eyes and bruises, or just busy in there.

"Who was that?"

"A Mr. Simon Riger. He wanted to sell us a pit bull guard

dog. She looked mean enough to chew up nails and spit out tacks."

Abilene frowned after the departing pickup. "They can be really nice dogs, unless some idiot gets hold of them and teaches them to fight or attack."

"Is that so?" I murmured. I wasn't convinced of that, but I was convinced tenderhearted Abilene could find good in any of God's creatures.

Frank Northcutt finally returned about 5:30. I was pulling weeds in some scraggly flower beds at the edge of the yard. His shoulders slumped with weariness. Impulsively I asked if he'd like to join us for dinner.

"It'll just be chili and corn bread from the freezer, but it will save you having to fix something."

"Sounds good," he said instantly. The lines in his fore-head relaxed a fraction. "Just let me go in and clean up first, okay?"

I'd invited him because he looked as if his spirits needed propping up, but I had to admit to an ulterior motive as well. I wanted to find out what had happened with Sgt. Dole and the medical examiner, and Frank's reaction to their conclusions.

14

Frank showed up at the motor home twenty minutes later, package of Sara Lee cheesecake in hand. "I found this in the freezer. I think all you have to do is thaw it out."

I eagerly accepted the frozen package. My best friend Thea and I had enjoyed many a Sara Lee cheesecake back on Madison Street in Missouri. "Thank you. I didn't have anything planned for dessert."

"I don't know what I'm going to do with all the stuff in the house," he said after I motioned him to a seat on the sofa and handed him a glass of iced tea. "The freezers are full, the cupboards are overflowing, there's enough food and toilet tissue in there for two people to hole up for a year." He paused. "Of course, that's probably what Jock and Jessie had in mind."

"Can't you just take the food home and use it?"

"Some of it, I suppose. The store-bought stuff. But there's a lot of unidentified meat and other unlabeled packages in there. Mikki would have a fit if I dumped all that on her."

"Did your father hunt?"

"I don't think so. But Jessie may have taken it up. She had a bow and arrow that looked as if it could bring down an elephant. And she was gung-ho on the idea of living off the land. Some of the packages in the freezer may be emu meat." In a disgruntled tone he added, "Considering what they paid for those dumb birds, the meat should be worth thirty or forty bucks a pound."

The dinette could seat four people, but anything over two put your elbows in each other's ribs, so we ate outside. I offered a blessing, but I resisted asking nosy questions about Frank's day. The cheesecake was a perfect ending for the spicy meal, lusciously cool and creamy. Afterward, Abilene gathered up the dishes and took them inside to wash.

"Well, I've got a lot to do, so I guess I'd better get at it." Frank put his hands on his knees as if he were going to stand up, but he didn't move. I sensed a reluctance to get at it, whatever "it" was.

"You didn't have any problem finding Sgt. Dole?" I asked.

"He's stationed over in Horton, where the courthouse and jail and medical examiner and everyone are located. The sheriff's department doesn't keep anyone stationed out in Dulcy." He sighed. "It's been a hard day," he added on a weary note.

"We'll be glad to do whatever we can to help."

"I had to identify the bodies." His throat moved in a convulsive swallow, and he sounded a little dazed. I'd had to identify a body once, so I knew the dazed feeling. "Though I don't think there was ever any doubt about who they were. Just one of those formalities, I suppose."

"Sgt. Dole told you about the . . . circumstances of the deaths?"

Frank nodded. "He showed me the note. A double suicide. Although, technically, they call it a homicide/suicide. At least now we don't have to worry about some maniac killer running around loose. He said I can get the gun back later, though I'm not sure I want it. He gave me Jessie's earrings and wedding ring."

"You recognized your parents' signatures on the note?"

"They're easy enough to recognize. Jock's never was readable. Looks like the graph of a wild day in the stock market. Jessie always put those little triangular dots over the *i* in her name, though her signature was the only place she ever used them."

Small distinctions in the handwriting of each parent that made them easy to identify. And also might not be difficult to fake? But I kept the thought to myself. Frank apparently had no reservations about the official findings on the deaths, and, as Sgt. Dole had pointed out, there was nothing at all to suggest that this wasn't exactly what it looked like: a suicide pact.

Nothing except my suspicions. And Abilene's. Both of which, I had to admit, were founded more on old mystery plots than concrete evidence. Although there was also a not-quite-definable ripple of what my good friend Magnolia from back on Madison Street would call "vibes." Vibes that raised questions.

"Was what they did totally unexpected? A complete surprise to you?" I explored lightly.

"A total shock, that's for sure." Koop came around and sniffed at Frank's shoe. Frank casually put out a hand to stroke the cat's back, and Koop suddenly shot into the air like a fur ball version of a champagne cork. He hissed and spit, flipped a somersault, and shot into hiding under the motor home.

"What's with him?" Frank asked, obviously astonished. He inspected his hand for damage.

"Do you smoke? Koop has kind of a thing about smokers."

"Apparently he doesn't give credit if you're trying to quit," Frank muttered, obviously not appreciative of Koop's inclination toward instant judgment.

"No, I guess not." I couldn't see any scratches on his hand.

"That was about how Jock and Jessie felt about smoking too. I didn't smoke until Mikki and I got married, and, the way they carried on, you'd have thought I'd taken up axe murder as a hobby."

"Were either of them having health problems?"

"I don't think so. I was up one weekend last winter when Jock was cutting wood for the fireplace, and even at his age he could out-chop me."

"Drugs?"

"Jock took some medication to lower his cholesterol, but that's all. Oh, you didn't mean that kind of drugs, did you?"

"No."

"They may have been into the drug scene when they were hot in Hollywood. I think pot and cocaine were the chips-and-dip of their crowd. But they were much too health conscious for anything like that now."

"Did they seem depressed?"

"No. What they were was . . ." Frank paused, eyebrows drawn into a frown. "Paranoid."

I immediately wanted to ask more, but he went on before I could think how to phrase a tactful question.

"Is it possible to be surprised and shocked about something, and yet at the same time realize that deep down what you're feeling is, *This doesn't really surprise me*"?

I nodded thoughtfully. "Yes, I think that's possible."

"In one way it strikes me as unbelievable they'd do this. Take their own lives. Kill themselves. Yet in another way, there seems a certain . . . inevitability about it. They were so disillusioned about everything. So suspicious of everyone."

"That's more or less what their note said."

"I'm still sorting it all out. I guess I will be for a long time."

"I'm so sorry." I paused, not wanting to ask upsetting questions but still curious. "Did the medical examiner determine a time of death?"

"I don't think he pinned it down exactly. But approximately two to three days before you found the bodies. Apparently the door was unlocked when you arrived?"

I had to explain, then, about how we'd discovered the bodies. I was afraid Frank might be disturbed about our method of entry, but instead he nodded gratefully.

"I'm glad you were concerned enough to go to all that trouble. No telling how long it would have been before the bodies were found if you hadn't." He looked off toward the old barn. "I guess the only thing that really surprises me is that Jock was the one who carried it out. I'd have thought Jessie would be more likely. She was . . . the stronger personality. More decisive. And hotter tempered too. I remember them telling how at some script conference, she got mad, piled up all the copies of the script she could grab, and set fire to them with a cigarette lighter. That was back in the days when both of them smoked like chimneys, of course."

I was rather appalled, but Frank smiled fondly. "She was quite a legend around Hollywood. She was a better shot than Jock too. We target practiced one time I was here, and she could outshoot both of us. Although I have to admit it doesn't take much to outshoot me."

We sat there in silence for several minutes. He seemed deep in thought, and I mulled over what he'd said about Jessie and guns. Abilene came out and sat in a chair off to one side. Koop, still keeping a disapproving eye on Frank, jumped in her lap.

Finally I said, "A man came by earlier today. He said he'd heard your parents were interested in buying a guard dog, and he had a couple of pit bulls with him." On a tentative fishing trip I added, "I've been wondering if they were afraid of something. Or someone."

"Oh, they were afraid, all right. They thought somebody, maybe everybody, was out to get them. More of their nutty paranoia. I'm just glad they hadn't already bought some ferocious beast, which would have been another problem I'd have to deal with."

"Are you suggesting . . ." I paused, trying to decide how to phrase this tactfully. "That they may have been . . . mentally disturbed?"

"Oh no, not in any true sense of needing psychiatric help or anything like that. They just thought the worst of . . . everybody. And they took world and national problems very personally."

"You mean events such as 9-11?"

"Right. They were in New York when it happened. It was actually what pushed them into moving here. If something happened . . . No, in their thinking, *when* something happened, they figured they had a better chance of survival here in the woods than in L.A. But even before that they were all shook up about Y2K. Remember all the doom-and-gloom prophecies about how the world was coming to a screeching standstill when 1999 rolled over into 2000?"

A lot of people were apprehensive then, I remembered, although it hadn't worried me. I figured it was a man-made dating of time, and I was secure in God's time line.

"And since 9-11 there have been Afghanistan and Iraq, which I'm sure reaffirmed their fears and suspicions."

120

"They thought the country was in danger of attack? Another terrorist strike or maybe even nuclear war?"

He nodded. "At any moment. Virulent disease organisms planted in public water supplies. Destruction of the power supply. Some Star Wars–type attack that would simultaneously destroy every big city in the U.S. Although they worried just as much about our own government, I think. That it was either going to become an all-powerful 'Big Brother' controlling every thought and action, or the whole system was going to collapse into anarchy, and it would be every man for himself." He looked at me and smiled wryly. "I figured they were way off base, but listening to them for a while, you began to think maybe *you'd* better start stockpiling food and guns and ammunition."

"But taking their own lives . . . Doesn't that seem a rather extreme reaction to world events, even if they are scary and troubling?" I asked cautiously.

I didn't want to turn his thinking toward a different possibility about his parents' deaths, but I couldn't abandon my own doubts about the official conclusion. Now I had these additional chinks in the armor of the suicide pact theory: why *hadn't* Jessie rather than Jock carried it out? And wasn't it possible the Northcutts feared some specific individual, rather than having generalized fears about a collapsing civilization, that prompted their interest in a guard dog?

"There were things other than world events that affected them too. They were really down on the government after a couple of IRS audits cost them hundreds of thousands of dollars. And they felt they'd been blackballed by Hollywood after they filed a lawsuit against one of the big studios." He paused thoughtfully, fingers scratching a mosquito bite on his neck. "Although I've wondered if it wasn't so much blackballing as the fact that Westerns went out of style, and there just wasn't a market for the kind of stuff they wrote."

121

"Did they have enemies in Hollywood?"

Unexpectedly he laughed. "Enemies? You better believe it. They never minded climbing over a few backs to get where they wanted to go. Jessie said all being *nice* in Hollywood got you was a ticket to nowhere."

I stayed silent, hoping he'd reflect on his own words and start thinking about enemies. But he just kept kind of smiling to himself, apparently at memories, and I said, "You mentioned an Oscar?"

"Sometime back in the sixties. Best original screenplay for a Western called *Ride Fast, Die Hard*. It and most of their other old movies still show up on cable or satellite TV occasionally, so they were still bringing in pretty good money."

I'd never heard of their Oscar winner, although I didn't mention that fact.

"And then there was my brother Evan's death years ago. Maybe their paranoia started way back then. He was shot by the police during a confrontation in a stolen car. They were convinced the officer wasn't justified in shooting him and, when the officer wasn't prosecuted, that the police and entire justice system were corrupt and rotten. Maybe that was easier than admitting their golden boy was really a rotten little punk."

A sudden bitterness in his voice jolted me, and an ugly thought reared up. Maybe Frank Northcutt was so willing to accept his parents' deaths as suicide because he'd helped set up the deaths to look that way. Who better to create a phony suicide note and then identify the signatures as authentic? Maybe he'd nursed an old grudge. Or wanted their assets and figured he had to do something before Jock and Jessie blew everything on emus and guns. And he'd been so quick to emphasize what a poor shot he was.

I instantly squelched that quagmire of suspicion. Frank might not seem broken up about his parents' deaths, true.

Even a bit resentful toward them. But I thought I sensed honest affection for them underneath the grumpy attitude.

I hastily jumped my thoughts in a different direction. "Were the emus part of their survival plans?"

"Oh yeah. According to them, emus were the key to making it through the desperate times. You could eat the meat and eggs. Emu oil would erase your wrinkles and cure your arthritis. No doubt grow hair on a bowling ball too. If some new world order needed hairy bowling balls. You could use the skins for leather to make shoes or clothing. Emus don't need as much space as other livestock, and they're more efficient at turning feed into meat than cattle or hogs. All-around wonder birds."

Frank was obviously not an emu admirer, and he gave a baleful glance toward the toothpick-legged birds standing behind their fence watching us. "The only problem is, their brains are about the size of mini-marshmallows, and one time when they got out it was like trying to round up ping-pong balls bouncing on a concrete floor. They'll steal your watch if they get a chance. Or peck your ears or your belt buckle. And they kick, you know. Kick forward, and those toenails can rip out something vital before you know it. Stupid birds," he muttered in rerun.

"They seem rather likeable," I protested mildly.

"I just hope someone shows up who likes them to the tune of a couple thousand bucks a pair, since that's what my folks paid for them."

The price startled me. Expensive meat. Or eggs. Or balm for bowling balls. "Did they plan to raise them commercially?"

"Beats me." His tone suggested he'd like to see them all between buns at an emu-burger stand.

"You're hoping to find a buyer for them as soon as possible, then?"

"Don't I wish. But that's one of my problems. Jock and

Jessie didn't exactly put their affairs in pristine order before they decided to . . . do what they did, so it appears that at the moment I can't dispose of anything. Not the stupid emus, not the Hummer, not this place. I need to find a will, and if I can't find one, settling the estate may stretch into the next decade. Those birds may die of old age before I can get rid of them."

I doubted the situation was that bad. Exaggeration and facetiousness were perhaps just Frank's way of coping with his loss. But I also had to wonder, why *hadn't* the Northcutts put their affairs in order? They'd worried about food and supplies for future survival. They seemed the type of people who would take orderly care of their final affairs before doing something drastic.

"You've talked to a lawyer?"

"That's one of the reasons I was gone all day. I called my lawyer down home, but he said I'd need someone here in Oklahoma. He gave me a name, and then I had to wait around over in Horton to get in to see the guy. Now I'm looking for a will, maybe a safe-deposit box key, plus papers on this property and all their other assets. About which I know nothing, of course." Again that simmer of resentment. He stood up abruptly. "So I'd better get at it. Thanks for dinner."

"Have you made funeral plans yet?"

"One thing Jock and Jessie did do a long time ago was set up a burial plan and buy burial plots next to Evan, so at least that's taken care of. I'm having the bodies shipped out to California and buried there."

"You'll go out there for services, then?"

"No, I don't think so. It'll be just a private, no-services burial. I can't see that it's going to matter one way or the other to Jock and Jessie." He gave me an apologetic glance. "I suppose that sounds harsh and uncaring, and I don't mean it to be. It's just that things are . . . unsettled. I have to take the kids back to their mother in a few days. We're trying to buy a new house, and Mikki would like to expand and upgrade her beauty salon. And now there are all these complicated details with the estate."

The suspicion reared its ugly head again. A wife, an ex-wife, two kids, a new house. Was he in need of big bucks, big bucks he figured he'd inherit if his parents were conveniently out of the way?

He strode off toward the house. I thought he intended to tackle the search for important papers immediately, but a few minutes later I heard noises and saw him trying to wrestle the bloody sofa out the sliding glass door.

He'd grimly gotten it that far by himself, but Abilene and I ran over to help him. Together, keeping our eyes away from the bloodstains and our breath held to avoid the scent, we managed to push the sofa off the deck. Something gave a loud *cr-a-ack* when it hit the ground.

Frank went back inside, dragged out the coffee table and bloodstained tan rug, and dumped them on top the sofa. Then he got a rope from the SUV, wrapped one end around the sofa and the other around the trailer hitch on the SUV. He unceremoniously dragged everything off to an old burn pile over toward the barn.

I could sympathize. I also wouldn't want the sofa as a bloody reminder only a few feet away if I were staying in the house. But I was relieved that forest fire danger meant he couldn't immediately set fire to it. Somewhere in the back of my mind was still the thought that the sofa could hold important clues.

Lights went on when Frank went back in the house, and they were still burning when I got up at 2:00 to let Koop in from his nocturnal wanderings.

125

By noon the next day, Frank was still holed up in the house. Despite my concerns about colored blobs on the trees and the strange footprint, Abilene went for a hike in the woods. The emus, making their odd, sometimes plaintive-sounding noises, trailed along the fence, following her as far as they could. I pulled more weeds. I'm not a great gardener, as my garden back on Madison Street would attest, but I get a real satisfaction out of annihilating weeds.

Frank hadn't mentioned our staying here longer, but neither had he told us to shove off, so I wasn't inclined to hurry away. I figured that as long as we were here, the Braxtons were less likely to catch up with me, and Abilene's fondness for the emus would keep her from taking off for parts unknown. But we had to do something about clothes for her. She'd washed everything by hand last evening and wrapped herself in a sheet, sarong style, for bed. The jeans were still damp this morning, but they were all she had to put on.

When Abilene returned from her hike she reported seeing

more colored blobs, plus several deer, but no more footprints. She got out mayo and a can of tuna to make sandwiches for lunch, and I went over to the house and knocked on the frame of the sliding glass door. Frank had it and all the windows open, giving the place a much-needed airing out. He opened the door with a sandwich in one hand.

"I was just going to ask if you'd like to join us for lunch, but I see you're already eating."

He waved the sandwich. "Canned corned beef. There are two cases of it. And two more of sardines. Unfortunately, Mikki hates 'em both."

"Are you making progress on finding what you need?"

"I've been going through the mess on the dining room table. The only thing useful I've found so far is a folder on the Hummer. Nothing on this property or other assets. Some old script contracts may come in handy, but most of the stuff seems to be research material and plot and character notes. It looks as if they intended to get away from Westerns and try a contemporary or maybe even futuristic adventure."

That apparently didn't strike him as significant, but it did me. They were hard at work on some exciting new idea, and they interrupted it to kill themselves? Another chink in the suicide classification.

Frank looked at his watch. "I was hoping to start home tomorrow, but the way things are going I'm not going to make it. Mikki will not be a happy camper."

"I won't keep you then. I hope you find what you need."

"Yeah. Me too. What I did find is that the basement is full of more food and enough supplies to outfit an excursion to outer space. My estimate that there was enough food here to last them for a year was about two years low."

I decided this was as good a time as any to get bold. "Are you thinking about what you'll do with this place until you can sell it? Abilene and I are available for caretaking, if you need someone."

He gave me a hesitant look. I saw myself as he undoubtedly saw me: one hundred pounds of five foot one LOL with possum-gray hair, wrinkles, and polyester slacks. I wished I could get down and show him a few one-armed pushups like tough guy Jack Palance did at the Academy Awards one year, but since that was out of the question I decided to appeal to him on the basis of money. "We'd be willing to do it very reasonably."

"You wouldn't mind being way out here all by yourselves?"

No, but . . . "You mentioned once that your folks had called 911 a couple of times. Do you know why?"

"One time the emus got out, and all that was left of one of them was some feathers and bones out in the woods. They were convinced some conspiracy of emu rustlers did it, but I figured someone just sneaked in and let the dumb birds out as a prank. Or maybe they managed to get the gate open on their own. They're sneaky," he muttered, as if the birds may have craftily plotted their own escape. Which hardly went along with being "dumb," but I didn't point out the discrepancy.

"Anyway, I figured a coyote or mountain lion or something got that one. Jock and Jessie finally had to hire some guy to come in and use a net to capture the last two running around out there. I don't know what their other 911 call was about. Actually, I think the ranch is a fairly safe place. You aren't going to get transients wandering through."

"We saw an odd footprint out in the woods," I said.

"What do you mean, 'odd'?"

"Barefoot."

I expected Frank to be disturbed by the idea of a shoeless stranger skulking around, but he shrugged it off. "Could be

128

Jock or Jessie's track. No telling what kind of survival games they were playing out there. When civilization collapses, you can't count on rushing to the nearest Wal-Mart and buying shoes, you know. You've gotta be ready to rough it."

Frank's explanation of the barefoot print was not totally out of reason, given the Northcutts' peculiarities, though his tone was facetious again.

"We both like it here. And Abilene is very good with the emus. Which, considering their value," I reminded him, "need good care so they don't get out and have something happen to them."

"Yeah, right. Those stupid birds." He frowned, but he got off that familiar sidetrack long enough to ask, "She's, what? Your granddaughter?"

I was tempted to say she was. Abilene and I hadn't known each other long, but already I had the feeling that if I'd had a choice in granddaughters, she'd have been mine. But, as usual, my aversion to untruths got in the way. "No, we're just friends."

"Was she recently in an accident or something?"

Yes, Abilene had been in both an accident and an "or something," but I just said yes without elaborating.

"Well, let me think about it. I probably can't risk leaving the place totally untended."

That sounded as if he was looking at Abilene and me as a last resort, but I didn't mind being a last resort if we could get the job.

Over the tuna sandwiches, I reported the conversation to Abilene. "Of course, I may have spoken too soon. Perhaps you aren't even interested in staying here for a while . . . ?"

"I'm interested." She smiled. "It's not as if the president

of General Motors is breathlessly waiting for me to show up in a power suit and claim some high-powered executive position."

"IBM is ignoring me too."

"Okay, then, if Frank wants us to caretake here, we'll do it?" She sounded genuinely eager, and I was pleased that she also seemed to accept the idea of herself and me as an "us."

"You don't mind sleeping all cramped up there on the sofa?"

"I don't mind. Though maybe, until the weather turns bad, I'll fix a place outside to sleep."

Outside? I thought about the close-by woods, the unidentified footprint, and the unknown reasons Jock and Jessie were interested in a guard dog. Although, after talking to Frank, I decided the guard dog may have been about protecting the emus from someone letting them out again, not a personal danger. "You wouldn't feel unsafe outside?"

"I feel a whole lot safer here, inside or out, than I ever felt with Boone," Abilene declared with a depth of feeling that told me again of the physical and emotional pain she'd been through. "And I like looking up at the stars at night. Sometimes . . . I think about God then."

She gave me a sideways glance, as if self-conscious about the admission, but I nodded my approval. "It's hard to look at all those stars and not think about God," I agreed. And I just might sleep outside myself, I decided. I liked looking up at the Lord's handiwork too, which unexpectedly now reminded me of Mac MacPherson and some stargazing we'd done together.

Abilene and I smiled at each other, pact made. Which was when I reluctantly realized I owed Abilene certain information before she committed herself to this. With insurance money providing Boone with a new Porsche, she was prob-

130

ably safe from him now. But she wasn't necessarily *safe*. Not when she was with me.

It took quite a while to tell her all about how I'd helped send one of the Braxtons to prison for murder and how the brother had vowed vengeance. How the Braxton clan had already twice tried to carry out that vengeance, once with an arson attempt on my house back in Missouri, once with a car bomb planted in the old Thunderbird I'd traded for the motor home. How the Braxtons had more recently picked up my trail and chased me into Oklahoma.

"I think I ditched them before I headed down this way to Dulcy, but I can't be sure. It's possible they'll show up right here. And I doubt they'd be concerned if someone else got caught in the crossfire of a scheme to do me in."

Abilene had stopped eating mid-story and was staring at me in astonishment.

"So it could be just as bad, or worse, than if Boone was after you. I won't be hurt or angry if you'd rather not stay in the danger zone around me," I added when she seemed speechless.

Finally she said, "You don't *look* like . . . uh . . ."

"A target for thugs? A magnet for murderers?"

"You look like someone's granny who sits in a rocking chair and knits scarves and booties."

I winked at her. "That's my disguise. Down underneath I'm really Ivy the Invisible Investigator, upholder of law and order, bane of crooks everywhere. Although, in a pinch, I can knit too."

She eyed me doubtfully. "You're sure about these people? There really is this mini-Mafia out to get you?"

A mini-Mafia. Oh yeah.

"I'm sure. I could drive you into Dulcy or Horton or wherever the bus stops, and help you get a ticket to . . . somewhere." No response to that, and it occurred to me her thoughts were perhaps running in the opposite direction. "Or maybe you'd rather *I* disappeared into the sunset, and you could stay on here to caretake alone?"

"What do *you* want?"

"I don't want to put you in danger."

"I've been in danger for the past six years." She rubbed the ridge above her wrist, an absentminded gesture but a powerful reminder of that danger. "I survived Boone all those years without you. You've survived the Braxtons without me. It looks to me as if together we could take on all of them, or anything else that comes along."

I beamed at her. "I think so too," I said.

High-fives may be old-fashioned these days, but that's what we gave each other anyway.

16

Frank came over a couple hours later. The temperature was close to ninety. Abilene was repairing a weak place in the emus' fence, but I was sitting on a lawn chair in the shade of the motor home, painting my toenails. I was embarrassed at being caught at something so personal and hastily stuck the cap back on the polish. Too late. Frank was already staring at my left foot.

"Is something wrong?"

"No! No, of course not. I guess I'm just surprised to see the toe ring."

Obvious were the unspoken words at the end of that sentence: on someone of your advanced years.

"My grandniece gave it to me. She's always trying to drag me into the twenty-first century."

"Oh. Well, it's, uh, very attractive."

"It took some getting used to," I had to admit, "but now it's quite comfortable." I wiggled my toes and thought defiantly, *And even LOLs can wear toe rings if they want to. So there.*

Frank plopped into the other chair, and I realized he looked frazzled.

"No luck finding anything?" I asked, glad to be away from the subject of toes and toe rings. I stuck my feet under the chair to let the polish dry.

"No safe deposit box key. No wills. No deed. I did run onto a box of cancelled checks covering the past couple of years, and maybe I'll find something useful there. But I'm wondering now if they have a private safe hidden around here somewhere."

"Wouldn't they have told you if they did?"

"I don't think Jock and Jessie were quite as paranoid about me as they were about everyone else, but they didn't exactly take me into their confidence."

"Have you decided yet how long you'll be staying here?"

"I'll probably leave tomorrow. Mikki called. She got home from the convention and says the kids are giving her a bad time so I'd better get home and referee until I take them back to their mother in Dallas." He sounded harried, as if juggling kids, wife, and ex-wife was a nerve-wracking job. "So, I want to talk to you about your looking after the ranch for a while."

"Both of us?"

"The lawyer says money can be released to pay the burial expenses and probably whatever is necessary for 'preservation of assets.' But I don't yet have any idea what cash is available, so I can't offer you much in the way of salary. The two of you could split it however you want." He smiled wryly. "What I can offer is all the food you can eat, all the toilet tissue and paper towels you can use, plus enough shampoo, toothpaste, dental floss, and Band-Aids to last into the next ice age. Also, should the need arise, an impressive supply of snake-bite kits and Pepto-Bismol. You shouldn't have to buy much while you're here."

"I have a long cord we can run from the motor home to the house for electricity, and hooking up the water hose is no problem. But we'd have to find some way to connect into the septic system."

"Jock and Jessie lived in a travel trailer here while the house was being remodeled, so there must be a way. We'll look for it."

The cash he then got down to offering was indeed not much, but he said he'd also pay electric and phone bills and set up an account at the feed store for emu food. I called Abilene over for a brief conference, and we accepted the offer.

"Is there anything we can do to help out now?" I asked, as I had before.

He reached in a pocket and pulled out a key ring fastened to a square of leather with Jock's name carved into it. "Right now I need a break. I thought I'd take a look at what's in these outbuildings."

He didn't invite us, but neither did he say the exploration was private, so I put on my shoes and we tagged along.

"I've been wondering what's in those big tanks," I said as we followed him to the first shed.

"The one labeled G is gasoline. The D is diesel. You may as well use whatever gas you need for the motor home while you're here. I think each tank holds a thousand gallons."

The labeling was logical enough, although I wondered about the safety of keeping such huge amounts of inflammable liquid around.

"Jock and Jessie didn't trust the Middle East oil supply in a crisis and figured on having a stockpile of their own. I'm not sure who they didn't trust when they bought all that corned beef. And six boxes of foot fungus powder." He stopped and

135

glanced back at us. "I'm sorry. You must think I'm terribly disrespectful."

"Frustrated, perhaps?" I suggested.

"Yeah, I guess that's it. Frustrated. Jock and Jessie and I had a lot of differences. We weren't really close, and sometimes I wanted to shake them for being so strange and stubborn. But that doesn't mean I didn't love them."

"Did your children know them?"

"We visited them out in California a couple times when Natalie and I were still married, and she brought the kids up here from Dallas to see them several times. Jock and Jessie weren't really grandparent material, but they tried, and they always liked Natalie." He frowned as if he found that baffling, and resented it as well.

"Did she share their . . . umm . . . survival interests, perhaps?"

"No, but she's always been big on fitness. Yoga and karate and weight lifting, even running marathons. Jessie admired that. It didn't make for a real cozy situation the time Mikki and I came up and Jessie kept raving about what fantastic shape Natalie was in and how she'd run all the way up to the lake and back when she was here. Sorry," he added apologetically. "I'm sure that's more than you ever wanted to know about my marital complications."

Not necessarily. Gossip isn't usually one of my shortcomings, but curiosity is.

He unlocked the padlock on the first shed, swung the door open, and switched on the overhead light. I instantly felt rather overwhelmed by all the *stuff*. I could identify a couple of big items on the concrete floor as generators because they bore a similarity to the generator in the motor home. With these, using the gasoline or diesel in the big tanks, the Northcutts were well prepared to take care of their own electrical needs in case of disaster.

Frank confirmed this, adding, "They intended to convert to solar power eventually, so they'd be completely independent, but they hadn't gotten started on installing solar panels yet."

Gardening tools lined one wall, apparently also for a future project, because I hadn't yet noted any actual gardening activity.

There were animal traps, a box of compasses and flashlights, five-gallon jugs of water, a Coleman camp stove and several lanterns, something I thought might be a solar cooker, and various other items I couldn't even identify. An electric meat saw looked big and powerful enough to cut up any creature currently roaming North America. Everything, it appeared, for the well-stocked do-it-yourself survivalist.

Including, I noted, a pair of snowshoes hanging on the wall. I'm fairly certain snowshoes are about as useful in southeastern Oklahoma as shark repellent, but the Northcutts obviously intended to be prepared for any contingency, up to and including a coming ice age. A tangle of webbed material in camouflage colors draped the wall beside the snowshoes. The emu-catching net, perhaps?

"Looks like all they were lacking is a rocket launcher and a nuclear submarine," Frank muttered.

I wasn't certain we might not yet discover those items. On to the next shed.

Here were several big boxes of an odd type of gun, not like those in the cabinet in the house. I could tell they weren't handguns, but neither were they rifles or shotguns. So what were they? I cautiously picked one up. It appeared to be constructed of sturdy plastic, with a canister attached on the bottom and a container, rather like a covered funnel, on top.

"Are they toys?" I asked, puzzled.

Frank bent over one of the boxes. "No, I don't think so."

More boxes held plastic bags of small, brightly colored round objects, somewhat like gumballs. Several jumpsuits in camouflage colors hung on the wall. Another box held a jumble of goggles and face masks. I jumped when I looked farther back in the shed and saw a bear.

No, not a real bear. The wooden, life-sized silhouette of one. Along with other silhouettes of deer, a mountain lion, and people in various kinds of uniforms. Holes pockmarked the silhouettes. After a moment I realized what they were. Bullet holes.

The whole setup jittered my nerves. What did we have here? Some terrorist cell accumulating a stockpile of strange, futuristic guns?

"Hey, I know what these are!" Frank held up one of the guns, unexpectedly smiling when he peered into the container on top. "They're paintball guns. I took Jeff and a couple of his buddies to a place outside Dallas where they rent them. They had a big field where you could go out and play games and shoot."

"At each other?" I asked, mildly appalled.

"Sure. They usually set up teams, with maybe a goal of capturing the other team's flag. You hide behind wooden or vinyl barriers, but sometimes you're out in the open running between them, and as soon as you're hit with a paintball, you're out. But it's not just for kids. Lots of adults get into it too. I did," Frank admitted. "It was fun."

He stepped to the door with one of the guns in hand, pointed it in the direction of a nearby tree, and pulled the trigger. A drippy red blob immediately blossomed on the bark. He grinned, obviously pleased with himself.

"Hey," Abilene said, "that's like all those blobs we saw out in the woods!"

I also realized now that what had looked like broken eggshells out in the woods were actually the remains of the outer coverings of the used paintballs.

"I remember Jessie saying something about some group that came here to practice war games out in the woods once in a while. I don't know exactly how many acres are here, but several hundred anyway. Plenty for a full-scale war. I was afraid that they might be shooting real bullets, but they must have been using paintballs."

My glance at the wooden silhouettes affirmed that at some time *someone* used real bullets. I'd heard about white-supremacy groups practicing war games in isolated places. So I came right out and asked.

"Were your folks into white-supremacy stuff?"

He turned and looked at me, his expression surprised. "Jock and Jessie racist? No way. They were truly passionate about civil rights in their younger days. Though I suppose, after they went paranoid, they were suspicious of people with different skins. Or creeds or anything else. It was an equal-opportunity paranoia. They were distrustful of everyone." He rested the paint gun against his leg. "Actually, I was surprised they let this group come on the place. But I guess they figured they needed more live bodies than just each other for moving targets to practice on."

Strange people.

Frank pulled the trigger several more times. Most of the paintballs missed the tree target, but a green one finally splatted it. "Bull's-eye!" he yelled.

Abilene picked up one of the guns and inspected it curiously. "How do you aim it?"

"They don't have a sight to aim through, like a real gun has. You just point it in the general direction and pull the trigger. You put the paintballs in that container on top—" He pointed to the funnel-shaped thing on the gun she held.

"And it feeds them into the gun. The propulsion power comes from the pressurized canister on the bottom."

I inspected one of the canisters. It was marked with the chemical symbol for carbon dioxide.

"Some of the canisters use pressurized air instead of carbon dioxide. They had a machine for refilling them at the rental place. I don't know if these carbon dioxide ones are refillable or not."

Abilene stepped around him. "How do you do it? Like this?" She pointed the paint gun in the direction of the woods, pulled the trigger, and splatted a bush. She gave a surprised grin. "Hey, that is kind of fun!"

She pulled the trigger several more times, rapidly catching on how to hit a target and honing in on a tree trunk with a couple of solid egg-yellow splats. She grinned again.

"Does it hurt if you're hit with one?" I asked.

"It stings a little if a paintball makes a direct hit on the skin, and it can make quite a bruise or welt if you're shot up close. But it's not deadly dangerous. Though a direct hit in the eye can be really bad. But that's what the face masks are for. The stuff washes off easy. It's water soluble. And it isn't poisonous or anything. I heard once you could even eat it and it wouldn't hurt you. Not that it's my idea of a good snack."

"How far do they shoot?" Abilene asked.

"I'm not sure. At least two or three hundred feet, I'd guess. I think these guns may be a little more high-powered than those at the rental place."

Frank stepped back into the shed and pulled a face mask over his head. "C'mon, put on a mask and we'll give it a try," he urged Abilene. He picked up a flag from a barrel in a corner. "I'll plant this over by the woods, and whoever captures it first wins!"

Abilene slipped on a mask, and, like kids discovering a new

game, they gleefully headed for the woods. Frank planted the flag at the edge of the clearing, where the faint trail took off through the woods. Abilene ran about a hundred feet to the left. Frank did the same on the right.

"First one gets hit is out!" Frank shouted as he disappeared into the brush.

"What does the winner get?" I yelled.

"Satisfaction!"

I didn't see how either of them could ever hit the other in the dense woods, but I heard a *splat* as Abilene's first paintball thumped something in Frank's direction.

"Missed me!" Frank yelled jubilantly.

I wasn't certain how I felt about this. Grown people shooting paintballs at each other?

Then I shrugged. Why not? I grabbed a mask and a paint-ball gun, checked to see the funnel was full, and headed for the woods.

I sneaked around to the right, circling Frank's position, and slipped into the brush. They didn't know I was in the game, which perhaps gave me an unfair advantage, but I decided to go with the old philosophy that all's fair in love and war. Especially paintball war.

My game plan was to work my way around to a point farther down the trail, from where I could see the planted flag. Then, when either of them got close to it, I'd blast 'em. I took tentative aim at a clump of leaves up ahead, just for practice, and astonished myself by dead-eying it with a pink blob. Hey, that *was* kind of fun!

After snagging my mask on bushes and getting whopped with one branch after another, I changed tactics. I slung the carrying strap on the paint gun over one shoulder, got down on my belly, and slithered under most of the brush. Being small, scrawny, and semi-invisible does have its occasional advantages. When I came to the trail, I cautiously got to my feet. Yes, there was the flag some twenty-five feet back toward the clearing around the house.

I couldn't see anyone, but somewhere in the brush I heard the occasional click of a trigger, the whoosh of a firing gun, sometimes the splat of a paintball hitting something. Then, there he was, Frank sneaking up on the flag!

I fired and then ducked so he couldn't see me. I missed, but I heard him get off several shots in quick succession. Not in my direction. He still thought Abilene was his only opponent.

I parted the bushes carefully. He was within three or four feet of the flag now. *Splat!* I got him, Pepto-Bismol pink right on the shoulder.

"Okay, I'm out," Frank yelled. He sounded mildly disgruntled. "You got me."

A moment later Abilene appeared from the opposite direction, ready to claim her victory. *Splat!* I got her too!

She whirled in a semicircle. "Hey, what's going on? Who's shooting with pink?"

I stood up and pushed through the bush. They both stared.

"Meet the champ," I said. I picked up the flag and waved it triumphantly as I marched out of the woods.

"Hey, that's not fair," Abilene protested. "We didn't even know you were in the game."

"Foul!" Frank cried. "Illegal player on the field!"

"I didn't hear anyone telling me I couldn't play, and I have the flag, don't I? And I don't see any paintball blobs on me—"

I didn't get to finish my victory proclamation before a barrage of paintballs hit me. Yellow blobs like raw egg yolks. Green blobs like slimy pond scum. I retaliated, of course, with pink blobs of my own and a satisfying number of hits.

"New game!" Abilene yelled. She grabbed the flag and headed down the trail with it.

"I think I'll retire winner and let you two battle it out," I said graciously, with as much dignity as is possible with a yellow blob decorating my derriere and both green and yellow spread across my front.

"Oh no, you don't," they chorused in unison. "You're in."

They ganged up on me in the next game, of course. The aim of the game wasn't capturing the flag now; it was Get Ivy. And get Ivy they did. I came out looking as if I'd tangled with a raw omelet of moldy eggs. Feeling like it too, with goopy stuff in my hair and soaking through my shirt and running down my neck. They'd have let me quit then, I think, but my competitive ire was aroused.

This time I grabbed the flag and planted it in a small clearing farther back in the woods. "Two hits before you're out this time!" I decreed. "No cheating!"

Something whizzed by my head and splatted the bush behind me. I got off a quick shot and dodged behind a tree. I peered through the bushes, but my opponents had instantly vanished. I knew better than to make directly for the flag. This called for a sneak attack.

I did the belly thing again, squirming along the ground using my elbows for propulsion, pausing every few feet to listen for giveaway rustles. The problem was, down on the ground, I quickly lost my bearings. The trees and brush all looked alike. That slimy pond was back here somewhere. I could just see myself slithering into a sea of green scum by mistake . . .

Cautiously I stood up. There, a flash of blue through the bushes! Abilene's blouse. I whipped up the gun and got off a shot.

I heard it hit, along with an *oof* of surprise.

Odd. That didn't sound like Abilene. Had I hit Frank instead? No, he was wearing a tan shirt. I stood there, puzzled. I didn't want to say anything and give away my position. I saw a flicker of movement and shot again.

I didn't hear the paintball hit, but suddenly something crashed through the brush, branches breaking, footsteps pounding.

"Abilene?" I called tentatively. "Frank?"

One paintball lobbed me from the left. Another hit me from the right. Neither came from the direction of the crashing brush.

"Okay, you got me," I yelled. "I'm out. But I hit someone. Who was it?"

No answer, neither of them wanting to give away their position. Upright, my sense of direction returned, and I headed for the flag. Around me, the bushes rustled as Frank and Abilene jockeyed for position. Abilene's defeat came first.

"Okay, I'm hit twice." She came out of the brush, plastered with the green of Frank's paintballs from this and the earlier games.

He appeared a minute later dripping yellow goo but smiling like a kid who's just gotten away with spitballing the teacher. "Didn't I tell you it was fun?"

I examined them both. More recent blobs had obliterated my earlier pink hits on both of them. So where was that last hit?

"Which one of you took off running when I hit you a couple minutes ago?" I asked.

"Not me."

"Not me."

"Then who?"

I led the way back to where I'd fired the last shot, then to approximately where I'd blobbed someone. The ground was

145

dry here, no footprints visible, but there were shards from my broken paintball on the ground.

Frank laughed. "You probably terrorized some poor deer into running for his life. There are lots of them out here."

"And when he gets back to the other deer he'll be ostracized because of the big pink blob between his eyes," Abilene suggested. "He'll probably have to go see the local deer psychiatrist because he's so traumatized."

Obviously they were not taking my claim seriously. Was it possible I'd mistaken a deer for a human? Misidentification was how deadly hunting accidents happened. Hunter mistakes a person for a deer, and I'd simply done the reverse. But I'd been so certain I'd seen that flash of blue, not once but twice, and I'd never heard of a deer wearing blue.

"C'mon, let's go get something to drink," Frank said. "There's frozen juice, canned juice, bottled juice, you can have your pick."

We trooped out of the woods. Frank seemed in high spirits now, and Abilene was actually laughing, which was good to hear. Okay, I had to admit it, splatting paintballs was fun, even if we did all look as if we'd been in a frat house food fight. I shrugged off the matter of my mysterious target. Maybe there was a pink-splatted deer out there somewhere thinking, *This is it. I gotta get out of this redneck country.*

"Come on over to the house as soon as you get cleaned up," Frank said.

I looked at Abilene, drippy with blobs. "We'll have to run into town first. Abilene doesn't have any clothes to change into."

"Nothing?"

"Nothing."

I suspected that puzzled him. A woman without a closetful of clothes? But instead of asking questions he surprised me by saying to Abilene, "You're not much taller than Jessie. Maybe something of hers would fit you."

Abilene looked shocked. "Oh, I couldn't—"

"Yes, you could," I interrupted firmly. At my age, you've learned to be practical about these things. A dead woman's clothes are just as wearable as any others.

Frank echoed that practicality. "In fact, c'mon over and take anything you want. I may be able to make use of some of Jock's stuff myself, but I'll have to get rid of Jessie's things sooner or later anyway, so you might as well have whatever you can use. I don't think the lawyer will make a fuss about my giving away a few clothes."

"Wouldn't your wife like to have some of your mother's things?" Abilene asked.

"No, Mikki isn't going to want any of them."

"You're sure?"

"I'm sure."

"Maybe just a pair of jeans, then, if there are any," Abilene agreed hesitantly.

I changed out of my paintball-daubed clothes, sloshed a wet washcloth over my hair, and we went over to the house. When I knocked, Frank yelled at us to come on in. Abilene took off her splattered shoes. She'd wrapped a towel around her shirt so the paintball residue wouldn't get on anything in the house.

"In here. Down the hallway on the left," he called.

I decided there was no point in telling him I was already familiar with the bedroom. I took a quick peek toward the gun cabinet when we entered the room. It was closed now, but the crossbow was still leaning beside it.

The large closet was divided into his and hers sections, but neither was crowded with clothes. If Jessie had ever been one for glamour, she'd abandoned it when she left Hollywood. What Frank pulled out of the closet and tossed on the bed were jeans and other work or casual pants, sweat-

147

shirts, hooded and plain. Denim and khaki shirts, plain cotton blouses, and T-shirts. No Hollywood sequins here.

"Take whatever you can use." Frank added a plaid jacket to the growing pile.

"Actually, there isn't room in the motor home for a lot of clothes," I said reluctantly. I would've liked to see Abilene take advantage of this largesse, but space was definitely limited.

Frank paused. "You know, now that I think about it, there's no point in the two of you being crowded into that little motor home and the house sitting here empty. Why don't you just move in here instead? There are two bedrooms upstairs, so you can each have a room of your own, and this bedroom will still be available if I need it."

I didn't hesitate. I hadn't minded living in the little motor home these past months. By now I even felt a comfortable affection for it. The size eliminates a lot of housekeeping chores. But the idea of temporarily spreading out in a real house made me feel a little giddy. All that space!

I looked at Abilene, who didn't say anything. "Sounds good to us," I said for both of us.

Abilene tried things on in the bathroom. The jeans rode a bit high on her slim ankles, but they were wearable, and everything else, except for the shoes, fit fine. She kept on one of the more faded pairs of jeans and a red T-shirt, and we carried the other items upstairs.

I told her to pick whichever bedroom she wanted. She chose the smaller one with patchwork quilts on the two single beds. I was pleased with the other room, identical except for the flowered spreads on the beds and enough extra space to accommodate a beautiful rosewood desk and a love seat.

I offered to fix dinner, to which Frank gladly agreed. It was dark by the time we finally sat down to mystery-meat meatloaf at one end of the still-cluttered dining room table. A minute later the headlights of a car flashed across the windows.

"Are you expecting anyone?" Frank asked.

"Not us," I said, although a scary possibility occurred to me. Would the Braxtons dare drive boldly into this isolated spot and start pumping out bullets? No one within miles to see or hear . . .

I jumped up. "I'll get the door." I was certainly not eager to clash head-on with Braxtons, but neither could I let Frank go out to meet them in total ignorance of the danger.

I heard steps on the deck and cautiously called through the door, "Who's there?"

I jumped to the side in case the response was a blaze of gunfire but instead heard a female voice demand, "Who're you?"

"I'm . . . working here."

"Where's Frank?"

"He's here."

By that time Frank was beside me. He yanked the door open, apparently recognizing the voice. "Mikki! What a . . .

nice surprise." He sounded more startled than welcoming, however. "What are you doing here? I mean, I'm *glad* you're here, but the kids—"

"I decided to take the kids back to Natalie early and just come on up here to be with you." She cupped Frank's chin in a big squeeze and made a kissy moue with her mouth.

Frank's head jerked back, and his eyes did a widening-in-alarm thing. "What did Natalie . . . uh . . . say?"

Mikki's smile held satisfaction. "She wasn't rolling out the mint juleps in welcome, that's for sure. I think she and that high-powered boyfriend had somethin' planned." Her voice wasn't full-blown Southern, but it held a hint of drawl. She gave me a wink over Frank's shoulder. "If you know what I mean."

"Well, uh, let me introduce everyone. Ivy Malone, my wife, Mikki. Mikki, Ivy is one of our new caretakers here."

Mikki looked me over. So soon after his parents' deaths seemed an unlikely time for a wife to be suspicious of her husband's activities, but I got the impression she was relieved to find I was a gray-haired LOL rather than some local femme fatale cavorting with her husband. For a caretaker, however, she apparently had stiffer standards, and her cool inspection told me I was coming up short. Too few muscles, too many years.

But fair's fair, and I did a critical appraisal of my own. Shoulder-length blond hair, stylishly tousled and expertly colored to a tawny rather than brassy look. Flattering makeup, though a little heavy on the eyeliner. Long, perfectly manicured nails, delicately peach-pink. Impressive diamond on her left hand. Unexpectedly shrewd blue eyes in a baby-doll face.

Frank had said she wouldn't be interested in Jessie's clothes, and now I could see why. Partly because Jessie's wash-and-wear wardrobe was designed for chopping wood and raising emus, and Mikki's elegant, raw-silk white pant-suit said "expensive boutique, dry-clean only." But perhaps even more because there was no seamstress in the world who could alter Jessie's slim clothes to Mikki's spectacular Dolly Parton proportions.

"Honey, do you really think you can live way out here in the middle of nowhere? I mean, it might be okay when we're younger, but as we get older . . ." She squeezed my arm as if she were sympathetically aligning her much-younger age with my declining years, but we both knew she was only emphasizing that I was way too far over the hill for the job. "And those awful birds or whatever they are." She shuddered delicately.

Whatever their problems, and I detected some edgy undercurrents here, Frank and Mikki were in agreement about the emus.

Frank didn't give me time to defend my caretaking abilities. "And in here—" He led the way to the dining room, apparently not troubled by crossing the bare spot where the bloody sofa had once stood. "This is our co-caretaker, Abilene Tyler."

Mikki paused before following him across the bare spot. Aware something was missing, I supposed, but not certain what. I detoured the space. I still had too clear a vision of dead bodies occupying it.

Mikki now turned those shrewd eyes on Abilene. Abilene still had discolored bruises and the strange haircut, but she was unmistakably very attractive anyway. Frank didn't strike me as an irresistible hunk who'd attract women like Brad Pitt in a convertible, but Mikki's brows edged together, and I got the quick impression she regarded any attractive woman as a potential rival.

"Would you like to join us for dinner?" I invited quickly. "There's plenty of food."

151

She gave me an airy wave. "Oh no, honey, I've eaten."

She didn't actually pick up a piece of silverware to examine it, but I could see her looking it over. I wondered if she was disappointed to see that it was only inexpensive stainless steel, not sterling silver.

Frank started to slide into his chair at the table. "I'll bring your suitcases in as soon as we've finished dinner."

"Oh, honeybun, I'd really like to have them now, if you don't mind." She smiled sweetly.

I thought the request to interrupt his dinner rude, and I suspected Frank *did* mind. But he merely frowned and headed for the door.

"Perhaps just a cup of coffee?" I suggested. I motioned toward the coffeemaker on the counter, can of cut-rate coffee beside it.

Mikki wrinkled her nose. "Not right now, thank you, hon." She turned and surveyed the huge living room and gave another of what I now suspected were trademark shudders. "Jock and Jessie were absolute *dears*, but they sometimes had such *odd* taste. And I never could understand why they didn't get rid of that glassy-eyed deer head and those *dreadful* horn chandeliers."

Okay, I had to agree with that, though I didn't say so. With Frank outside, I expected a rapid third degree in questions, but after that one comment, Mikki ignored us. She made a quick tour of the living room, stopping to inspect the piano and an antique sewing machine I hadn't noticed before, then leaning over to study a Navajo rug. Perhaps it was unkind of me, but I had the impression she was efficiently setting a dollar value on everything. Then she disappeared down the hall to the master bedroom, apparently assuming that was her rightful place in the house.

Frank came in lugging two suitcases, plus a cosmetics case tucked under his arm. I could hear conversation in the bedroom, though only an occasional actual word came through. All of which, spoken in sweet/sharp tones—*Natalie, assets, lawyer*—were Mikki's.

"Perhaps Abilene and I should wait until later to move into the house?" I suggested when Frank finally returned to the table. By then we were almost through eating, and the gravy had congealed on his mashed potatoes.

"That would probably be best. I don't think we'll be staying long. I may have to run into Horton and rent a trailer. Mikki wants to take a few things home with us."

"Some of the canned and frozen food?"

"Well, no, not really. Jessie has a nice collection of Navajo squash blossom necklaces and other turquoise jewelry—" He broke off and laughed a little too heartily. "Though that wouldn't take a trailer to haul, would it? But some of the Navajo rugs are old and quite valuable. Things Jock and Jessie picked up when they were filming on the reservation years ago. A few pieces of the antique furniture are quite good also. Plus there's the Oscar and the piano, of course. It's an old-fashioned player type, possibly quite valuable."

I hadn't realized before that it was a player piano.

"We'll be taking things just for safekeeping, of course. Everything will have to be inventoried and declared as part of the estate," he added hastily, as if he thought I might suspect them of trying to conceal assets.

An ulterior motive to taking things home with them, other than Mikki's general acquisitiveness, hadn't occurred to me before, but . . . hmmmm.

It also struck me that Mikki seemed rather familiar with the house and its contents considering that Frank had said she'd been here only once.

Abilene and I loaded the dishwasher, retrieved some of the clothes she'd chosen from Jessie's closet, and retreated

153

to the motor home. Lights burned long into the night in the house.

Abilene had fresh clothes to put on next morning, but she still needed shoes and undergarments, so we put things away in the motor home and drove into Dulcy, then on to Horton. I was perfectly willing to pay for whatever she needed, but she insisted on extracting the dollars from the narrow fold of bills in the leather pouch that still hung at her throat. Her selections were plain and practical: white panties, simple bra, cotton pajamas, sturdy socks, and jogging-type shoes, not an expensive brand name.

Horton was considerably larger than Dulcy, but it was still a small town. I enjoyed the novelty of shopping with someone even though we both had to watch our dollars. I did splurge on a new Patricia Rushford Christian mystery. I used my prepaid phone card to call the mail-forwarding place in Little Rock that I was using as an address, gave them my password, and asked them to forward my mail to General Delivery in Dulcy. We finished the shopping tour with cones at an ice cream shoppe, Abilene's raspberry sherbet, mine black walnut.

We made one last stop at the supermarket for milk and eggs, plus some fresh vegetables and fruit. Abilene stopped at the rack of greeting cards.

"Did you want to send someone a card?" I asked.

"I don't know if I should."

"Would it be to someone back in the area where Boone lives?"

"Oh no. It's just that Lily has a birthday next week. I don't want her to think I've forgotten her, but I don't want to intrude on her new life . . ."

"They're where with their mother?"

"In Kentucky. I have the address." She touched the cord at her throat again.

"Then I don't think it would hurt to send her a nice card."

"Should I tell the kids where I am?"

I considered the question. Given the hostile state of affairs between the children's real mother and Boone, it was unlikely they'd be in touch. But it never hurt to be extra careful.

"Maybe later on, okay?"

Abilene picked out a cute card shaped like a kitten, and we stopped in Dulcy to buy a stamp and mail the card. Before sealing the envelope she carefully took two one-dollar bills from the ever-thinning fold and tucked them inside. I shouldn't have been watching, I suppose, but I was, and I saw her sign the card, "With big barrels of love from your other Mom." She swiped a knuckle across her eyes.

Frank's SUV was gone when I pulled the motor home into our parking place, but the sliding glass door on the back side of the house was open so I assumed Mikki hadn't gone with him. Her big Lincoln had been pulled into the carport beside the Hummer. Abilene and I had a quick sandwich, and I went over to the house and knocked.

Mikki came to the door wearing blue shorts and white T-shirt, the Dolly Parton proportions on full display. She had a cup of coffee in one hand—apparently she'd decided it was cut-rate brand or nothing—and cigarette in the other. The morning appeared to have taken a toll on her hair and makeup. Dust smeared her blush, and a strand of spider web dangled from her disheveled ponytail.

"I was wondering if I could help sort or pack or something?" I said.

She waved the cigarette. "Frank went into town to rent a trailer, and I'm taking a break. I guess we won't be able to take the Hummer this trip. I can't believe Jessie didn't leave things more organized." Not quite a pout, but she sounded put-upon.

"Like their wills?" I ventured.

"Well, I suppose it would be asking too much, but they *could* have pinned them to that note and saved us a lot of trouble." She gave me an appraising glance, hip cocked against the door frame. "You're the one who found the bodies, aren't you?"

"Yes."

"It must have been pretty awful?" An uplift at the end made it a question, as if she was looking for lurid details.

I didn't offer them. All I said was a noncommittal, "Not pleasant," and asked a question of my own. "Were you surprised by what Frank's folks did?"

"Surprised? Oh no. Absolutely not!" Blond tendrils bounced as she shook her head.

The vehemence of her answer mildly surprised me. I hadn't thought she'd known them that well.

"I mean, they just didn't *think* like the rest of us. All this awful *hoarding*. Have you seen how much toilet tissue is in the basement? And hiding things and playing war games and being so suspicious of everyone. And then to complicate everything for Frank by not even leaving *wills*. I just can't believe they'd be so . . . thoughtless."

I got the impression Mikki was more annoyed by this *thoughtlessness* than heartbroken over the loss of her in-laws. Although perhaps she was hiding her grief. Hiding it well.

"It does seem that people like Jock and Jessie would want to tie up loose ends before . . . doing what they did."

She gave me an odd glance. "What do you mean?"

"Nothing in particular. Just that it seems odd. Out of character."

"Surely you don't think it was something other than

suicide?" The shrewd blue eyes took on an unexpected alertness.

"Deputies and the medical examiner were here. There didn't appear to be any doubts about the manner of death. Homicide/suicide, I believe it's referred to technically, in Jock and Jessie's case."

"Frank mentioned that everyone seemed quite professional and competent. I'm sure their conclusions can be trusted. And there was the note, of course. That doesn't leave any doubt."

Yes, the note. My nagging suspicions about murder still weren't totally squelched, but, given the note, suicide seemed the only possible conclusion. I detoured that subject, however, and said, "Frank mentioned he thought Jock and Jessie might have had a private safe hidden here somewhere, and the wills could be in that."

"Not in this house, there isn't a safe," Mikki declared. She crossed over to the kitchen sink, dumped the remainder of her coffee, and squashed her cigarette in a saucer. "I've looked behind every picture, under every rug, in every cubbyhole—"

She broke off as Frank's SUV, pulling a U-Haul trailer, came around the house. At the same time the phone started ringing. Mikki made no move to answer it.

"The . . . uh . . . phone's ringing," I pointed out.

Mikki lifted a dismissive shoulder. "Natalie calling to belly-ache about something. She called earlier. She's such a hotshot real estate agent . . . she even bought the apartment building they live in, did you know? . . . but *we* wind up penny-pinching because she's always demanding more child support or something extra for ballet lessons or soccer camp or some ridiculous thing. She even hit Jock and Jessie up for money a few times. When what those kids *really* need is more attention and discipline from her. It's no wonder they're so ill-behaved, they're

157

on their own so much. Now I suppose she's trying to figure a way to grab some of the estate."

The phone kept ringing persistently. Mikki just as persistently ignored it. Finally I said, "Perhaps I should answer it just in case it's someone other than Natalie?"

Mikki shrugged, and I walked over and picked up the phone. "Hello?"

A female voice that sounded both wary and doubtful said, "Mikki?"

"No. This is Ivy. We're helping out here for a while."

"Oh. I see. This is Natalie Northcutt?" An upswing at the end seemed to ask if that meant anything to me.

"Yes, of course. What can I do for you?"

"I heard about Jock and Jessie's deaths. I was just wondering about services. I'm thinking the children and I should probably be there, although . . ." The thought ended on another doubtful slide, although I wasn't sure if she was doubtful about her own welcome at her ex-parents-in-law's funeral or about the wisdom of taking the children to such an event.

"Frank said there will be only a simple graveside service at the cemetery out in California where they'll be buried. I'm not sure of the date, but I could have Frank—" I realized Mikki was watching me like a hawk-eyed salesclerk suspecting someone of shoplifting, and I rephrased the statement. "I could ask Frank about the date and call you back."

"No. That's okay. We wouldn't be able to go out to California anyway. But thank you for your helpfulness. I'm sure Frank is quite devastated. They were wonderful people."

She hung up, and Mikki, sounding triumphant, said, "See? It was her, wasn't it?"

"She just wanted to know about funeral services. Is that what she called about earlier?"

Mikki hesitated, and I realized she probably hadn't given

the ex-wife a chance to say much of anything on the earlier call. Another shrug. "I don't know. She asked for Frank, and he was about to leave for town. So I told her she'd have to call back."

And then when Natalie did call, Mikki wouldn't answer the phone. I suppose I was feeling a bit snide at Mikki's attitude, and I jumped back to the subject of the will with a suggestion I doubted would soothe her.

"Maybe the wills might show Jock and Jessie left part or all of the estate to the children."

Mikki's mouth actually dropped open. She stared at me. She'd obviously never thought of that.

Actually, I regretted the comment as soon as the words were out. What if Mikki decided that the complication of no wills was preferable to wills that left Frank's kids in control? Might something "accidentally" happen to such wills if they were found?

That would be a drastic, even illegal step, but somehow, looking at the horrified expression on Mikki's face, I wouldn't put it past her.

19

Frank backed the U-Haul trailer up to the deck, and Abilene and I spent the afternoon helping Frank and Mikki load it.

First item on Mikki's agenda was the largest piece, the player piano, and it took all four of us to huff and puff it out to the deck and into the covered trailer.

Next came an antique, pedal-style sewing machine, the rosewood desk from my upstairs bedroom, several small antique tables, and, stuffed in around them, the Navajo rugs. Also in need of "safekeeping," as Frank had earlier phrased it, was a heavy, metal tea service, probably silver but possibly an incredibly valuable platinum. An antique-looking lamp, two boxes of piano player rolls, the Oscar, and quite a collection of film memorabilia, plus numerous boxes with contents unknown to me.

One thing to be said for Mikki: she didn't just give orders. The temperature was in the nineties, sultry enough to raise a sweat just lifting an eyebrow, but she was right in there packing and lugging and stuffing, eyeliner smudged to jungle-trail rings around her eyes and T-shirt glued to her back with perspiration. During a break, when Abilene went to check on a noise in the emu pen and Frank was at the refrigerator getting ice, I remarked to Mikki that she seemed quite knowledgeable about antiques.

It was a euphemistic way of saying what I was really thinking, that it looked as if she was expertly scooping up anything of value that could be dragged, carried, or pushed out of the house. By now I'd also observed that the music box and the lovely perfume bottles in the bedroom were gone, and I was sure Jessie's squash blossom and turquoise jewelry collection would never be seen here at the end of Dead Mule Road again.

"I have an antique corner in my beauty salon where I sell a few things. It's just too bad the player piano isn't grand-piano style. They're much more valuable—" Mikki broke off suddenly, gave me a sharp look, and added hastily, "But the sentimental value is what really matters, of course. These are heirlooms Frank's children may want someday."

She was sweating like a plow horse for *sentimental value*? I gave a silent *ha!* to that. I was reasonably certain most everything in the U-Haul would turn up in her "antique corner" eventually. If not sooner.

Mikki also, to my surprise, emptied the gun cabinet, rolled the guns in blankets, and loaded them into the trailer. I would have expected guns to activate one of her delicate shudders, but she seemed surprisingly knowledgeable about them, tossing a couple of small handguns aside as "cheap Saturday night specials." I finally remarked on her unexpected expertise.

"My former husband and I ran a sporting goods store in Oregon for several years, so I couldn't help but learn a little. We wouldn't want these to get into the wrong hands," she added, her tone virtuous as she stuffed a heavy, deadly looking handgun into a pillowcase.

161

I suspected Mikki's interest in the guns was based more on monetary value than safety worries—she didn't seem concerned about whose hands those "cheap Saturday night specials" might fall into—but it was none of my business, of course. One thing I learned as I helped in the wrapping process was what those objects I hadn't been able to identify in the bottom of the gun cabinet were. Mikki knew. Silencers. Even Frank looked startled at that revelation, although I couldn't tell if he was startled by the news that his parents owned silencers or that Mikki could identify them.

It was close to 8:00 by the time the trailer and SUV were both as tightly packed as pills in a bottle. I thought Frank and Mikki would rest up and start for home in the morning, but Mikki announced they were taking off now because driving would be cooler at night. The plan was that Frank would go ahead and Mikki would follow in her car, in case he ran into any problems with the trailer.

"I've had the mail forwarded down to our address, and I've notified Jock and Jessie's Hollywood agent and everybody else I could think of about their deaths. If you get phone calls from anyone who hasn't heard yet, you can just refer them to me," Frank said as he stood beside the open door of the SUV. He looked as enthusiastic about this drive as a tired soldier on a forced night march. "And give me a call if you run into any problems."

The cluttered mess of folders on the dining room table had been swept into boxes, but I knew Frank still hadn't found any of the important papers he needed. Hesitantly, because I wasn't certain he'd want me poking around in private matters, I said, "I have some experience with filing and such. If you'd like me to try to get things organized . . . ?"

"I would be forever grateful for any organization you can give anything here." He made an exaggerated bow of gratitude. "Keep an eye out for a safe deposit key or letters from a lawyer, anything like that, okay? And I still think there may be a safe hidden around here somewhere. Though probably nothing big or we'd have found it by now."

"Have you looked into the computer files?"

"I tried, but I couldn't get past the password. But if you're into computers . . . ?"

"My grandniece showed me a few things."

"You're welcome to give it a try. There isn't an Internet connection, however. I suppose Jock and Jessie were afraid someone would hack into their stuff and steal their emu records or something." He grimaced, then slid into the SUV and gave me a smile and wave. "Don't forget to eat a lot of corned beef."

He took off down the driveway, the big SUV pulling the heavily loaded trailer without difficulty.

"I won't bother locking the house," Mikki called from the deck as dust billowed behind the departing vehicle. Frank had already put the suitcases in her car along with an overflow of boxes. "You'll be moving in right away, won't you?"

I was relieved by the question. I hadn't been certain she knew we were going to live in the house, that Frank might have avoided telling her because he thought she'd disapprove.

"Yes, we will."

"Well, good luck living here. If I were you, I'd stay out from under those antler chandeliers." She rolled her eyes. "They look like disasters waiting to happen."

"I keep thinking they'd make the perfect instrument for an 'accident' in a murder mystery. *The Horns of Death*, perhaps. Or *Assassination by Antler*."

Then I realized that bit of levity was in very bad taste, considering her in-laws had recently died in that very same room. But she didn't seem to notice my gaffe. She laughed.

"Right. *The Case of the Deadly Chandelier*. Wouldn't you know,

Frank just loves the ghastly things? He thinks we're going to take one down and put it up in our new house." She rolled her eyes. "I've got news for him."

"Who knows?" I said. "Maybe they'll accidentally fall and break into a zillion pieces."

"One can only hope," she said, and we smiled at each other in conspiratorial agreement.

Not that I'd ever actually *do* anything to the chandeliers, of course. I was here to take care of things, not destroy them.

Mikki slid into her car, then rolled down the window, her moment of lightheartedness cooling to tight lines around her mouth. "If that ex-wife of Frank's shows up, don't let her in the house. Or anywhere else."

"Why would she come here?"

"Because she's greedy and ambitious and pushy. A friend in Dallas said she and the boyfriend bought some old folks' home and are turning all the people out in the street so they can put up high-priced condominiums. All heart, you know? She'll try to glom onto anything she can here, with some oh-so-noble story about doing it for the kids."

Well, the ex-wife wasn't going to get any antiques, that was for sure. Nor any of Jessie's collection of Navajo jewelry. Mikki had already "glommed" onto all that herself. With her own self-righteous claim of saving heirlooms for Frank's children.

I waved her off. I was, I had to admit, glad to see them go. They weren't unpleasant people, but a tense, before-the-storm atmosphere swirled around them, and the place seemed much more serene and peaceful with them gone. Just me, Abilene, Koop, and the emus now.

Frank had found the septic hookup his folks had used for their travel trailer, so with Abilene guiding me I moved the motor home over there and emptied the holding tanks. The logical thing would be for us to move into our new rooms immediately, but the day had been hot and sultry, and it didn't feel as if the night was going to cool down much. Abilene decided to sleep outside, so I did too.

We spread our blankets and sheets on the grass near the deck. The mosquitoes were already out, and I was grateful the Northcutts had hoarded a good supply of mosquito repellent. The crescent moon had already gone down by the time we went to bed, and only the stars, like incandescent grains of sand, decorated the sky.

I crossed my hands behind my head, remembering what Abilene had once said about looking up at stars. Koop had planted himself on my midsection, his purr motor rumbling. "Are you thinking about God now?" I asked Abilene.

"Mostly I was thinking about the kids." There was a bobble in her voice that made me reach across the grass between us and pat her hand in sympathy. "We used to do that wishing on a star thing. You know, star light, star bright, first star I see tonight, I wish I may, I wish I might . . ." An audible swallow. "Whatever. Something like that."

I knew what she was wishing right now. Nothing for herself. Just for a safe life and good things for the kids.

"You really believe in God?" she added reflectively.

"Oh yes, and that he sent his Son to make a way for us to spend eternity with him."

"I'd like to believe in God and eternity and that he really cares about us and all that, but . . ."

"But?"

"But sometimes it all seems kind of like . . . tooth-fairy stuff." She crossed her hands under her head as she looked up. "A feel-good fairy tale about this all-powerful being who loves and cares about us. I've never seen much real sign of that. And all that stuff about a miraculous virgin birth, and Jesus being crucified and then coming back to life. It's hard to believe."

"I thought you said you didn't know anything about God," I teased lightly. "And already you know these important truths."

"You come across things when you read." I heard a shrug in her voice. "Doesn't mean I think any of it's the *truth*. From everything I've seen personally, dead is . . . dead."

"Sometimes I've had doubts too," I admitted. Mosquitoes hummed around my head, but the repellent was working. "But I can always look up at the stars like this and go back to the beginning."

"The beginning?"

"Do you think all this popped into existence by itself? That the orderly design of sun and planets and galaxies, and then us too, along with all the animals and plants on earth, just accidentally came into being?"

"That's hard to believe too," she admitted.

"Which is why the first words in Genesis make so much sense. 'In the beginning God created the heavens and the earth.' And if God could create all this, if everything started with him, surely he can do anything he wants with any of it. Virgin birth, resurrection, miracles . . . piece of cake!"

"You think he knows . . . right now . . . everything we're saying and doing and thinking? That he's in control of everything?"

"Oh yes. He's had his hand in history all down through the ages. He has his hand in each of our lives today."

"You think he controls every itsy-bitsy little thing that happens to us?" She sounded skeptical. "Like if someone gets a hangnail?"

"Well, I don't know that every time I get a hangnail or a flat tire or have a bad hair day that it's something he choreographed. Sometimes a hangnail is just a hangnail. But we never know how God may choose to work in our lives, and if he has a *purpose* for a hangnail or a flat tire, he can certainly provide one."

I thought she was considering that, but suddenly she jerked upright. "What's that?"

"What's what?"

"I heard a noise out in the woods."

"Probably just the emus."

She sat there cross-legged in her new pajamas, head cocked as she listened. Me, I was worn out from lugging around piano, guns, and Navajo rugs. I tried to listen too. I heard frogs croaking, insects chirping, and Koop purring, once a scuffle from the emu pen. But somewhere along in there I just fell asleep.

I'd already decided to drive into Dulcy for church the next morning, but I didn't mention it to Abilene until we were eating breakfast in the big house. Considering our encouraging discussion under the stars, I hoped she'd come along. But she said she was going for a hike.

"A hike?" I repeated, instantly alarmed. "Do you think that's a good idea?"

"I never did hear anything more last night, but I still think I heard *something—*"

"All the more reason not to go prowling in the woods," I said.

"I want to check it out. I could take a gun," she added. "Mikki left a couple of them."

I didn't think toting a gun was any improvement on the hike idea itself, and, as it turned out, a gun wouldn't have done much good anyway because we couldn't find a bullet of any size or kind anywhere. Which made me think ammunition must have been what was in some of those heavy boxes we loaded into the trailer. A distinct relief, I decided. Bullets were what made guns dangerous.

"I'll take a paintball gun, then," Abilene decided. "They look pretty realistic."

"Murderers tend to be able to tell real guns from phonies," I pointed out. "And what do you do when he starts shooting bullets and all you have is paintballs?"

"According to the authorities, there hasn't been any murder. Ergo . . . that's a word I found in some books I read, and I kind of like it, don't you? Ergo, ergo. Anyway, ergo, no murderer."

Ergo or not, I wasn't convinced hiking out in the woods was a good idea. Nor was I totally persuaded there wasn't a murderer. "Somebody left that bare footprint," I pointed out. "And we've seen movement out there in the woods and you heard something last night—"

"Probably just a deer."

"I hit something with a paintball that I'm sure wasn't a deer."

But by then I was mostly talking to myself because Abilene was at a kitchen drawer picking up the shed keys Frank had left there.

"See you later," she called from the door. "Don't worry. Say a prayer for me if you want to."

I did exactly that, both then and later in church. I was disappointed she didn't come. *But these things take time, don't they, Lord?*

It was a good service, with a strong message centered on Romans 8 and friendly people talking to me both before and afterwards, including a big welcoming hug from Margaret Rau. She was appalled by the Northcutts' deaths and seemed concerned when I said I was staying on for a while as a caretaker.

"All alone?" Her tanned forehead creased into worry lines. "It's so isolated out there."

"There's another caretaker. I won't be there alone." I didn't elaborate. I doubted hearing that the other caretaker was a young stray I'd picked up would relieve Margaret's concerns.

"Good. I'm glad to hear that. Has that strange Ute guy ever showed up out there again?"

"No. Why?"

"Someone said they saw him over in Horton a couple days ago."

"I can't think of any reason he'd come to the house. He's surely heard about the Northcutts' deaths. Maybe he's working for someone over in Horton now."

"Could be, I suppose." Her face brightened. "Maybe you could come in on Wednesday evenings too? We have a potluck and then Bible study."

"I'll try."

The gas was getting low in the motor home, but I didn't stop at a station. I intended to take Frank up on his offer to let us use gasoline out of the big storage tank. We hadn't discussed our using the Hummer, but it wasn't anything I wanted to drive anyway.

Abilene wasn't around when I got home. I fussed with moving things from the motor home to the house, putting towels in the shared bathroom, and watching Koop prowl the new surroundings. I turned on the computer but, like Frank, couldn't get past the password block. I even walked as far back into the woods as the bare footprint, although deer tracks obscured it now.

But mostly I worried. Worried about everything from Abilene getting lost to being stalked by some vicious wild animal to encountering some long-haired, wild-eyed owner of the barefoot print.

However, when she dropped the paintball gun on the deck and walked into the kitchen at the big house about 2:30, it appeared that the worst that had happened to her was that she was tired, sweaty, and had a backside covered with enough mud to plant petunias. Also a powerful scent of muddy swamp. Which I can guarantee is never going to be up there with White Diamonds as a best-selling perfume.

"How'd that happen?" I inquired.

She brushed at the mud blotch. "I spotted a big yellow and black butterfly. I guess I . . . forgot to watch where I was going."

I laughed. Leave it to Abilene to be so entranced by a butterfly that she tumbled into a muddy swamp.

But she also had news, and her expression turned sober when she announced it. "I found something else back there."

"Like . . . what?"

"Somebody's been camping way back there in the woods."

"You saw someone?"

"No, but there's a flattened place in the grass where a tent's been pitched. And there are empty tin cans and Styrofoam plates. He's a big chili and sardines and ramen noodles eater, and he swigs a lot of Dr Pepper. Plus an occasional beer."

"Not exactly your neighborhood gourmet, then."

"He does like Oreo cookies."

"Maybe it isn't just a 'he,'" I suggested. My first jumpy thought, of course, was that this could be a Braxton, but I didn't want to overreact to something that could be quite innocent. "Maybe it's a family that hiked into the wilderness to vacation on the cheap."

"I saw only one set of footprints."

"Barefoot?"

"No. He has shoes. Big, heavy boots, actually. And there were heavy tire tracks where he'd been parked."

"Tire tracks?" I repeated, startled. "How could anyone get a vehicle way back in there?"

"There's an old road coming in from the other side. I don't know where the property lines are, so I don't know if the campsite is on this property or someone else's or maybe government land." She went to the little closet at the far end of the kitchen and yanked out a broom. "Could you sweep me off? I feel like I have swamp creatures crawling on me."

We went outside to the grass, and I briskly whopped the broom across her backside. The mud was mostly dry now. I didn't see any swamp creatures, but smelly dust and chunks flew as I swept.

"I'll go shower and put on something clean."

I had iced lemonade—courtesy of about fifty cans of the stuff in one of the freezers—ready when she returned dressed in a pair of Jessie's old shorts and a blue T-shirt. She climbed onto a tall stool at the counter separating kitchen and dining room and took a thirsty gulp of lemonade.

"So, do you think this guy's been sneaking over here? That he's who we've seen and heard, maybe even the 'deer' I paintballed?"

"I found enough trampled grass and bushes with broken branches and footprints . . . footprints going both directions . . . to know he's definitely been over here. That's how I found the campsite, in fact, following the trail he left."

Not Ute then. My second uneasy suspicion, linking Abilene's news of a camper with Margaret Rau's comment that Ute had been seen in the area, was that he might be sneaking around out here with something nefarious in mind. But Ute was too much of an expert at survival-style living to leave a trail that could be so easily followed. He'd survived six weeks in the wilds with only a pocketknife and matches, and this camper/skulker sounded as if he'd starve without a can opener.

"Generic weirdo?" I suggested. "Peeping Tom?"

Abilene twisted hula-hoop rings on the tiled surface of the counter with her icy glass. "Maybe."

She sounded skeptical, and I couldn't give my suggestion much credence either. There must be easier ways to peep than sneaking through miles of brush and swamp.

"Maybe he didn't camp there specifically because it gave him access to this place. Maybe he just wandered over here in his spare time, out of curiosity."

"It's a long way to wander."

"How far?"

"Probably three or four miles. Though it feels like about ten, going up and down hills and around the swampy places and brush that's too thick to get through."

"Maybe he's out for the exercise, then."

"If he wants exercise, it would make more sense to hike on that old road than to thrash around in the brush."

Okay, both of those more-or-less innocent possibilities shot down. "Was he using a campfire?"

"No. I found a couple of empty books of matches near a stump, so he probably had one of those propane or Coleman stoves set up on it. At least he's conscientious about fire danger."

Okay, conscientious about fire or not, this was worrisome. What was the guy doing? I've been known to be overly suspicious, but this guy obviously wasn't making neighborly jaunts to borrow a cup of sugar or deliver welcoming brownies.

"Maybe he's a transient looking for something to steal," I suggested, still hoping for something generic, something not connected to *us* to explain his presence.

"Or maybe he had something to do with the Northcutts' deaths."

"Or maybe," I suggested slowly, "both."

"Both?"

"Maybe he wants to steal something he didn't get when he killed them."

Which could mean *we* were standing between him and his goal.

About as secure a position as standing between a bull and a red flag.

"But, officially, there isn't any murder," Abilene reminded me.

"Right. But we might notify the sheriff's office about someone illegally camping or trespassing, and see what they come up with. That Deputy Hamilton seemed nice. We could talk to him."

"They're in the middle of their big murder and drug investigation. I doubt they're going to be too concerned about some guy dumping sardine cans."

True. Then I brightened. There was an important point we were ignoring here, no matter who our camper/skulker was.

"But the tent wasn't there, you say. Just a flattened place where it had been. So maybe it's been days, even weeks since he's been there, and we're worrying about something that's long over."

"I don't think so. I found part of an old newspaper just a couple days old."

Not good. But there was still my main bright point.

"But however recently he may have been there, he *is* gone now. Right? So we really don't have anything to worry about." I also thought this departure eliminated a Braxton camper/skulker. The Braxtons, when they located me, tended to do something drastic about it.

There was only the barest hesitation before she agreed

with my optimistic conclusion. "Right," she said, and drained her glass.

Abilene went out to repair a loose place on the deck railing.

As I put a load of clothes in the washer, another possibility occurred to me. The sheriff's nephew had been murdered, possibly because of a drug involvement. I'd heard of such things as movable meth labs, labs actually set up in a car or van.

Could that be what our camper/skulker was up to, perhaps with some connection to the murdered nephew?

But if that were true, why would he be sneaking around *here*?

Unless he knew something we didn't.

21

We moved the rest of our stuff from the motor home to the house, and I fixed salmon patties for dinner. Cans of salmon were also in abundant supply, as if there'd been some great migration from the sea to the Northcutts' basement.

I discovered a couple of peculiarities while looking around down there. One was the Northcutts' apparent paranoia about a coming crisis in the world supply of toilet tissue. A veritable mountain of it reached almost to the ceiling in one corner. The mountain didn't look too stable, and I stayed away from it. I didn't want my obituary to announce that I was the first woman in history to be decimated by an avalanche of tumbling toilet tissue.

Koop, always interested in sticking his nose into new places, had followed me down the stairs. I wasn't paying much attention as he wandered among big plastic cartons of beans and rice and laundry detergent, until I heard a muffled meow.

"Koop?" I called. "Kitty, kitty?"

Another muffled meow, this time sounding rather crotch-ety, as if he was not pleased at being wherever he was, but I still couldn't see him. I was suddenly excited. The Northcutts were the kind of people who'd invest in a secret passageway or hidden room. Had Koop discovered it?

Another series of meows, these impatient, and I placed them as coming from a top shelf. I grabbed a step stool and planted it near the sound, which I had by then decided was regrettably too close to suggest Koop had wandered into a hidden room.

"If you got in there, wherever you are, can't you get out the same way?" I grumbled. Unhappy yowl from Koop.

I climbed on the step stool and started removing cans. This was an area of true survival-type food, cans of pow-dered cheese and dehydrated fruits and vegetables and eggs, all packed, according to the labels, in "inert nitrogen" for long-term storage.

The surprise came when it didn't take long to reach Koop because, although the top shelf looked full, it had only a single row of cans up front with a large empty space behind. A space that Koop had somehow managed to squeeze himself into.

I dragged him out and deposited him on the floor, then climbed up to inspect the space more closely. It could have been left because the Northcutts hadn't yet acquired enough survival food to fill the shelves completely. Yet there was something so purposeful about the careful arrangement of cans around the empty space. For *what* purpose?

An obvious answer.

For hiding something.

Something that had never been put there?

Or something that had been there but was now missing?

After dinner I took Abilene down and showed her the odd space. Koop had gotten into it, we decided, by starting at the end of a shelf a good ten feet away and squeezing along the narrow space between the cans on the top shelf and the ceiling above. Once in the large empty space, pure cat self-importance had apparently made him demand help rather than squeeze back the way he'd come.

"Did Mikki bring anything up from down here?" Abilene asked.

"Not that I know of."

"Maybe Jock and Jessie were reserving it as a place to put something special."

Given the Northcutts' peculiarities, "something special" might mean anything from mummified emus to spare body parts. I decided I'd rather not speculate and headed for the stairs.

We tried the TV in the "great room" that evening. Frank had said that was what Jock and Jessie called the big room, and it did seem appropriate. This TV had a clear, sharp picture, no doubt due to the huge antenna atop the house, which went up much higher than the antenna on the motor home. Yet my eyes kept straying from Diane Sawyer on the TV screen.

"Does that deer head over the fireplace bother you as much as it does me?" I asked finally.

Abilene glanced up at the impressive spread of antlers. "It is a little glassy eyed."

"And crooked."

"Um, well, yeah, that too." Abilene didn't sound particularly concerned, but she added, "If you want to fix it, there's a stepladder out in one of the sheds."

"I do."

She got the keys again, and we trooped out to the survival-equipment shed. She grabbed one end of the ladder, and I took the other. We set it up by the fireplace, and I put a foot on the bottom rung.

"Oh no. I'll do it," Abilene said.

"I am perfectly capable of climbing a ladder—"

"You might be capable of dancing on the rooftop too, but that doesn't mean it would be a smart thing to do."

Abilene politely forearmed me aside. She climbed to the top of the stepladder and leaned over to straighten the wooden plaque to which the deer head was attached. "How does it look—" She broke off as she peered more closely at a point under the deer's jaw.

"What?" I asked.

"Maybe you should look at this."

"Okay, come down and I'll climb up and—"

"No, I'll bring it down."

She lifted the plaque off the bracket holding it and wrestled the big antlered head down the ladder. She set it on the floor.

"There." She pointed to a small, neat hole in the animal's once-powerful neck. "What does that look like to you?"

I knelt and fingered the hole. It had clean-cut, distinct edges, hairs sliced with almost scalpel precision.

"It's a bullet hole, isn't it?" she asked.

With a certain reluctance, I stuck my finger in the hole. I couldn't feel a bullet, but my finger didn't go in very far.

"I suppose a bullet hole is logical. The deer probably didn't die of old age," I said.

But I knew we were thinking the same thing. Also doubtful that a taxidermist would leave an open bullet hole to mar his work. And besides, this hole looked sharp and fresh.

"So how did it get there?" Abilene asked.

"Good question."

She knelt beside me and tilted the head so we could see

the back side of the plaque. A splintered spot bulged outward, as if the bullet was still lodged in the wood.

"I wonder if it's from the same gun that killed the Northcutts?" My gaze followed Abilene's as she glanced the long length of the room to the bare spot where the sofa and bodies had once stood. "But I don't see how a stray bullet could have come this way. Jock was facing the other direction when he shot Jessie."

"And he certainly couldn't have missed with a first bullet when he shot himself."

Again I knew we were thinking the same thing: *If* he shot Jessie. *If* he shot himself. But then, as usual, I bumped into the familiar block wall: the note. How could anyone have forged the signatures so expertly that Frank didn't doubt their authenticity? Unless Frank himself had counterfeited the signatures, and then neatly protected himself by identifying them as genuine . . .

I backed away from that thought. I didn't want to go there. I liked Frank. I thought that whatever his messy wife/ex-wife problems and his differences with Jock and Jessie might be, he'd honestly cared for them.

But if his money problems went deep enough . . . I knew about Mikki's pricey tastes, an expensive new house in the works, and the ex-wife hounding him for more support money. Maybe even larger financial difficulties I knew nothing about. And if Frank had thought all Jock and Jessie's assets would conveniently flow to him if they were dead . . .

Murder had certainly been done for less. And I didn't really know Frank all that well.

"Maybe we should contact Deputy Hamilton," I said.

This time Abilene nodded.

I doubted we could get hold of the officer on a Sunday evening, and I was right. The woman at the sheriff's office helpfully suggested I talk to a different officer, but I said no, I wanted Deputy Hamilton and left my name and number.

Much to my surprise he called only a few minutes later.

"This isn't an emergency," I said quickly. "We just happened onto something odd and would like to talk to you when it's convenient."

"Now's as good a time as any. If you don't mind some chewing noises in your ear. I picked up a hamburger on my way back to the office."

He didn't say back from where, but I could guess that the sheriff was still keeping everyone hopping on his nephew's murder. I identified myself and my relationship to the Northcutts' deaths, in case he didn't remember me, but he broke in to say, "I know who you are, Mrs. Malone. And Ms. Morrison too."

I thought about correcting that to the Tyler name Abilene had reverted to, but I decided it would be better to stay away from irrelevant distractions. So I just told him we'd stayed on as caretakers at the Northcutt place and had found this bullet hole in the deer head.

"And you think this may have some . . . ah . . . significance?" He sounded puzzled.

"Possibly. A third shot, in addition to the two that killed the Northcutts, might suggest some . . . irregularities in the situation as a suicide."

He didn't need diagrams. Probably he remembered both Abilene's and my imaginative excursion into the possibility of faked suicide. "As in a double murder, you mean, not a mutually decided upon homicide/suicide?"

"Possibly."

"All the evidence points to suicide. The note—"

"I don't suppose a handwriting expert was called in to verify that the signatures on the note were genuine?"

"I don't believe it was even considered. The son did personally identify the signatures, you know."

So, back to that. Did I want to start accusing Frank?

"And there is the fact that gunshot residue was found on Jock Northcutt's hand," Deputy Hamilton added. "They tested for that."

"Oh. Well, that's . . . good."

Suddenly Deputy Hamilton laughed. "Look, I know finding a stray bullet hole might be disconcerting. It isn't the norm for your average suburban home. But, you know how Greeks celebrate by breaking plates?"

"I've heard of that, yes."

"It sometimes seems to me that what Oklahomans do instead of breaking plates when they want to celebrate or let off steam is drag out the ol' six-guns and blaze away. A holdover from the Wild West days, maybe. One cowboy out at a local ranch celebrated getting a new pair of boots by putting his old ones on top the hood of his pickup and using them for target practice. Making quite a mess of both boots and pickup, I might say, since he was a lousy shot. Another time, some new people were concerned about all the shooting at a neighbor's house, and I found it was an old guy celebrating his birthday. He said he always shot off as many rounds as he had years. Since he was ninety-two, it made quite a commotion."

I smiled. So it wasn't all murder and drugs in a cop's life. "I get the picture."

"And the Northcutts," he added, "were known to be, well . . ."

"Trigger happy?" I suggested.

"There've been rumors about war games in the woods out there. So maybe they were just . . . who knows? Playing some strange indoor game. Or one of them may have been cleaning a weapon without checking if it was loaded first. They did keep a lot of guns around. Perhaps you've heard about the confrontation between Mrs. Northcutt and a visitor?"

"Yes, but she didn't actually fire the crossbow. Or whatever it is you do with a crossbow."

"True." Pause, with chewing and gulping noises. "Look, Sheriff Howell has me pretty busy on this murder and drugs case, but I'll try to get out your way in the next couple days. We'll have a look, okay?"

"Thank you. We'd appreciate that."

Abilene set the mounted deer head in a corner where it would be readily available to show Deputy Hamilton, and we carried the stepladder out and parked it on the rear deck.

Next morning we plunged into housecleaning. All the packing and moving had left a trail of dust balls and debris. I vacuumed and Abilene mopped, and we both tackled spider webs and dust. Koop kept out of the way and tried out various pieces of furniture for their level of snoozing comfort.

About midmorning we took a break. Abilene went out to water the emus, and I made an impulsive decision to call good friend Magnolia back on Madison Street in Missouri, where we were neighbors for so many years.

I used my prepaid phone card, punching in the long string of numbers to do it. I was pleasantly surprised when Magnolia actually answered, because she and Geoff are so often on the road in their motor home. Magnolia is deep into genealogy, and they're frequently off investigating genealogical connections. (Rattling the family tree to see what nuts shake out, as Geoff puts it.)

"Ivy, it's so good to hear from you!" Magnolia exclaimed. "I don't suppose you're going to tell me where you are?"

"No." I always figure it's better no one knows; that way they're honestly ignorant if Braxton cohorts try to finagle the information out of them. "But I'm fine."

"That's good. I worry about you, you know."

I didn't want to worry her further with details about my encounters with more dead bodies. I also realized how much I missed her. And her creative changes of hair color. "What's with your hair these days?"

"My hair? Oh, I'm letting it go natural."

"Which is?"

"Silver, of course. Though I do have a few streaks to give it, you know, character. And a bit of pizzazz."

"What kind of streaks?"

"Um, rainbow, I suppose you might call them."

Which sounded as natural as a purple cow. But no doubt, on Magnolia, looked quite lovely. She has the flamboyant personality to carry off rainbow streaks.

"Mac called a couple days ago," she added. "He asked about you."

"Oh, did he now."

Mac is Mac MacPherson. Magnolia introduced us before I left Madison Street. It would be stretching things to say Mac and I have a bumpy relationship. Mainly because it would be a stretch to say we even have a relationship. But we once spent fun time together at something called a Meteor Daze festival, and he stopped to visit me when I was staying with my niece in Arkansas. So I suppose we're a little more than acquaintances. There seems to be a vague *something* between us. But the man also seems to think I might be laying a sly husband-snare for him, which makes me a bit huffy.

"He's still traveling the country, I suppose, writing his travel articles?" I asked.

"Actually, I think he's stopped in one place for a while."

"With one of his daughters?"

"No, he's in . . . let's see, where was it? Some man's name . . . Oh, I know. Hugo. Hugo, Oklahoma."

I concealed a gasp of surprise. Hugo was, what? Only sixty or seventy miles from where I was right now sitting.

184

"What's he doing there?"

"Recuperating, I believe. He suffered an attack."

"What kind of attack?" I asked, alarmed in spite of my huffy feelings toward him. "Heart attack? Stroke?"

"No, some sort of animal attack."

"An animal attacked Mac?"

"I don't know the details, but he isn't badly hurt. Nothing life threatening. But he injured his wrist and back, and he can't drive long distances for a while. I thought he sounded depressed, stuck there in a strange place all alone, not knowing anyone."

"Mac never goes anywhere without immediately knowing all kinds of people," I declared. Mac is one of those people who can find something to talk about with anyone. And the thing is, it isn't phony politeness. He's always genuinely interested.

"That's true," she agreed. "But you know what I mean. Too bad you aren't close enough that you could go visit him. Although, since you're on the road anyway . . ."

I recognized that tone. Dear Magnolia, playing on my sympathies. Mac *needs* you. Matchmaking again.

"And I do believe he may have worked his way through some of those commitment issues that were bothering him before."

"Magnolia, his problems with commitment are none of my concern. I am not in the market for a husband."

"You weren't in the market for a cat either, were you? But now you have one."

A small touché, I suppose, though I chose to ignore it.

"Actually, I can't get away right now. I'm caretaking on a ranch, and there are animals here."

"Oh." She sounded mildly frustrated by that roadblock but then brightened. "Well, then, you can at least call him! I almost forgot. He has a cell phone now. You know, you

185

should get one too. I'll get the number. I wrote it down here somewhere . . ."

She set the phone down before I could decide whether or not I wanted Mac's number, so I was left twiddling my thumbs and watching my prepaid minutes fizzle by.

"Well, who'd have thought I'd write it on the back of this note about some Swedish cousins of Geoff's in Toronto? Anyway, here it is."

She read off the number, and I obediently scribbled it on a notepad by the phone.

"And you will give him a call, won't you? I think a familiar voice would do so much to cheer him up. And you surely owe him that much."

Owe him? The man has sent me maybe three or four post-cards since the last time I saw him. However, hearing Mac had suffered some mysterious animal attack did concern me. And being incapacitated and alone in a strange place might well be depressing, even for a man as light-footed as Mac.

"Okay, I'll call him."

"Good. Now repeat the number back to me so I know you have it right." I did, and then she said, "Oh, something else."

Something in her tone put me on alert. "Yes?"

"Remember I told you a development outfit was nosing around about buying up houses here so they could put in a big motel and convention center? Well, they made us a definite offer. A very good offer. And I-I think we're going to take it." Her voice gave an uncharacteristic quiver, but she also sounded resolute.

"Sell out? Leave Madison Street for good?" I could hear the dismay in my voice.

"It's all different here now. Everyone's gone. Including you."

"But I'll surely be coming back!"

186

I wanted the Margollins to be there on Madison Street, even if I wasn't. They were right. The area was different now, no longer the everybody-knows-everybody neighborhood it had once been. But as long as they were there, a certain foundation of my life remained, a solid root, proof that I could go home again, that I wouldn't always be running from the Braxtons.

"But where would you go?" I asked.

"We might just live full time in the motor home, like you're doing. Or maybe we'll find some wonderful new place where we want to settle down."

I had the feeling she was trying to convince herself they were doing the right thing, and, even though I hated to see them leave Madison Street, I didn't want to undermine that decision.

"God filled the world with wonderful places," I agreed.

"Maybe they'll make you a good offer too."

Me, sell *my* house on Madison Street? The thought opened a hollow spot in the pit of my stomach. However many wonderful places there might be in this world, Madison Street was *home*.

And then I reminded myself, as I sometimes have to do, that the foundation of my life is not in a place, or people, or anything else that is of this world. It is only in the Lord, and wherever I am, he is there too. *He* is my foundation, and with him is my true home. Everything else is temporary.

"Just let me know if you sell out and leave, okay?" I said. I gave her the name of the mail-forwarding outfit in Little Rock. "I don't want to lose touch with you."

"And you'll call Mac?" she asked again.

"Yes, I will."

I sat there holding the phone after she hung up, and I felt a powerful urge to jump in the motor home and barrel right down to Hugo. *Now where did that come from?* I wondered, quite startled at myself.

Hastily I punched in the long string of numbers again, then the cell phone number Magnolia had given me.

Mac answered on the first ring, as if he'd been sitting there with the cell phone propped in his lap. You surely can't tell much from a one-word hello, but he didn't sound like his usual upbeat self.

"Hi, Mac. It's Ivy Malone."

"Ivy!" He instantly brightened, which gave even this well-worn heart a short swoop on the ol' roller coaster. "Hey, what a nice surprise to hear from you."

"Magnolia tells me you were injured in some animal attack?"

"No big deal. Just a few problems with my wrist and back. But I can't sit for long, so I'm using this chair the doctor prescribed. You kneel instead of sit on it. An ergonomic chair, he calls it."

"I had a friend who used one at her computer. She liked it."

"It's more comfortable than it looks. But no help as far as driving goes. I don't suppose you're anywhere in the vicinity of Hugo, Oklahoma?"

"You know I'm living in a motor home now?"

"Magnolia told me you'd decided to take up traveling for a while. So if you're anywhere near Oklahoma . . ."

"And if I were?"

"Maybe you could stop in for a visit. Or even stay a while. This is a great RV park. Nice swimming pool. Nearby video store and a drugstore that delivers. Reasonable rates, and they run a van downtown daily." He paused after the sales pitch. I stubbornly remained silent, and he finally made the big plunge. "I'd really like to see you again, Ivy."

I wouldn't mind seeing him too, but I perversely didn't admit that to him. "It's been a while, hasn't it?"

"Too long. But I guess you're too far away to come?"

"Actually, not all that far. But I can't get away." I explained about caretaking the Northcutts' ranch. "How far could you drive?"

"I'm not sure. Do you have something in mind?"

I hesitated. Did I have something in mind?

Ummm, well, yes. Maybe. But the prospect jiggled my nerves for a couple of reasons. Did the Braxtons' tentacles extend far enough that they knew about Mac, and he might inadvertently lead them to me? Was my subconscious slyly working on some devious husband-snaring agenda unknown to my conscious self, some scheme the conscious me would toss like a rotten tomato?

"Ivy?" Mac said tentatively into my silence.

I determinedly kicked Braxton worries aside and told my

subconscious to take a hike. Mac was a friend who needed someone right now, and I wasn't going to turn my back on him.

"There's plenty of room here to park, with a septic hookup for an RV. It's only about seventy miles or so from Hugo. If you could drive that far . . . ?"

"Yes, definitely," he interrupted eagerly. "If my back gets to hurting, I can just pull over for a few hours."

"Although you might find it's too isolated here. Doctors and hospital and stores are a long ways away. There's nothing to write a travel article about. And I wouldn't want you to do anything that might make your back problems worse."

I was backpedaling, the appalling thought occurring to me that if he showed up maybe I'd revert to some starry-eyed adolescent state and fall head over heels in love with him. He recognized the retreat immediately.

"So is this an invitation or not?" he demanded.

"Yes, it's an invitation," I said firmly. "Although I'll have to okay it with the owner first. I'll call you back, okay? Oh, hold on, I hear something." I stood up so I could see out a window. "A car from the sheriff's department is here, so I'll have to go now."

"And the sheriff's department is visiting you because . . . ?"

"Well, umm, there were a couple of dead bodies here when I arrived. And we just found another bullet hole. Not a brand-new one," I added hastily so he wouldn't think killers were standing in line to take potshots at us.

Moment of silence before, sounding resigned, he said, "Why doesn't any of this surprise me?"

"These things happen, you know," I said defensively.

I thought I heard *Only to you, Ivy Malone,* but perhaps I imagined that. I quickly said, "But the bodies are gone now, and it's quite peaceful and beautiful here."

"Good. I'll be ready to head out whenever you call. You can explain the dead bodies to me when I get there."

"Fine. You can explain your animal attack."

By that time Deputy Hamilton had pulled around to the backyard, and I opened the sliding glass door for him. He was in khaki pants and short-sleeved shirt, gun holstered on his lean hip with various other pieces of cop equipment dangling from his belt. He looked around as I led him across the great room to the deer head. I thought he was wondering what had happened to the bloody sofa.

"Frank moved it to a burn pile out toward the barn." I waved in that direction. "It's still out there, if you need to examine it."

Deputy Hamilton looked at me blankly, and I realized the sofa was not what was on his mind.

"Abilene is outside somewhere," I said.

Deputy Hamilton had too much law-officer self-control to blush, but his self-conscious smile told me I'd guessed correctly about what he was thinking.

"Perhaps she'll be around later," I added. Although I doubted that. Abilene was still skittish.

He squatted by the deer head and inspected the hole. Koop came over to look too, did the cigarette sniff-test, and decided the deputy was okay.

"It's a bullet hole, all right." Deputy Hamilton pulled out a pocketknife and dug into the back side of the plaque. The bullet fell out on the hardwood floor with a small clunk.

"So, what do you think?" I asked.

He bounced the lead lump in his hand. "Peculiar."

"But it doesn't mean anything?"

"I wouldn't say it doesn't mean anything. But I don't think

191

it proves anything. There's no telling how long it's been in there." He glanced upward. "That bracket over the fireplace, that's where the head was hanging?"

"Yes."

"Were there any other bullet holes?"

"We never looked," I said, aghast that I hadn't thought to conduct that elementary bit of investigation.

Deputy Hamilton carried the stepladder in from the back deck and, starting at the left corner, searched the wall up high. I searched the lower section, partly on my hands and knees. I found a 1989 penny and a mean-looking spider, plus the knowledge that LOL knees are not meant for this type of sleuthing work.

"I think we can safely conclude there are no other bullet holes," Deputy Hamilton said when we reached the far corner. He was standing on the floor now, and Koop was up on the ladder inspecting the situation.

"That's good, I guess. I'm sorry we bothered you," I added.

I was by now embarrassed that I had so quickly jumped to the conclusion that the bullet in the deer head would lead to some important revelation. Was I infected with that RHS malady common to mystery readers everywhere? Red Herring Syndrome. Seeing clues where none exist.

"That's okay. I needed a break from murder and drugs."

"No suspects in the nephew's murder yet?"

"Oh yeah, there are suspects. But the more we investigate, the more rabbit trails we run into. And more drugs. Pot, meth, cocaine, even heroin. You name it and we've got it. The meth is mostly a local, do-it-yourself industry, but the other stuff is coming in from outside. We just haven't found the pipeline yet."

"But Eddie Howell was definitely tangled up in it."

Without responding, Deputy Hamilton picked up the

antlered head and started up the stepladder with it. Koop jumped down.

"Oh, you don't need to bother. We can do that."

"I just want to see—" He grunted the heavy head into position, then looked toward the far end of the room.

"Did the bullet come from back there where the sofa was?" I asked.

"Hard to say, but it's possible. The trajectory appears to be coming from that direction and headed slightly upward."

Which is what it would be if someone sitting on the sofa had fired at a standing person. Although that didn't fit any scenario of suicide or murder that I could imagine. I thought about asking Deputy Hamilton if he was convinced the homicide/suicide conclusion was correct, but I knew he wasn't going to confide doubts about an official position to an outsider.

So instead I detoured and asked, "How did they happen to test Jock Northcutt's hand for gunshot residue?"

He bounced the bullet a few more times but finally said, "I thought the information might be helpful."

Bingo! So he'd requested the test because he *hadn't* been convinced the tidy, straightforward conclusion was the right one. Or at least he hadn't been before the gunshot residue test reinforced the suicide scenario.

I made a cautious fishing trip. "Did you know Ute, the guy who worked here for the Northcutts for a while?" I asked.

"I stopped him once for no taillight on that old van of his."

"I don't suppose that warranted a background check?"

"Actually, I did run his name through the system," he admitted. "But I didn't come up with anything on him. Or on the buddy who was with him."

"Buddy?" I was surprised. "Another of the shaved head variety?"

"No. Just an ordinary-looking guy. With an ordinary name. Joe Michaels. With a California driver's license. Ute's full name is Dave Uteman."

"You have a good memory."

"A cop needs one. Although in this case, maybe I remember them because something just didn't seem right. They were both extremely nervous. I really wanted to search the vehicle, but I didn't have probable cause to do it." He sounded frustrated.

"Something didn't seem right because . . . ?"

"Now, Mrs. Malone, you know I can't make incriminating comments about people who did nothing to suggest they were anything other than your basic, upstanding, law-abiding citizens," he chided.

"You just had this gut feeling the van might be loaded with drugs," I guessed.

Deputy Hamilton neither confirmed nor denied that. "Ute was very polite and cooperative and said he'd get the taillight fixed immediately."

"A prudent stand for someone with a van full of drugs," I suggested, again to no comment. I took a new tack. "There were some hard feelings between Ute and the Northcutts. Their son was suspicious of him."

"In connection with their deaths?"

"Well, only before he knew the circumstances of the deaths," I had to admit.

"Was he satisfied with the official conclusion?"

"Yes, I think so."

We looked at each other for a moment, and finally he tossed the lump of lead to me. "Then probably you and I should be satisfied with it also."

I noted that he included himself in the advice, which suggested he might still have a smidgen of doubt, but I didn't press the issue. I walked him out to the rear deck. He paused to survey the grounds. No sign of Abilene. I momentarily thought about mentioning our camper/skulker, but there didn't seem much point in it now that the man had moved on.

"Thanks again for coming," I said.

"You tell Ms. Morrison I hope she's feeling better now, okay?"

"I'll do that."

It seemed the appropriate time to go, but he lingered. "I understand you were in church on Sunday."

"Were you there? I didn't see you."

"No. Margaret Rau told me. She's been after me to go for months now."

"Maybe we'll gang up and both nag you."

He took another long look around, from the motor home to the emu shed to the old barn. No Abilene.

"Will Ms. Morrison be with you at church?"

"I'm hoping so."

"Maybe I'll do it one of these days."

I didn't think Frank Northcutt would be home during the day. I was prepared to leave a message on an answering machine so he'd call back later, so I was surprised when he picked up the phone himself. I explained the reason for my call.

"Sure, fine with me if your friend wants to park there. Probably good to have a man around. Everything going okay? Emus behaving?"

"The emus are fine. I don't suppose you know anything about a bullet hole in that deer head over the fireplace?"

He surprised me by laughing. "No, but it sounds like something Jessie'd do. Maybe a fly was annoying her, and she just took a potshot at it. I once saw her break a cup going after a cockroach." Again he sounded fond of his mother's unconventional personality.

"There have been a couple of phone calls. I gave them your name and number."

"Thanks." He didn't elaborate on whether anyone had called.

"Is everything okay?" I asked. He was sounding a little distracted even as we spoke. "I thought you'd probably be back at the post office by now."

"I decided to take a couple more days off to go through these old checks and some other papers I brought home, and I've run into something . . . puzzling."

I wanted to know what, but asking seemed too nosy, so I remained silent. Knowing even as I did so that sometimes silence can be even more effective than a question. And who could possibly interpret silence as nosy?

"It's about some of these checks. Several of them are made out for large amounts of cash. I can't imagine what Jock and Jessie needed it for. I mean, who walks into a bank and asks for forty or fifty thousand in cash? And does it several times?"

"All from the same bank?"

"No. They were using accounts at several different banks, spreading the withdrawals around. It all adds up to several hundred thousand dollars, maybe more. I never knew exactly how much they got out of their Hollywood Hills place, but it must have been a bundle, with a lot left over even after they bought the ranch and the Hummer and everything else."

Puzzling indeed. And taking the cash out of several different banks suggested a calculated decision. One such transaction might raise eyebrows, but several such withdrawals at the same bank could well set off alarms. Which meant . . . what?

"Perhaps they needed cash to buy all these supplies and food," I suggested. "There's shelf after shelf of survival-type stuff in cans down in the basement. And that mountain of toilet tissue."

"There are cancelled checks for all that. Some survival-food company was probably sending its executives on bonus trips to Hawaii, considering all the business Jock and Jessie did with them." The words were on the sour side, but he still sounded more distracted than annoyed. "What I'm thinking . . ."

I let silence work again.

"What I'm thinking is that maybe they were being black-mailed."

"Blackmailed!"

"Although I have no idea by whom. It's just the only reason I can think of for all that cash."

"But blackmail wouldn't be any motive for someone to murder them. Killing the people you're blackmailing cuts off the source of income." A question instantly bounced into my head. Could Ute have had something incriminating with which to blackmail Jock and Jessie? And when they'd finally said "no more," he'd simply killed them to keep them from going to the authorities?

Frank was in a silence of his own for a few moments, perhaps thinking silence would encourage me to expand my thoughts, but finally he said, "But no one murdered them. They committed suicide, remember?"

My brilliant response was, "Ummm."

"What I'm wondering now is if they did it because they just couldn't see any other way out of a blackmail situation."

What he said made a certain appalling sense. A ruthless blackmailer driving them beyond the limits of endurance. Although given what I'd heard of Jessie's temper, her killing the blackmailer appeared a more likely possibility.

"And what I want to know is, who could have been black-

197

mailing them? And why?" Frank sounded belligerent and angry now, but frightened too, and I suspected he must be wondering if this unknown blackmailer was going to come after *him* now. Make him pay up or they'd reveal some devastating or incriminating fact about his parents.

"I don't suppose you have any idea what they could be blackmailed for?"

"Not a clue. Although I think it would have to be business connected, not some . . . personal indiscretion involving one of them, because sometimes one and sometimes the other signed the checks for cash. They weren't concealing anything from each other. I used to think it was just paranoia when they hinted they had big enemies in Hollywood, but maybe they really did."

"Look, I haven't gotten around to trying to organize anything with their old files, but I'll start right away. Maybe I can find something."

"I'd appreciate that." He paused. "If you do find anything, let me know directly, would you please?"

He didn't say it in so many words, but I got the drift. *Don't pass the information through Mikki.*

I wrapped the chunk of lead in plastic, labeled it, and put it in the drawer of a nightstand in the master bedroom for safekeeping. Then I called Mac again, told him Frank had okayed his parking here, and gave him instructions on how to find the Northcutt place. He said he'd get started first thing in the morning.

"I'm looking forward to peach cobbler," he said. The first time I'd met him, I'd had a peach cobbler in hand. Interesting that he remembered.

I spent a frivolous amount of time that afternoon thinking about Mac, so it wasn't until I was getting dinner—corned beef hash and green salad—that a totally different perspective on those big checks for cash popped into my head. One "industry" always dealt in cash. An industry known to be operating locally. An industry in which it might take a considerable amount of cash to get set up and started . . .

I made a roll call of possible characters in this industry.

Right at the top, Jock and Jessie Northcutt themselves.

Not necessarily users but perhaps knowledgeable about the drug world from their Hollywood years. Maybe with useful connections to that world. Now dead. Had they horned in on someone else's territory . . . and been eliminated?

Eddie Howell, the sheriff's nephew. Probably both a user and dealer, now also dead. Were the Northcutts Eddie's source?

Young man, name unknown to me but a friend of Eddie's, also in the dead column. Killed in an unexplained rollover accident. A fatal connection or irrelevant coincidence?

Ute. Drug connection unknown but highly possible in his work with Jock and Jessie. Deciding he wanted all the action for himself and getting them out of the way with a murder neatly disguised as a homicide/suicide? If anyone was in a position to come up with genuine signatures and somehow turn them into a suicide note, it was surely Ute.

Our unknown camper/skulker. Perhaps a curious but innocent bystander fond of ramen noodles and an occasional barefoot stroll. But perhaps someone with a less innocent agenda. Possibly Ute's buddy, working with information supplied by Ute about drugs or cash hidden in the house or sheds? The space behind the cans of survival food was empty—emptied by the killer?—but was there another hiding space, *not* empty, a space the camper/skulker was scheming to gain access to? Although, so far as we knew, the camper/skulker had picked up and moved on.

Confusing.

I'd pretty well eliminated Frank Northcutt from suspicion, but I know it's a mistake to eliminate anyone until the true culprit is nailed down. So, even though he was down to bit-player status, he was still in there. And there were any number of unknowns. Old enemies of the Northcutts from Hollywood. New enemies in the drug world.

Faces in the shadows.

So where was I with all this? Cleverly outthinking the authorities with my deductions and connections, or muddling around in overcooked red herrings?

At dinner Abilene and I discussed this, to no conclusion, and then I remembered I had news about Mac's coming arrival the following day. Her eyes lit up in a way that said teasing about a boyfriend was imminent, and I quickly derailed that by bringing up Deputy Hamilton's solicitous good wishes about her health.

"It seemed like something more than professional interest," I stated with the wide-eyed innocence only an LOL can produce.

Abilene blushed lightly, but then she tossed out an unconnected but startling bit of news of her own that instantly derailed me.

"I found an egg today."

"An egg? An emu egg?"

"I've never seen one before, but it was in the emus' pen, so that must be what it is."

"What does it look like?"

"You'll just have to come see. It's . . . impressive."

"Is one of the emu hens sitting on it?"

"No. I remember those people who raised them saying that the females don't even sit on the eggs. The males do the sitting. I saw several of them looking it over, but no takers so far." She gave me a sideways look. "We could . . . you know . . . try to hatch it ourselves."

"I'm not into sitting on eggs, emu or otherwise."

She gave me an injured, this-is-not-a-joking-matter look and came up with a plan so quickly that I knew she'd spent some time concocting it.

"We could make a nest out of a towel or blanket, and I saw a heating pad in the bathroom closet that we could rig up to keep the egg warm."

"Or we could make an omelet out of it."

"Ivy!" she gasped, horrified.

"You eat eggs all the time," I reminded her.

"This is different."

Immediately after dinner, she led me out to see the egg. It wasn't in a nest or even a depression in the ground, just lying under a tree in the wooded part of the pen. It looked enormous, about six or seven inches long, and it was green, a dark bluish-green.

"Are you sure it's an emu egg?" I asked doubtfully. The emu flock had followed us, but none of them seemed interested in claiming the egg. They just wanted to peck at my watch and try to untie my shoelaces. "Maybe we'll hatch it, and some Jurassic Park monster will leap out."

"That's ridiculous," she scoffed, but she didn't sound positive, and we were both still staring at the egg when a motor home pulled into the yard.

Mac!

I deserted Abilene and the egg and dashed out to meet him. He swung out of the motor home, hair still thick and silver, now with nicely trimmed beard to match. Belly still flat, knees still knobby in tan shorts, no perceptible glitch in his movements, although there was an Ace bandage wrapped around his wrist.

"I didn't expect you until tomorrow!"

He grinned. "Maybe you're so irresistible I couldn't stay away a minute longer."

"Maybe Hugo has an Oklahoma version of the Blarney stone, and you've made one too many visits to it."

"You're so cynical, Ivy Malone," he chided.

"I don't even have a peach cobbler made for you yet."

"That's okay, you look better than any peach cobbler." He grinned again and held out his arms. I stepped into them. A very nice place to be.

But right in the midst of our big hug, I looked over his shoulder and there was Abilene hurrying toward the house, large green object cradled in her hands, her clutch on it suggesting this was a priceless treasure, her hurried gait suggesting the future of the emu species depended on getting this egg inside with all possible speed.

Hey, wait a minute. We haven't actually decided we're going to do this hatching thing, and doing it in the house was never even mentioned . . .

Mac turned around when I broke the hug, his expression puzzled until his gaze followed mine. "Who's that? And what's that thing she's carrying?"

"That's Abilene. It's an emu egg."

Then I had to explain about Abilene and who she was, and by that time the hug was forgotten and we were standing at the fence looking at the long-necked, heavy-bodied creatures. One of them tried to peck through the fence at the motorcycle tattoo on Mac's arm. He jerked his arm back. A thought occurred to me.

"I hope it wasn't an emu that attacked you?"

"No. It was a . . . yak."

"A yak?"

"They're kind of like oxen, only with long, shaggy hair. And big horns."

"And this yak attacked you?"

"I don't know that you'd call it an actual *attack*." He sounded defensive. "I was with a tour group at an exotic animal farm. I was working on a magazine article, so I talked the guide into letting me inside the pen with the yak herd for some better photos. I guess they're usually peaceful animals. But a bee stung one on the nose, and it kind of went berserk, and I was in the way." He broke off and gingerly rubbed the area of his tailbone. "Anyway, it tossed me about ten feet, and I landed in an . . . awkward position."

203

"I see."

"Ivy Malone, you're trying not to laugh," he accused. "And you're not doing a very good job of it."

"I am not laughing! Why would I laugh?"

"You're thinking, *Mac was attacked by a yak. A berserk yak attacked Mac. Mac had a yak attack.* Tee-hee."

"I never tee-hee," I stated primly.

"Well, here's something else to laugh about. Guess what I landed in?"

"A water trough?"

"I should be so lucky. With all these cow-like creatures around, I'm sure you can imagine what there were piles of all over the ground."

Oh. "Look on the bright side. If you'd landed on a rock or stump you'd have been hurt much worse than landing in a pile of . . . soft stuff."

"Still looking on the bright side of things, I see." He sounded grumpy about it.

"I try."

"I suppose there was a certain humor in it," he muttered. "The local newspaper thought so. Unbeknownst to me, there was a reporter in the tour group, and, sure enough, he had his handy-dandy camera ready. They headlined the photo 'Mac Encounters Yak.' And there I was on the front page, with a very surprised look on my face as I sat sprawled in the pile of 'soft stuff' as you put it, with a yak staring at me."

"You're recovering from your injuries satisfactorily?" I managed more primness.

"The wrist doesn't work quite right, but I don't have any problem getting around. Though I'm probably not up to mountain climbing yet. It's just that I can't sit comfortably for any length of time. I have to go back for more X-rays next week. Just make me one promise, okay?"

"Which is?"

"No Mac yak attack jokes. Everyone in the RV park was having a heyday with them. There was even a knock-knock one going around."

I crossed my heart. "Promise." Though I had to admit I hadn't promised not to snicker a bit to myself. *A Mac yak attack, a yak attacked Mac. A berserk yak went on attack.* Say it five times, and it had a catchy rhythm. Music to hatch emus by?

By the time Mac and I got inside, Abilene had the egg snuggled into a matching blue-green bath towel in a box in the corner of her bedroom. She was trying to arrange the heating pad over it.

Mac jumped right in to help, rolling up more towels to keep the heating pad in a position so the egg would stay warm but not overheat.

"I think maybe it needs something that would imitate a heartbeat." Abilene fussed with a fold in the towel. "Wouldn't the little emu in its egg be able to feel a real emu's heart-beat?"

Then they were off on a how-to-simulate-a-heartbeat discussion, and whether a lightbulb might work better than the heating pad. Me, I was just thinking, and finally asking, "What if the emu lays more eggs?"

I had visions of a row of big green eggs encased in bath-towel nests lining the wall from corner to corner, like some science-fiction nursery. Then another thought. "What happens if this thing actually hatches? How big will it be? Will it have to live right here in the bedroom?"

No one paid any attention to me or my concerns. "I still think it would make a nice omelet," I muttered. "A nice, *big* omelet."

"I wonder how long it takes an emu egg to hatch?" Mac asked.

Abilene didn't ignore that as she did my omelet suggestion. "Yeah, we need to know, don't we? You'd think the Northcutts would have some pamphlets or books or something about raising them."

I remembered a book on the coffee table. The one under the blood-spattered note. Something about emus and survival.

I went downstairs to look. I couldn't find the book, and I was feeling a little grumpy about the whole emu-egg thing anyway. Next thing, Abilene would probably be naming it. So by the time Abilene and Mac came down a few minutes later I had a peach cobbler started. Fresh peaches make the best cobbler, of course, but the Northcutts provided a plentiful choice in the canned variety: halves, slices, or chunks.

Abilene went outside, hoping for more eggs, I suspected. Mac brought his ergonomic chair in, and we caught up on events since we'd last seen each other at my niece's in Arkansas. He told me about his grandchildren and where his travels had taken him, and I told him about the Northcutts, dead and alive, and my latest narrow escape from the Braxtons.

When the cobbler was done I called Abilene, and we sat out on the deck in the lovely evening dusk eating big dishes of cobbler and ice cream. I was relieved she hadn't found more eggs. She went to bed fairly early, but Mac and I talked until late.

"I'm glad I didn't wait until tomorrow to come," he said when he finally picked up his chair to go.

"I am too."

We smiled at each other, and I thought he was considering a good-night kiss, but about that time the phone rang. He raised his eyebrows.

"You have friends who call at midnight?"

"Calls for the Northcutts can come at any hour," I explained.

So he settled for a smile and a squeeze on the shoulder instead of a kiss. I wavered between relief and disappointment as I went to answer the phone.

The man didn't identify himself, but when I told him the Northcutts had recently passed away, he said, "But they were supposed to have a treatment to me by this weekend!" He sounded indignant, as if they had died purposely to circumvent this obligation.

"Treatment?" I repeated, puzzled. "What kind of treatment? Medical?"

He groaned, managing a groan-tone that insinuated if I were any dumber I wouldn't have known how to pick up the phone.

"Whatever this treatment is, you'll have to discuss it with their son." I gave the man Frank's number in Texas. "Have a nice day," I added.

My acerbic tone apparently reminded him he wasn't exactly putting on a good show of etiquette here, and he finally muttered, "Sorry to hear about the deaths," before adding hopefully, "I don't suppose you know anything about the treatment?"

"No, we don't treat anything. We just hatch emu eggs with a heating pad," I said and hung up. Let him figure that one out.

Next morning I fixed bacon, eggs, and biscuits for breakfast. Afterward we got Mac's motor home hooked up with electricity, water, and septic system. It was a blue-sky day, with just a hint of fall coming. The kind of day that made me remember how school on opening day always smelled, that wonderful blend of chalk and floor polish and new shoes. Do schools still smell that way, or is that something that disappeared with the coming of backpacks and computers?

"This is a terrific place," Mac enthused. "My grandkids would love it. I wish you could meet them." He gave me what felt like a thoughtful inspection. "Sometimes it gets a little old being on the move alone all the time."

"I think Frank plans to sell this place as soon as he can get the legal complications straightened out."

"And look at that old barn!" Mac motioned off across the weedy field to the weathered barn, where a picturesque cupola and the weather vane of a prancing horse decorated the top ridge. "You know, I have some other old barn photos around somewhere. Maybe I could put them all together and get a magazine article out of it. Want to walk out there with me?"

Mac got his camera, and we started toward the barn. I hadn't been out there before. The dry weeds were high except where the sofa had knocked them down when Frank dragged it to the burn pile, so we followed that easier path until I detoured sharply to miss the sofa.

"Let me guess," Mac said. "The sofa where you found the bodies?"

"Their son, Frank, dragged it out here to get rid of it, but we can't burn it until fire danger is over."

"The police weren't interested in it?"

"They're convinced the Northcutts chose to commit suicide together."

Mac gave me a speculative look. "But you're not?"

I hadn't mentioned those doubts earlier, but either Mac was shrewd and intuitive or I'm as easy to read as a large print edition of *Reader's Digest*. "I'm not as convinced as they are," I admitted. "But they're the experts."

We went on out to the barn. It was a wonderful old place. Sunlight shafting through cracks in the boards lit up a dance of dust motes, as if they were holding some private celebration. More sunlight through a hole in the roof spotlit a tangle of discarded harness on the dirt floor. Scents of dry earth and long ago animals mingled with a flutter of birds high in the eaves. We climbed up to the hay loft, where our feet raised dust and musty scents and bits of old hay.

"Wouldn't it be fun to come out here and listen to rain on the roof in a storm?" Mac said, and I had to admit that a man who thought that would be fun appealed to me.

We were walking back to the house, talking about where would be the closest place to get the film developed, when suddenly Mac stopped short.

"Hey, what's this?"

We were crossing the parking area behind the house, and I didn't see anything until he toed a glint on the ground. He leaned over to brush the dirt and gravel aside. We both stared in astonishment at what lay there gleaming in the sunlight.

24

"It's a gold coin!"

Mac wiped the coin against his tan shorts, then held it up between thumb and forefinger. A bearded man decorated one side, a horned animal, along with the date 1977, the other. Mac's identification as he studied the coin was more specific than mine. "It's a South African gold Kruggerand."

"You mean it's something someone would have in a coin collection?"

"No, I don't think they're considered collectibles. There's a troy ounce of gold in each one, so I think they're more like an investment. Some people prefer gold to bank deposits."

An investment for people who feared the whole system of government and banking and paper money might collapse any minute. A description that fit Jock and Jessie Northcutt like a ski mask.

Abilene, on her way into the house, saw us standing there and came over to see what was going on. Mac showed her his find.

"Wow! But what's it doing out here?" she asked. "And why didn't we ever see it before? We've all walked back and forth across here dozens of times. And so have lots of other people."

It did seem odd we hadn't spotted the coin before. Yet . . . "Once, back on Madison Street, I found an earring I lost out in the garden at least a dozen years earlier. And I'd worked in that garden, never seeing the earring, every one of those years."

Mac nodded. "I did a human interest article about a guy who lost his class ring on the school football field, and it wasn't found until almost eighteen years later."

So the coin may have been hidden there in the dirt and gravel for years. The 1977 date certainly made that possible. But the coin didn't look as if that was where it had been all that time. The gold surface was still as shiny as if newly minted, neither dented nor scratched, the outlines of both the horned animal and the bearded man precise.

"Maybe someone just recently lost it," I suggested slowly. "Someone who was carrying a large number of gold coins from the house to a vehicle and accidentally dropped it. Someone in a hurry . . ."

Abilene and I exchanged glances. Someone who'd just murdered two people . . . and stolen the coins from a hiding place behind cans of survival food in the basement?

"I'd better call Frank."

Mikki answered the phone. When I asked for Frank she said he'd gone back to work today. She also said she was at home only because an electrical meltdown at the beauty salon had shut down everything from hair dryers to curling irons. "Last week it was the water system. Now *this*." I could envision a roll of blue eyes. "Always something with that miserable building. I think it's as old as the Alamo."

Would she soon be holding a garage sale of antiques to raise repair funds? Or gritting her teeth until Jock and Jessie's larger assets became available?

"I can take a message for Frank." She laughed. "But if it's about those dumb birds, my solution to any problem with them is simple. Stewed emu, emu fricassee, Southern-fried emu, or maybe if you're feeling really fancy, emu cordon bleu."

I'd bet she'd be all for emu-egg omelet too, which made me feel guilty for ever having considered it. I wanted to talk to Frank in private about the gold coin, but I could hardly say that to Mikki without ramping up her curiosity, so all I said was, "The emus are fine, and this isn't an emergency. I'd just like to talk to Frank about some things when it's convenient."

"I'll have him call."

I tucked the coin next to the chunk of lead bullet in the drawer of the nightstand in the master bedroom for safekeeping. Mac went out to the motor home to look for his other photos of old barns, and I used the free time to dig into the file cabinets and boxes of files. Maybe I could have something useful for Frank by the time he called.

Finding files helpfully labeled "Gold Investments" or "Blackmail" or "Drug Deals" seemed unlikely, and it didn't happen, of course. What I found was a jumble of information on survival techniques, everything from how to purify water to smoke meat, from reloading bullets to turning a semi-automatic gun into a fully automatic, from raising emus (which I set aside for Abilene) to worm farming (which I was grateful the Northcutts hadn't yet gotten into). Then there were research files on an esoteric variety of subjects: sharks, Atlantis, polar caps, hypothermia, which made me wonder just what kind of script Jock and Jessie were working on. Such a script could be hidden behind the password barrier in the computer, but I strongly suspected the ever-suspicious Northcutts would also keep a hard copy tucked away somewhere.

Which made me think, like Frank, that there must be a home safe, probably fireproof, where all the items they considered really valuable were stored. Was it possible such a safe held not only a script and wills but also a cache of gold coins? Could the coin Mac had found simply be one Jock and Jessie themselves had accidentally dropped? It was a more pleasant thought than the one about a killer and thief that kept tromping around in my head.

The phone didn't ring until I'd pretty well had it with files for the day. I was sneezing from the dust, had a paper cut on my finger, and was well frustrated by the Northcutts' disorganized filing system. No doubt they were the type of people who could lay hands on whatever they wanted in the mess at any given moment, but certainly no one else could.

"Sorry I'm so late calling," Frank said. "I didn't have a chance to get back to you until now."

Interpretation: he hadn't had opportunity to call without Mikki around. I told him about Mac's discovery of the gold coin. He leaped on the news with relief.

"So that's it! All that cash had nothing to do with blackmail. They were just using it to invest in gold! Which is exactly what they'd do, of course, being so paranoid about everything from banks to the stock market. And all on the up-and-up."

I was inexperienced in such matters, but so far as I knew, buying or selling gold was indeed legal. Dealing in cash could mean an attempt to conceal activities from the IRS, however, which was not legal. But it was definitely a logical explanation for all that cash.

213

"Now all we have to do is find where they've stashed all this gold!" Frank sounded excited.

We discussed how large a safe it would take to hold however many coins several hundred thousand dollars in cash would buy. He said he hadn't looked in the sheds and now wondered if a safe could be hidden among the survival gear out there.

I hated to bring up this other, far more grim possibility, but it had to be done. I told him about the odd space behind those survival food cans in the basement. "It's empty now, but a lot of *something* could have been hidden there."

"Surely Jock and Jessie wouldn't hide gold in a place as insecure as that," he scoffed.

"You knew them better than I do."

It was a long few moments before he said, "Actually, I suppose it would be just like them to hide something valuable in a place like that. I remember a movie they wrote once, about a crook who stole a fortune in diamonds and rubies and hid them right out in the open in a 'treasure chest' in his fish aquarium."

Another silence as his thoughts worked through some mental filtering system. He finally arrived at the bottom line, where I was waiting for him.

"So, if gold was hidden there, in that space behind the cans, and it isn't there now, what happened to it?"

"Good question," I agreed.

"The obvious answer is that it was stolen, of course. And the thief accidentally dropped this one coin as he was making off with the bags or boxes or whatever it was in."

"I think that's a likely possibility."

"Maybe not just a thief. Maybe a killer. I've been assuming the authorities were right when they said Jock shot Jessie and then himself, but maybe . . ." Then, more as if talking to himself than me, he said, "I wonder if Ute knew about the gold?"

Exactly what I was wondering.

We had mystery-meat stew for dinner, but the following evening Mac barbecued steaks over a charcoal grill.

The steaks were excavated from the freezer, supermarket packaged and nicely identifiable as filet mignons. The grill and a dozen sacks of charcoal came from behind three large garbage cans holding sealed sacks of wheat and rice in one of the sheds.

Following Frank's thoughts that Jock and Jessie might have hidden a safe out there, we'd all three spent most of the day digging through the clutter of survival supplies and gear. Hiding a safe away from the house seemed a logical possibility, but logic, I was becoming more and more convinced, was not one of the Northcutts' more prominent traits. (Was having a stainless steel pot big enough to cook half a bear logical? How about owning enough water purification tablets to sanitize the Mississippi?) And though we found no safe, Mac did discover the paintball guns. I doubted Frank would object to the expenditure of a few paintballs, so I showed Mac how the guns worked.

He took several experimental shots, getting that foolish grin that paintball splatting seems to bring to grown men. Okay, grown women and LOLs too. I confined myself to a few sedate shots at an uncomplaining tree, but Abilene experimented with an Old West, quick-draw style. And managed to splat her own feet and legs with an assortment of colors that we termed "Paintball Chic."

Mac turned out to be a barbecuer extraordinaire, and the steaks were deliciously charred on the outside, juicy on the inside. Abilene and I voted him "Grand Master of the Barbecue" and crowned him with a tiara of aluminum foil.

Afterwards, well-fed and content, we sat on the deck as the sun went down and the evening cooled. Mac, in his ergonomic chair, didn't have a satisfactory lap, so Koop draped himself around Mac's neck and purred in ergonomic satisfaction. Occasionally adding a tongue swipe at Mac's silver beard, to which he seemed to have taken quite a liking. The radio in the kitchen, tuned to a "Golden Oldies" station, played dreamy old Johnny Mathis songs.

Murder and suicide, drugs and gold and blackmail all seemed far, far away.

Later, there was even a good-night kiss. I'd never been kissed by a man with a beard. All I can say is, don't knock it till you've tried it. Koop knows a good thing when he sees one.

The next day Abilene hiked through the woods to the campsite and—good news—reported it appeared unoccupied since the last time she'd been there. That afternoon we took turns cranking the handle on an old ice-cream maker Abilene dragged in from the shed, and we consumed the product of our labor in considerably less time than it took to make it.

On Sunday morning Mac figured out the workings of hose and nozzle on the big gas storage tank and filled the tank of my motor home. Then he surprised me by going back to his own motor home and returning to the house dressed for church in dark slacks, pale blue dress shirt, and tie. Wasn't there some singer they used to call the Silver Fox? Mac and his elegant beard definitely qualified for the title today.

I briefly thought Abilene would come too. She asked some questions and seemed to be considering it. But eventually she backed out, with the excuse that we were, after all, caretaking here, so someone should stick around.

The people at church were friendly and curious. I introduced Mac as a friend up from Hugo, no further explanation. The pastor's message was about the Israelites' forty years of wandering before entering the Promised Land, relating this to how many of us do our own years of wandering before finding our way to the Lord.

"I suppose he was talking to me," Mac grumbled on the way home.

I'd also been thinking this message definitely applied to Mac. He'd been physically wandering the country in his motor home since his wife's death, spiritually wandering considerably longer than that. But I was a bit startled that a God-light had immediately clicked on in his head and spotlighted the connection for him.

"Could be," I agreed, very low key. I figure it's better for God to trickle a message into the cracks of someone's thought processes rather than my trying to jackhammer it in.

"I've been reading a chapter or two in the Bible now and then."

"That's good."

"I make notes about what I find doubtful or hard to believe."

My reaction was half groan, half laugh. The statement was so *Mac*. Mac the Doubter. Mac the *organized* doubter. Though not necessarily Mac the Total Unbeliever, I was fairly certain.

"Do you make notes about what you do believe?" I inquired.

He tapped fingers on the armrest. "I suppose, to be fair, I should do that, shouldn't I?" He sounded grumpy about that too.

"The thing is, if something is true, it's true whether we believe it or not," I pointed out. "The truth doesn't change just because we don't believe it. Like the world was always round, even when people believed it was flat."

"And tomatoes were always edible, even when people thought they were poisonous."

"A fortunate awakening," I agreed. "Otherwise we'd be making spaghetti sauce out of . . . what? Turnips?"

"I've been thinking sometime I might like to go to Israel and . . . get a feel for where all these events happened." A considered pause, then, Mac being Mac, he added, "If they did happen."

It's times like this when I wish I were eloquent and brilliant, able to come up with words that blaze like diamonds on black velvet. Because what came out of my mouth was, "I've known people who went there and were baptized in the Jordan. I always thought that would be nice."

Nice. A word with all the eloquence and brilliance of a third grader writing about his summer vacation. *We went to Yellerstun Park. It was nice.*

"Haven't you already been baptized?" Mac asked.

"Oh yes. But doing it again in the very river where Jesus was baptized, that would be . . . beautiful."

Which earned me a thoughtful look but no comment.

Mac's appointment for more X-rays was set for Tuesday morning, which meant he had to leave on Monday afternoon to drive back down to Hugo. When he returned depended on what the X-rays showed and what the doctor had to say. Possibly Tuesday evening, he said, but maybe not for several days.

On Monday morning Abilene and I decided that before he left we should take advantage of his presence so we could run into Dulcy without leaving the ranch untended. At the post office I picked up the mail I'd had forwarded to General Delivery. Some of it was well-traveled by the time it reached me, going first to the Madison Street address, forwarded to my niece's in Arkansas, again forwarded on to the mail-drop place in Little Rock, and finally here. The better to confuse Braxtons, just in case, because earlier incidents had suggested they might have a spy-eye in the postal system.

However, the most important item among those well-traveled missives was only a notice that it was time to have my teeth cleaned. Less traveled but more important was a chatty letter from my grandniece, Sandy, telling me she'd won several more gymnastic medals and asking if I was wearing the toe ring she gave me.

We went to the feed store to pick up emu food, then on to the grocery store. The Northcutts' well-stocked shelves and freezers were supplying most of our needs, but we still wanted some fresh fruit and milk and, since emu eggs seemed to be off limits, fresh eggs in a carton. At the checkout counter, Abilene stepped over to the magazine rack while the cashier slid our items across the scanner. Then I remembered something.

"Abilene, I forgot cottage cheese," I called over to her. "Could you run back and get a carton?"

The cashier glanced up. "Are you Abilene Morrison?"

Abilene dropped the copy of *Farm and Rancher* in surprise. My fingers fumbled on the ten dollar bill I was digging out of my purse.

"I-I'm Abilene Tyler."

"Oh. Some guy was in here a couple days ago trying to locate an Abilene Morrison, and I told him I didn't know anyone by that name. But Abilene is kind of unusual, you know, and when I heard her—" she nodded toward me, "call you that—"

She broke off, I suppose because we were both staring at her as if she'd just pointed a finger at Abilene and yelled, "There, that's her, that's the Wicked Witch of the West."

"Yes, it is an unusual name, isn't it? But parents name their children all kinds of strange things these days, don't they? Butterfly and Tiara and Orion, even Lizara. Wouldn't that be awful? It practically invites being called Lizard-face or something like that." I was babbling, of course, trying to distract the cashier but at the same time figure out how to find out more from her.

Abilene was more direct. "Did he give his own name?" she asked.

"I don't think so . . . ummm, no, I'm sure he didn't."

"What did he look like?"

"Oh, medium height. Kind of wiry built, I guess." She shrugged. "I think he was wearing a baseball cap. Just kind of everyday looking, you know?"

I glanced surreptitiously at Abilene. The description could fit anyone from the guy behind us in line to the killer on last week's TV news. But I had the uneasy feeling it also fit a specific someone she knew.

"Did you see what he was driving?" Abilene asked.

The cashier looked mildly annoyed at this barrage of questions, as if she wished she'd never mentioned a guy asking for an Abilene. She reached for my ten dollar bill. "No."

"Did he say why he wanted to find this Abilene Morrison?" I asked.

"If she"—jerk of cashier's thumb at Abilene—"isn't Abilene Morrison, what difference does it make?"

"Just curious." I gave her my sweetest LOL smile.

"It was something about needing to get hold of her because her parents had been killed in an accident."

"Well, that . . . that's certainly too bad for . . . that Abilene." I glanced at Abilene, my own reaction a little shaken. Her jaw had clenched, but she didn't show any other reaction. "How long ago was this guy in here?" I added.

"Oh, three or four days, I guess." The cashier was already working on a stack of frozen TV dinners the guy behind us had tossed on the moving conveyer.

I picked up one of our plastic sacks. Abilene grabbed the other one. She turned toward the phone just outside the door.

I silently held out my phone card, but she shook her head. Instead she put the call through collect, using the Abilene Morrison name when the operator asked who was calling.

The call didn't last long. Abilene never spoke another word except to say, "Thank you," at the end.

"No one answered?" I asked.

"Oh, there was an answer, all right." Her tone was bitter. "My stepfather. When the operator asked if he'd accept a collect call from me, he said, 'Nobody here wants to talk to her,' and hung up."

Perhaps not as shocking as if she'd learned her parents were actually dead, which they obviously weren't, but still shocking. The stepfather must know by now that she'd disappeared, but instead of being glad to hear from her, *this* was his response.

"I'm sorry." I put an arm around her waist and squeezed. "Would you like to use the phone card and try again a little later? Maybe you could get your mother."

"No. Let's go on home." She grabbed the sack at her feet and strode toward the motor home.

I hurried after her. I'd spotted a small beauty salon on

the far side of the grocery and had been thinking maybe I could talk her into getting her hair styled, but this wasn't the time for that.

So here we had it. The good news and the bad. The good news was that her parents weren't dead after all. The bad news was that her stepfather was still as big a jerk as ever. And the second bad news, the much worse bad news, was that Boone had been right here in Dulcy looking for Abilene, complete with a phony story he'd concocted to arouse sympathy for the search.

Neither of us spoke until we were off the main road.

"It had to be Boone, didn't it?" I said. "And you figured he was lying even before you called your folks."

Abilene nodded. "I know Boone. It's the sneaky kind of thing he'd do." She looked under control, but her voice broke when she said, "But how did he find me?"

"He hasn't found you yet," I reminded her. *And he isn't going to if I have anything to say about it.* "Would his former wife . . . what was her name? MaryLou? Would she tell him anything?"

"No . . . Well, I suppose she might, if he gave her a sob story about my parents being killed and he needed to get in touch with me to let me know," Abilene said reluctantly. "But she didn't know anything *to* tell him. I didn't put a return address on the card I sent to Lily—"

"But there would have been a postmark."

An incriminating postmark. And MaryLou, wanting to be helpful to Abilene in the loss of her parents, had told Boone where the card had been sent from.

"Is there any chance that could have been Boone camped out there in the woods and sneaking over to spy on us?"

Abilene gave me a startled glance. It was obviously a possibility she hadn't considered. But after a moment she shook her head. "No. Boone doesn't have that kind of patience.

If he actually knew where I was, I-I'd probably be dead by now."

Abusive husbands didn't always go on to kill their wives, of course. But some did. And after Boone's threats and what he'd already done to her arm . . .

"Which means he must not have found out anything helpful when he was snooping around Dulcy asking questions. So it's quite possible he's decided you were just passing through when you mailed the card to Lily."

"Yeah. Maybe."

The *yeah* was hopeful, but the *maybe* held dread.

This also suggested, since Boone had come looking for her, that our optimistic brainstorm that the insurance had bought him a new Porsche was mistaken. Or he was out for vengeance anyway, simply because that was the kind of guy he was.

"So, what do we do now?" I asked when I made the last turn onto the rough gravel of Dead Mule Road.

"About what?"

"Boone. Do you want to move on?"

She hesitated, as if she were tempted, but then she shook her head. "I can't just up and leave. Frank is depending on me to look after the emus. And I don't think you should be out there at the house alone."

Actually, I was thinking about *both* of us picking up and disappearing into the night. But she was right; we'd made a commitment to Frank. I admired her sense of responsibility and appreciated her concern for me, but surely taking care of emus and the Northcutts' place wasn't more important than Abilene's life.

What do you think, Lord? Should we stay or move on? I need some advice here. A thought came.

"I have an idea," I said slowly. "We could send the kids something else. Maybe you could draw them a little picture

223

or something. Except we'll have Frank Northcutt mail it from down there so it will have a Texas postmark. Then, still trying to be helpful, MaryLou will probably pass that information on to Boone."

"Or I could send something directly to Boone, so he'll be sure to see the postmark!"

That sounded even better, and we did it. Abilene still had a key to the wrecked Porsche. It probably wouldn't be of any use to Boone, but we wrapped it in a piece of paper and put it in a stamped envelope addressed to him. Then we put that inside another envelope addressed to Frank, along with a note asking Frank to mail it the next time he was in Dallas.

Would the key postmarked from Dallas send Boone off on a wild goose chase? Maybe! Dallas was a big place to look.

Mac left right after lunch. We gave him the envelope addressed to Frank, and he said he'd mail it from Hugo. Before he left, Mac donated a little present to the emu egg in its bath-towel nest: an old-fashioned ticking clock to give it a sense of heartbeat.

Which gave me a warm view of the caring behind Mac's own heartbeat.

"Watch out for attacking yaks," I called when he waved from the motor home.

"See you in a day or two," he called back.

"I'm looking forward to it."

But a peculiar lightning bolt ripped across my mind even as I said the words. *Nope, never gonna happen.* I brushed the jolting thought aside, annoyed with the groundless negativity, and replaced it with an energetic wave. "We'll make strawberry ice cream next time!"

26

Mac was hardly a noisy person, but the place felt unnaturally silent after he was gone. I scoffed at the idea that what I really meant by *silent* was *missing him* and industriously applied myself to organizing the manila folders and looking for anything that might help Frank Northcutt. I ran across a file with several articles about the coming worthlessness of paper money, with ideas for other investments. Gold was most often suggested, lending credence to the idea that the Northcutts may have invested all that cash in gold coins. Also suggested were diamonds and other precious gems (easily transportable, but beware of widely different values depending on cut and clarity), and platinum. Stay away from silver (too bulky) and antiques, which would be worthless in hard times.

No doubt excellent advice, although on my Social Security income I was hard put to invest in anything more than a good buy on toothpaste.

I did have to give the Northcutts credit for being organized in one area. They had a folder containing receipts and guarantees on everything from the freezers to a chain saw to an expensive pair of sterling silver nose-hair clippers. I wondered if Mikki had appropriated that item. Actually, I hoped so. I wasn't eager to run into used nose-hair clippers, sterling silver or not.

Abilene came in from doing yard work at about 4:00. She brought cold lemon sodas for both of us and dropped into a chair at the dining table. I could tell she had something on her mind, and I was afraid I knew what it was: Mac. She wanted to know more about our relationship and how I felt about him, and I wasn't certain myself.

My mind was on Mac and that hazy relationship, and it took me a moment to follow when she plunged into another subject entirely.

"Someone has been watching us. I found a place up at the end of the clearing where brush has been piled up so he'd be concealed but could see out."

"You mean this is where the guy who was camped back there in the woods was spying on us?"

"Maybe. But someone has been there more recently than that." She looked back over her shoulder toward the woods as if eyes might even now be probing us.

My instant suspicion, as usual, was spying Braxtons. Yet it seemed unlikely they'd have been watching all this time and not done anything yet. "How recent?" I asked.

"Probably today. I found a beer can. It was empty, but there were still a couple drops of liquid around the top. They'd have evaporated if the can had been there long."

This was disturbing news, but I was also impressed. "That's good detective work."

"I read it in a mystery. Mysteries can be quite educational." In an absentminded way she added, "I learned from one that a crocodile can't stick out its tongue."

Probably not a terribly useful bit of information, but if

226

some scaly, big-toothed creature stuck its tongue out at me and claimed to be a crocodile, I'd now know it was an imposter.

We sipped our lemon sodas and contemplated crocodile tongues and the return of the camper/skulker.

"You think it's the same person?"

"Same brand of beer. I think he may be camping in a different place now. Maybe he realized that other spot had been discovered and decided to move. I can probably find the new—"

"No," I said hastily. "I don't think that will be necessary."

"I don't think we should just ignore him."

"But what's he *doing* here? What does he want?"

"I think he's probably watching for a time when everyone is gone so he can do whatever it is he wants to do. Search for something, steal something, whatever."

"You don't think he's a personal danger to us, then?"

"I think if he gets tired of waiting he'll go ahead with whatever it is he wants to do, and if we get in his way . . ." She held a finger against her head and clicked an imaginary trigger.

Which gave me a really bad image of Jock and Jessie, dead on the sofa. If the guy had killed once, he probably wouldn't hesitate to do it again.

"Maybe we should contact Deputy Hamilton," I said.

"Deputy Hamilton already thinks we're strolling in the Twilight Zone."

The kind of people who turn simple suicides into complicated murders. The kind of people who see bizarre connections between a bullet in an old deer head and bullets in dead bodies. Although Deputy Hamilton had seemed to have some doubts about the suicide scenario himself. But my bullet-in-deer-head call probably hadn't raised our credibility level.

"I'm wondering . . ." Abilene gave me a sideways glance

that suggested she suspected I might not like what she was about to say. "I'm wondering if we could capture him ourselves."

"Capture him?"

She was right. I didn't like it. This may be a spy/thief/murderer, someone who could be equipped with anything from a machete to an Uzi. We were one LOL and one emu caretaker equipped with . . . what? One green emu egg and an oversupply of imagination.

One guess about who was most likely to capture whom.

I managed to keep from erupting like an egg in a microwave and say with relative calm, "How could we possibly capture him? We don't have a gun, and even if we did—"

"There are other ways. Just come out and look at the place where he's been hiding. Maybe we can think of something."

I did not want to get involved in planning a capture, but curiosity about the place where he'd been spying on us got to me, of course. Abilene led the way through the weedy grass to the far end of the clearing. Koop came along, sidetracking now and then to do a capture of his own with a grasshopper. By the time we ducked into the woods I had enough seeds and stickers caught in my socks to sabotage the Garden of Eden.

I didn't even see anything until Abilene said, "Here we are. This is it."

Brush had been so carefully stacked in gaps between live bushes and trees that from the outside it looked like part of the natural landscape. The hiding place was like a small room, with the stacked brush on three and a half sides, the entrance on the side away from the clearing. Overhead, branches dipping from surrounding trees dappled the space with a green canopy of shade. The unknown occupant had spent enough time in the brush-enclosed room to trample the ground to bare earth. It appeared he was either a nervous pacer or he practiced flamenco dancing in his spare time. The beer can lay where Abilene had found and left it, half-hidden in the brush.

Koop sniffed out a few crisp yellow crumbs on the ground. Cheetos? The ants were industriously working on them, but they hadn't made off with all of them yet—another clue that it hadn't been long since the skulker had been here.

Peering through peepholes cut into the brush gave a clear view of house, yard, emus, and motor home. And us. The stars of this skulker's private peep show. In spite of the heat I felt a spider-tap-dancing-up-the-spine chill as I realized how easily he could pick us off with a rifle from here.

A less crucial point was that I was glad we weren't inclined toward such watchable activities as nude sunbathing.

"So, what do you think?" Abilene asked.

"What happens if we do figure a way to capture him? What then?"

I had various uneasy thoughts, central to which was the idea that this looked way too much like catching a tiger by the tail. We had no idea what kind of "tiger" we might catch, or how vicious or well-armed he might be.

"If we caught him, then we could call Deputy Hamilton," Abilene said.

That sounded better, quite reasonable and sensible. "But what if Deputy Hamilton arrives, and our capturee turns out to be, say, some innocent bird or squirrel watcher?"

"Innocent bird and squirrel watchers," Abilene declared, "do not build hiding places and then sneak around peering through peepholes, watching normal people do normal things."

True.

"Do you think he comes at night?" I asked.

"It's possible, if what he wants is to get in one of the sheds. But since he hasn't already done that, I think he wants to get in the house, and he wants to do it when no one's home. He wouldn't figure we'd both be away at night, so he's watching during the day for a time when we're both gone."

"We could just leave a note letting him know we're on to the fact that he's spying on us. Maybe that would scare him off." I realized the hopeful foolishness of that even as I said it. We might as well leave a picture of a gun and a sign saying "Bang! You're dead."

"You're against trying to capture him, then?" Abilene sounded disappointed.

"Well, no, not necessarily. I just think there are a lot of unknowns involved, and we'd better give it more thought. If we lie in wait for him out here, we may find ourselves captured by our skulker, rather than the other way around."

"We could, you know, dig a pit and cover it with branches and leaves so he'd fall in. There are shovels and other tools in the shed."

I jabbed at the ground with the toe of my shoe and made no more dent in the hard, summer-dry earth than I would poking a toothpick at a concrete sidewalk. Even with Abilene's youthful strength and determination, I doubted we could dig a hole deep enough to capture any skulker more than two feet tall.

"I guess that would take too long." Abilene sighed. "Maybe I'd better go read a few more mysteries for ideas."

"I think we should forget any capture-the-crook scheme. If we're always around, maybe he'll eventually give up and go away."

"Unless he decides to get *us* out of the way."

Yes, there was always that.

I couldn't sleep. Abilene's theory that our skulker probably wanted to sneak into the house when we were gone during daylight hours was comforting. My hope that he'd give up and go away could also be right. But I kept hearing noises that suggested he might boldly try a different stratagem. Thumps. (Burglar crawling through a window?) Creaks. (Murderer coming up the stairs?) Crackle/crinkle. (That one baffled even my fertile imagination until I decided it could be a burglar/murderer crinkling the paper wrapping on a Snickers candy bar.)

Several times I got up and prowled the hallway, stopping at Abilene's open doorway to listen for any outside sounds coming through her open window. All I heard was the tick-tocking clock in the emu-egg nest. I hoped the sound was more comforting to the egg-enclosed emu than it was to me. To me it had an ominous ticking-down-to-doomsday, time-is-running-out sound.

By morning doomsday had not arrived. A radiant sun bloomed in a clear blue sky, and after breakfast Abilene said she had work to do outside.

"You're not going to try to find where that guy is camped now, are you?" I asked, both suspicious and alarmed.

"Oh no," she assured me. "I wasn't thinking of that at all."

Which should have given me a clue that she was thinking of something else I'd find equally worrisome, but a few minutes later I was excited about a find of my own. It was a manila folder labeled, with unambiguous clarity, Important Numbers. Inside was a single sheet of paper with a short series of numbers separated by dashes.

I could think of only one series of numbers that might warrant an Important Numbers file. The combination to the lock on a safe!

Abilene came in for lunch. She had scratches on her arms, bits of leaves and twigs in her hair, and sweat soaked through the back of her shirt, but, again, I was too excited about my find to think about these peculiarities. I showed her the numbers, and we spent more time looking for a safe built into wall or floor somewhere. Mikki had said she'd looked behind pictures, but we looked again, behind pictures, under furniture, and on the back walls of cabinets. We even found a way into a cramped attic over the bedrooms, and Abilene boosted me up so I could look around. I met enough spiders to get a good start on arachnophobia, but I didn't find any safe.

By evening I was too tired to worry about safes or prowling burglar/murderers or even creepy-crawly things. I fell asleep the minute I hit the bed and stayed asleep.

Until at daybreak I found myself upright beside the bed, body rigid as an icicle, heart jackhammering.

I knew something had wakened me, but what? Explosion? Gunshot? Emu egg hatching?

More noises now. Coming from outside.

Crashing, breaking, whomping noises, all punctuated by a series of blood-chilling screeches. Koop jumped to his feet, back arched and hair standing up along his spine.

Pink-pearl dawn showed at the window, its serenity at odds with the clamor. I dashed into the hallway in my nightgown and met Abilene throwing on jeans and sweatshirt over her pajamas as she hopped and stumbled and ran down the hall.

"Hey, wait, where're you going? What're you doing?" I yelled after her.

"To see what we caught!"

"What do you mean, *caught*?" And what do you mean, *we*?

"I set a trap!"

"Come back! We said we'd call Deputy Hamilton if—"

"He might get away before Hamilton could get here."

Abilene was already disappearing down the stairs. I debated a moment about calling Deputy Hamilton, but I was suddenly edgy about the legalities involved here. From what I've read, authorities tend to take a dim view of citizens acting on their own in matters such as this. And, from those weird sounds, I wasn't even certain what Abilene had in her trap.

I ran back to my bedroom, scrambled into clothes, and tore after Abilene. Koop wanted to come along, but I shut the door to keep him inside. I caught up with Abilene near one of the sheds as she came out carrying a baseball bat. Noises were still exploding from the brush enclosure. Thrashing, scuffling, and, as we got closer, panting sounds. And definitely human, unless one of the local four-legged fauna had somehow acquired a fertile vocabulary of ear-burning epithets.

Abilene slowed as we approached the brush-enclosed space. Dust billowed above it. She put a finger to her lips, and we quietly circled to the entrance on the back side. She held the baseball bat aloft, at attack readiness as we crept ahead. Then we both stopped and stared in astonishment.

The green canopy of branches that had been hanging over-head had crashed to the ground and now tangled around a struggling figure. The scrabbling feet churned up the earth as they circled the head in some strange, stuck-in-place race. Shifting branches revealed a body encased in a net like an oversized grasshopper caught in a spider's web. A rope flailed the bare dirt around the man, each twist of his body flinging it like some deranged lasso. Dust swirled around everything, including us, as if trying to escalate into a tornado.

Abilene lowered the bat. "Hey, it worked!" She sounded both astonished and pleased.

At the sound of our voices, movement within the net ceased. The body went rigid, but I suspected I was more scared of whoever was within the net than he was of us.

234

"What worked? What did you *do* here?" I gasped.

"Remember that camouflage net they used to catch the emus when they got loose? I figured, no reason it wouldn't work on a person too. So I dragged it out here and rigged it up in the tree with a rope . . . that rope . . ." She pointed to the thing now lying limp on the ground like an over-long rattlesnake. "Then I needed something to draw his attention, so he wouldn't look up and maybe see the net overhead, so I put a package of Oreo cookies inside on the ground. And then I tied a barrier of dental floss across the opening so that when he ran into it the rope would let the net drop on him. And it did! I guess the branch the net and rope were attached to broke . . . but it worked anyway!" she finished triumphantly.

"Did you get directions for this scheme out of some mystery novel?"

"No, I figured it out by myself."

I didn't know whether to congratulate her or roll my eyes. Abilene had built a trap. Baited it with Oreo cookies. Sprung it with dental floss. I could see bits of crushed cookies littering the ground now. The ants were probably thinking there really was an ant heaven. Were the police going to congratulate us for Abilene's creativity . . . or throw us in jail?

"And then you rigged it up all by yourself?"

"I suppose I should have told you—"

"Yes, you should have!"

"I was afraid you'd just worry yourself to death about it. Or have a hissy fit or something."

I drew myself up to my full five foot one. "I do not have hissy fits," I proclaimed.

"Will you people stop jabbering and get me out of here!" a male voice, apparently having heard enough, suddenly yelped from the tangle. He thrashed again, arms and legs flailing, rope whipping. The voice went panicky as he went into a hissy fit of his own. "Get me out of here! I'm suffocating! I can't breathe!"

He sounded so close to hysterics that Abilene dropped the bat, and we plunged into the cloud of dust and started yanking branches and vines off the jerking figure.

A figure whose only line seemed to be, "Get me out of here!" which he kept shrilling at the top of his lungs. Lungs that, so far as I could hear, did not appear to be suffocating.

Abilene picked up the bat again when we could see his nose poking through the web. "I don't think you're in any position to make demands," she pointed out.

Now I could see an eye surrounded by a red, sweating face peering through the web of camouflage netting.

"I'll sue you! I'll sue both of you for everything you've got. You can't just go around setting booby traps for people!"

He might have a point there. Abilene, however, was not intimidated.

"I set the trap," she said. "And what you see is what you get." She stretched the old sweatshirt out from her body and lifted one foot to expose her cheap jogging shoes. "So sue away."

A shaft of sunlight gleamed on the bald head above the angry eye. No, I realized, not bald. Shaved. I'd never seen him before, but instant recognition hit me. "Ute?" I said.

The shaved scalp strained against the camouflage netting as he tried to turn his head to get a better look at me. "So?" He sounded belligerent in spite of his trussed-up position. "Do I know you?"

So it really was Ute. I'd dismissed him as our possible skulker, thinking he'd never have left the kind of trail Abilene could so easily follow back to his campsite. Even now it seemed incredible that an amateur booby trap constructed of an emu net, Oreo cookies, and dental floss could have captured a man who had survived six weeks in the wilds with nothing but a pocketknife and matches. Yet it obviously had, because here he was.

"Why are you lurking around here spying on us?" Abilene demanded.

"Let me out of here!" he repeated. "This is killing me. I'm going to explode."

His face was red enough that he indeed looked near detonation. "Maybe we'd better do something," I said.

Abilene handed me the baseball bat. She stepped forward and yanked on the net, rolling his body several times like a hot dog on a grill. It didn't free him, but loosening the net unpinned his arms from his sides and allowed him to spread-eagle his legs.

"Is that better?" I asked. I could see now that he was wearing camouflage-colored shorts, dark T-shirt, and heavy boots. Age is difficult to determine through the barrier of a net, also camouflage color, but I guessed him to be twenty-eight to thirty.

"I want out of here."

"Not until we find out what you're doing spying on us," Abilene said.

He eyed me warily. "What are you planning to do with the bat?"

"Make one false move and you'll find out," Abilene growled.

Hey, I thought, pleased, *we're doing good cop, bad cop here.*

"We just want to know what you're doing here," I said in soothing, good-cop tones to counter Abilene's threat.

He made a stab at dignity. "I've been employed here—"

"You're not employed here now. We are. Frank Northcutt hired us to take care of the ranch and the emus after—" Abilene broke off, her glance at me questioning.

I nodded approvingly. Best to find out what Ute knew before giving our position away.

Ute muttered what seemed to be a unanimous opinion, except for Abilene's, on the emus. "Stupid birds."

"So you're not here to steal emus or give them IQ tests," I said and repeated our question. "Why are you here?"

"I . . . needed to find something."

"Something that belongs to you?" I asked skeptically.

"They owed me money." It's difficult to make out an expression on a face concealed under a camouflage net, but he looked like a man who, as soon as he's spoken, realizes he may have made an incriminating statement. People are dead. They owed him money. Not good.

The net changed shape like some weird blob of camouflaged bread dough bubbling with yeast as he punched with hands and feet against the restraining strands.

"I'm dying here, I tell you," he panted.

Abilene was not moved. "How much money did they owe you?" she asked.

"Forty dollars. And I sure wouldn't kill someone over forty dollars!"

"Who mentioned killing?" Abilene challenged.

"Maybe you should tell us about the Northcutts' deaths," I suggested. He could know Jock and Jessie were dead from news reports, of course, but somehow this sounded like a more personal knowledge. "We understand you had a disagreement with them, and they fired you."

"Yeah, which is why they owed me forty dollars. But I didn't kill them! They committed suicide, the two of them together. At least that's what the note said."

"You saw the note?" Abilene asked.

He struggled to sit up. Abilene lifted the net to help him. Within it he swiped his hand across his mouth. "Yeah, I saw it," he muttered.

"I think you'd better tell us about this," I said.

"Here? Now?"

"Why not? We have plenty of time. We're not going anywhere."

The sun had crested the wooded hills and mountains to the east, but a few fluffy clouds still glowed cotton-candy pink. A songbird trilled from a nearby treetop, and a tiny wren peered with beady eye out of the stacked brush, then swooped down to capture an Oreo crumb.

Ute's shoulders moved in what might have been a shrug of resignation as he apparently figured out that he wasn't going anywhere.

"Okay, Jock and Jessie fired me. I didn't like their stupid job anyway. They were just using me for grunt work. Taking care of those stupid birds. Fixing fence. Mowing the stupid yard. Jessie handed me the pay I had coming, and I left."

"Why did they fire you?"

"I complained about having to gather up the emu droppings and put them on a compost pile."

"They were acting normal at that time? The Northcutts, I mean, not the emus."

"As normal as they ever were."

Probably an astute observation, although I didn't comment on it. "And then what?"

"When I got to Dulcy I looked at the money and realized Jessie had shorted me forty dollars on what I had coming. At first I was just going to let it go, but then I started getting mad. What a couple of cheapskates! And after I'd done everything from wash the Hummer to crawl under the house looking for termites. A week or so later I came back."

"And how did the Northcutts react?" I asked.

"They didn't. They were right there on the sofa. Dead." The words came out flat and emotionless, but I saw his throat move in a big, convulsive swallow. Shock at finding the bodies? Or something else, something much more sinister, such as guilt?

"How did you get in?"

"I had a key to the gate. They'd made me give back the one they knew I had, but I'd had another one made that they didn't know about."

"You left the gate open when you came in?"

"No, I closed and locked it behind me. Jock and Jessie were real sticklers about that. The gate always had to be locked." His eyebrows scrunched together, as if he were annoyed with himself that he'd followed their rules even though he was both fired and angry.

"You had a key to the house too?"

"No, they'd never let me have a key to the house. Or sheds. I parked around back and knocked, but there wasn't any answer. The Hummer was here, so I figured they were out in the woods. Shooting at each other with paintballs or some stupid thing. I tried the door."

"And?"

"It was unlocked."

"So you decided this was an invitation to go inside?"

Ute ignored the sarcasm in Abilene's question, though he sounded defensive when he said, "They owed me the forty dollars. I figured I'd just go in and take it out in groceries. They had so much they'd never miss a few cans of stuff. But when I-I looked around to make sure no one was in the house—" Another of those convulsive bobbles of his throat. "There they were. On the sofa, blood and . . . and brains all over."

"You didn't call the police?"

"I thought about it. I really did," he said, his tone defensive, as if we'd accused him of dereliction of duty. "But then I figured, even if it *looked* like they'd killed themselves, and the note *said* they had, maybe I'd get accused of something. I hadn't been . . . shy about telling people how Jock and Jessie had cheated me. A lot of people knew I was teed off about it.

240

So I figured it would be better if no one knew I'd even been near the place since they'd fired me."

"You just quietly left?"

"Well, no," he admitted reluctantly. "I was thinking about the money they owed me, and how the job wasn't what it was supposed to be. They wouldn't even let me stay in the house, can you believe that? I had to sleep in my old van."

"So all this entitled you to . . . what?" I asked.

"I decided I'd look around a little. They owed me."

"So you stole their gold coins?" I suggested.

"What gold coins?" He sounded so astonished that even I had to believe he didn't know anything about gold coins. If there were gold coins. Maybe there'd never been any more than that lone coin Mac found. "I never saw any gold coins."

"Drugs, then?" Abilene asked.

"There weren't any drugs. Except for that herbal junk Jock thought was going to bring back his hair and Jessie thought would take away her wrinkles. That ginkgo stuff, and ginseng and St. somebody's wort and vitamins I never heard of." He sounded scornful or perhaps miffed by their lack of interest in real drugs, I couldn't tell which.

I remembered the packages of herb medications I'd seen in the bathroom cabinet, and we'd since found an even larger variety in the kitchen cupboards. I also remembered the medicine cabinet looked as if it had been rifled.

"So you went through their medicine cabinet, looking for something more interesting? Or saleable?"

"I felt sick to my stomach. Who wouldn't? All those flies and blood and smell. I was about to throw up. So I looked for something to take. I wasn't about to use any of that herb junk, but I did find some Tums."

Yes, I remembered that open bottle of Tums.

"Were they dealing drugs?" Abilene asked. "Real drugs?"

241

"Dealing drugs? Jock and Jessie?" He gave a snort. "No way. They were peculiar, suspicious of everyone and real cheapskates. Except when it came to buying all that survival food and gear, and the herbal stuff, of course. But a half ounce of pot on the property would've sent them into orbit. They made that plain when they hired me. No drugs. And no cell phones."

An odd combination, but I could believe it of the paranoid Northcutts. Though I did wonder if they were concerned about brain-eating cell phone waves or overheard conversations. I also had my doubts about total compliance with these drug rules from our shaved-head, net-wrapped acquaintance here.

"But you figured some drugs would be okay, maybe a little buying and selling to make a buck on the side, as long as Jock and Jessie didn't know," I suggested. "A local deputy stopped you once."

He squinted through the net at me as if curious how I knew about that, but he apparently decided not to question it. "I had a bad taillight on the van. No big deal."

"That's all?"

"What do you mean?"

"You were nervous. Like you were worried the deputy might search your van and find something incriminating."

"I may have been a little nervous," Ute admitted. "I didn't know what my buddy might have on him. Turned out he didn't have anything. But he was nervous because he thought maybe I did. We got a good laugh out of it."

One of those things where you had to be there, I guessed. "Who was this buddy?"

"An actor friend from California. He was between jobs, so he headed to New York to look for stage work and stopped to see me on the way."

Abilene and I looked at each other. Ute wasn't quite living up to our dark and dangerous expectations. Although he could be sitting there lying through his teeth, of course. Being trussed up in a net didn't necessarily guarantee honesty.

"I'm dying of thirst here. How about a drink of water?"

It was a ways across the clearing to the house, and Abilene said, "I'll go get it."

She ducked out the opening, and I watched through a peephole in the brush as she jogged toward the house.

"Hey, who *are* you people anyway?" Ute asked, his tone complaining.

"I'm Ivy. My friend is Abilene."

"Okay, Ivy, you seem like a reasonable woman. How about helping me out of this net? We both know I'm an innocent victim here, and I've got ants crawling all over me."

Clever Ute. Divide and conquer. Was he really as innocent as he was trying to make us believe?

I picked up the bat and made a decisive thump on the ground. "I don't think so," I said. "Abilene and I are a team. We work together."

28

Ute muttered something unintelligible, although I was fairly certain he was not complimenting me on what a sweet and gracious person I was. After that he sat in hostile silence.

Abilene returned with a tall glass clinking with ice cubes. Ute hadn't, at least, been lying about being thirsty. He drank the glass almost empty before stopping for breath. Then he extracted an ice cube and rubbed it on his face. His face had cooled a shade now, dropping from explosive firecracker red to old brick.

I gave him a minute to finish drinking and then continued the questioning. "So if you weren't searching for gold or drugs after you found the bodies, what were you looking for to make up for what Jock and Jessie owed you?"

"Doesn't matter. I didn't have time to find anything."

"Why not?"

"Because the stupid doorbell started buzzing. I didn't know there was anyone within five miles, and all of a sudden someone's right outside the door. Worst doorbell I've ever heard. Like a cross between a jackhammer and a whoopee cushion. Then this person starts hammering on the door. And I'm trapped in there with two dead bodies."

"But they were suicides. You've said so yourself."

"Yeah, well, that's right. But I was still . . . spooked."

I knew the feeling. I'd been spooked too, when Abilene and I found the bodies.

"So you didn't go to the door."

"No. I figured whoever it was would give up and go away in a minute or two. But instead, whoever it was started rattling the doorknob and trying to get *in*. I was so spooked by then that I jumped and rammed right into the wall. Practically knocked myself out. And then the stupid phone started ringing."

The thump and then the ringing phone I'd heard! Ute. So that was me rattling the doorknob. I started to protest that I hadn't really been trying to get in, but then I decided there was no need for Ute to know the details. Or even that it was me at the door.

"But whoever it was finally went away. I waited a few minutes to be sure they were gone, then I ran out through the kitchen door and jumped in my van and got out of there." He lifted his shirt beneath the net and wiped sweat off his forehead as if he were still feeling the nerves and exertion of that day.

"But the door was locked when we got here," Abilene said. "Did you lock it?"

"I don't know . . . Yeah, I guess I probably did. It just seemed like the thing to do, you know, them in there . . . dead and all."

A decent thing to do, I decided, even if some of his other actions hadn't been so decent.

Now I realized why the lock had been on a different side of the gate when I came back the second time. Ute had fas-

245

tened the chain and lock from the inside when he entered the gate, and I'd come along not long afterwards. After I left, he'd gone out, moving the lock to the outside of the gate, which was where it was when Abilene and I came back the next day. I also realized that if I'd come around the house that first time, I'd have seen his van.

"So where's your van now?" Abilene asked.

"Couple of miles back in the woods." His thumb poked through the net as he motioned. "There's an old road back there."

"Why did you move from where you were camped before?"

He looked mildly alarmed to realize we'd known where he was hiding out earlier. I'd figured the camper/skulker was sharp and observant enough to recognize someone had prowled in his camp, but I was beginning to think Ute might not be quite the expert outdoorsman he'd made everyone believe he was. Or maybe he'd never gone back to that camping place.

"It was too far to hike," he admitted finally. "I didn't like having to plow through all the brush and stuff to get here. Look, I'm getting really tired of sitting here wrapped up in this stupid net. It's making me itch." He scratched his arm as evidence.

"Tough," Abilene said.

He gave a much put-upon sigh.

"Somehow I don't think you've been spending all this time spying on us just so you can sneak in the house and grab forty dollars worth of chili and sardines," I said.

"I had something else in mind," he admitted grudgingly.

"Like what?"

He shifted on the hard ground. The sun was shining into the brush enclosure now. Sweat beaded his forehead. He had a couple of scratches on his face where a fallen branch had scraped him. I moved over to shade him with my shadow.

"I'd given Jock and Jessie some ideas for the new script they were working on. That was what my job was supposed to be, a research assistant. Anyway, once I realized they were . . . gone, I couldn't see that they'd have any use for the script. So I thought I'd just find a copy of it, or at least the treatment."

The word rang a bell. I remembered that bewildering late-night caller who'd been so indignant about not receiving a "treatment." "And a 'treatment' would be . . . ?"

"It's a short document that tells what the proposed story is about. Who the characters are, the concept, the setting, how the plot works out. A little like an outline or synopsis, but not exactly. More high-powered maybe. Stronger on concept." He spoke with a certain loftiness, a person with inside Hollywood knowledge we ignorant outsiders didn't possess.

If he was trying to impress, it didn't work with Abilene. She hit the bottom line. "And after you found this script or treatment, whatever, you were planning to pass it off as your own?"

He shifted uncomfortably on the ground. "Probably the best stuff in it *is* mine," he said defensively. "And now that they aren't around, I figure I'm as entitled to the script as anyone."

"There are legitimate heirs," I pointed out.

"Yeah. The wimpy son. The greedy wives. The bratty kids. None of them could tell a decent script from a sitcom dog. But I could make something really worthwhile out of whatever Jock and Jessie had started. It was my idea they go futuristic, with mutant sharks invading after atomic weapons demolished the ice caps and raised the sea level. A really great idea."

"So you and the Northcutts were kindred souls, survivalists/writers united together." After a moment's reflection I added, "With a mutual touch of paranoia?"

"I'm not paranoid. Although I could get that way around you two," he muttered. "Would you please stop thumping and twisting that bat like you're just waiting for a chance to whop me over the head with it?"

I hadn't realized it, but I was stirring up a small cloud of dust of my own. "Sorry. So that's what you've spent all this time here for, waiting to get into the house to steal Jock and Jessie's movie script or treatment?"

"I haven't had anything better to do, and it's cheap living in the van out here." He sounded defensive again. "I haven't sold anything except one short story in the last year. My agent just dumped me. This looked like my best shot. And I don't think it's fair to call my wanting the script 'stealing.' I mean, that mutant shark was my idea, and I'm pretty sure they used it."

Probably so, considering both what I'd seen in the files and what I'd heard earlier from Margaret Rau about the Northcutts' odd interest in shark attacks. Which I doubted gave Ute the right to claim the entire script, however.

"Perhaps you prefer the term *plagiarism*?" I suggested.

The word *stealing* hadn't seemed to upset him, but *plagiarism*, the word that applied distinctly to the written word, apparently did. He shifted uncomfortably on the net wadded beneath him and rubbed the back of his neck. His gaze darted to the line of ants industriously carrying off Oreo crumbs.

"You made yourself a good hiding place here. Very competently done. Apparently, even if you and the Northcutts had some differences, you are an expert survivalist?"

He jiggled his shoulders in an indecisive motion.

"I heard you spent six weeks alone in the wilderness with only a pocketknife and matches."

He scratched the side of his nose. "I may have . . . exaggerated somewhat."

"Exaggerated how?"

"I kind of . . . made that up."

"To impress the Northcutts?"

"I wanted to learn something from them working here. They hadn't had any big successes lately, but they were good writers. But I doubted they were going to hire just any old writing hopeful who wandered in from L.A. So I beefed up my resume to what I thought would interest them."

"Bought some camouflage clothes and an old van, got a tattoo, and turned yourself into a survivalist." We hadn't seen the tattoo yet, but I assumed it was there.

"I already had the van." He didn't deny my other accusations.

"But basically you deceived the Northcutts about who and what you were."

"I didn't really deceive them," he protested. He was sweating more now, maybe not just from heat. "It was more like playing a part. I'm interested in acting on the screen as well as writing for it. You remember the *Digby and Son* TV show?"

"No, I don't think so." I glanced at Abilene, and she shook her head.

"It lasted only part of one season, but I was a waiter on one of the episodes. A good one too. So with the Northcutts I just kind of acted the part of . . . a survivalist. One of *them*."

"But you're not."

"If I were really some survivalist expert, would I have gotten caught in your stupid trap?" He fist-jabbed the net, tore his thumbnail, and looked at it like a little boy about to run to Mama with a boo-boo.

We'd gotten sidetracked here, I decided. And maybe Ute was acting even now, trying to throw us off. I jumped to a new subject. Surprise, according to the mysteries I read, is

249

always good. So I surprised him with, "Do you think there's a chance Jock and Jessie were being blackmailed?"

"Blackmailed?" He indeed sounded astonished, but after a moment's thought a one-shouldered shrug followed. "They'd probably pulled enough shyster tricks over the years to warrant blackmail. Ethics were not a high priority with Jock and Jessie. Look what they did to me. But I don't know that they were being blackmailed." He paused, absentmindedly working his jaw back and forth as if checking for damage. "Actually, if you want to talk blackmail, I'd be more inclined to think they were the blackmailers, not blackmailees. I'd bet they knew all kinds of dirt on any number of Hollywood big shots."

Logical, except that it didn't jibe with the disappearing cash, which said they were paying out, not receiving, money. Information I didn't intend to share with Ute, of course. I offered a possibility that fit with his. "And perhaps this person or persons who were being blackmailed decided to end it by killing them?"

"How would I know? Besides, they weren't murdered. They committed suicide. The police and medical examiner and everybody said so. The newspaper ran several pieces on it."

Did he believe that? Or was he clinging to the suicide story because he was afraid if he didn't, if he expressed any doubts, he might wind up at the top of a sheriff's "People with Motives" list?

"That's what you thought when you first saw the bodies?" I asked. "That they'd committed suicide?"

"Right off, I thought somebody'd whacked 'em," he admitted. "But then I saw the gun and the note."

"Were you surprised then, that they'd done it?"

"I don't know. Yes and no, I guess. I mean, they were such fanatics about survival, you know? Why go to all that trouble

250

to survive, and then give up and do yourselves in? And yet they sometimes did things so impulsively. Like going down to Hugo one time and coming home with enough toilet tissue to t.p. New York."

Right. That mountain of it in the basement. I decided to hit him with another surprise. "Maybe the note was a fake. Maybe they *were* murdered."

"How could it be a fake?" he scoffed. "The newspaper said Frank identified the handwriting."

"You could have managed a fake note," Abilene said. "You're smart and clever and creative—"

Even the appeal to Ute's ego wasn't enough to make him admit, yeah, maybe he could have faked a note. He shook his head with all the vehemence of a small boy faced with a plate of brussels sprouts.

"Me? Hey, no." He struggled to rise within the net, but his knees jammed against his chin, and he wound up in an awkward toad-squat. "Don't try to pin this on me. Look at all the other people who had it in for them a whole lot more than I did!"

"Such as?"

"Someone they were blackmailing who was mad enough to kill them himself . . . or herself . . . or hire a hit man. Or maybe someone they wronged back in Hollywood had it in for them. What about whoever got those gold coins you were talking about? What about the son and that la-di-da wife of his? Maybe they decided to kill Jock and Jessie before they got cut out of the will. What about the ex-wife? She talked Jock and Jessie out of money more than once with some sob story about the poor deprived kids. I heard her myself. And what about those spoiled-brat kids? Or maybe Jock and Jessie really were into drugs, and I just didn't know it, and some druggie did them in."

It was quite a lineup of potential killers, I had to admit,

but Abilene jumped on a line buried in the list. "The kids?" she repeated. "You're saying the *kids* could have phonied up a suicide note and then shot their grandparents?"

"Well, okay, probably not the kids," Ute muttered as if realizing an off-the-wall charge about the kids really didn't strengthen an argument for his own innocence. "They're spoiled brats, but I guess they couldn't have pulled this off. But the son, now, he's a different story. And the wife too. She never got along with Jock and Jessie. They could have—"

"Wait a minute," I said. "Back up. You mentioned a will. Did you see a will? Or hear Jock and Jessie talk about one?"

"They were looking at something one time when they had me in the house trying to unplug the kitchen drain. I didn't actually see what it was, but it was typed on that long, crinkly kind of paper lawyers use, and I thought it was a will at the time. They were arguing about something in it. Maybe Frank and his wife thought they'd better protect what they had coming as an inheritance by getting rid of the old folks before they changed the will."

An ugly thought, but money often turned people ugly.

"But why would Jock and Jessie change their will? There were no other children to inherit."

"Who knows? Maybe they wanted their paintball war games group to have enough money to buy paintballs for the next fifty years. Maybe they decided to set up a paintball scholarship. Maybe they wanted their money to go to some 'Save the Emus' organization."

"Did the Northcutts have a home safe where they'd keep a will?" I asked. "Or maybe a safe deposit box?"

"I wasn't exactly their confidante. I wouldn't even know if they had a piggy bank."

"You thought you had something coming from them too," Abilene broke in to remind him. Bluntly she added, "Maybe Jock and Jessie weren't dead when you got here. Maybe they

252

refused to give you the forty dollars you thought they owed you. So you became angry and—"

"That's crazy! Sure, I was teed off about the money, but like I already said, I did not kill them over forty lousy bucks!"

"People have been murdered for forty lousy *cents*," Abilene said.

And what I wondered was: how many "lousy bucks" would it take for Ute to commit murder? Would several hundred thousand dollars worth of gold coins do it? Just because he'd denied knowledge of the coins didn't mean he didn't know about them. If they did actually exist.

"Have you ever run around here barefoot?" I interrupted.

"Barefoot?" Even through the net, Ute's expression came across as baffled at this peculiar change of subject. "You've got to be kidding. With snakes or who-knows-what crawling out of that swamp back there? And what's barefoot got to do with anything anyway?"

"We found a barefoot track back by the swamp. Maybe it was the killer's track." Abilene pointedly inspected Ute's feet as if measuring them for size or looking for incriminating mud.

"Oh. Well. That." His tone was dismissive.

"That," I repeated.

"I came back the day after I found the bodies. I drove around on the far side of the woods and hiked through so nobody'd see me coming out here. I thought maybe I could locate the script before anyone else found the bodies. Except the two of *you* were already here. Then *she*"—he jabbed a finger through the net in Abilene's direction and gave her a baleful glare—"she headed right toward me in the woods, and I ran. Only I fell in that stupid swamp and practically drowned—"

"There's only a foot or two of water," Abilene said.

"Yeah, well, there's about three more feet of mud down in the bottom. By the time I got out I was covered with about forty pounds of the stuff, and my shoes and socks were so full of it I couldn't even walk. So I took them off and kept going. I suppose I left some barefoot tracks."

Another small mystery explained. We were scared of what might be lurking out there in the woods that day, and it was just Ute. Belly-flopping in the swamp.

"And then I finally got up the nerve to come back later to see if the place was empty, but no, you were still here. And Frank too. The war-game warriors, chasing around out in the woods, shooting each other—and me—with paintballs."

Oh yes, I remembered my splat on a target that took off through the brush. Ute again.

So we now had explanations for several small mysteries that had helped fuel my suspicion that Jock and Jessie had been murdered. How the lock came to be on a different side of the gate. The odd thump in the house. The barefoot track. There were also the suspicious rumors we'd heard about Ute himself.

Okay, Ute wasn't the most noble character in survival land, that was for certain. A writer who was willing to pass someone else's creative work off as his own. A man with a much too large and colorful vocabulary of epithets. A man who pretended to be something he wasn't. A man who was willing to let dead bodies sit on a blood-soaked sofa instead of calling the police.

But probably not a murderer.

So, what did this mean? That the Northcutts' deaths really were a mutually agreed upon homicide/suicide, and Abilene and I were victims of our overactive, mystery-novel-fueled imaginations?

Could be.

"I guess we should turn him loose," I said reluctantly.

Abilene nodded with equal reluctance. She eyed the bat

as if she'd like to take at least one whack at him. I kept a firm grip on it.

"It's about time," Ute said.

We pulled and pushed, rolling him around like a lumpy log as we tried to get him out of the net. More dust billowed. More noisy complaints about our rough technique from Ute. We were all panting with the exertion. I did spot Ute's tattoo in the melee. It looked like a vulture to me, although I supposed the artist's intention may have been an eagle.

"We're going to have to cut him loose," Abilene said finally. "Do you have a pocketknife?" she asked Ute.

"I had one of those switchblade kind. But I accidentally hit the button on it, and it came open in my pocket. I was lucky I didn't cut my leg off. So I got rid of it."

"Figures," Abilene muttered, and I had to agree. Ute was no hardy survivalist ready for any emergency. He was probably fortunate he hadn't severed a finger using his can opener. "I'll go get something from the house."

"Did the emus ever lay any eggs while you were here?" I inquired while Ute and I waited. He'd scooted himself over to where the stacked brush offered more shade than I did. He scratched vigorously at a knee.

"I never saw any."

"Abilene found one."

He looked up with mild curiosity. "Yeah? What's it look like?"

"It's big. And green."

He wrinkled his nose in distaste. "Figures. Stupid birds."

Maybe what the Northcutts should have done with their money was organize an "emus aren't as stupid as you think they are" society, since the birds seemed in need of better press than they were getting.

Abilene returned with a butcher knife from the kitchen.

255

Ute eyed it warily as she hacked through the tough strands of netting.

"Thank you," he muttered when he was finally able to crawl out and stand upright. He brushed at dirt, twigs, and ants clinging to his shirt and shorts. A dirty imprint of the net crisscrossed his backside.

I watched him, thinking that if he'd been acting a part here, this was when we'd find out. I glanced at Abilene and knew she was thinking the same thing. She had a killer grip on the butcher knife. I surreptitiously picked up the baseball bat again.

He didn't, however, seem to have attack in mind. He ran a hand across his shaved scalp and disengaged a clinging leaf and a couple of ants.

"What are you going to do now?" I asked.

"Right now, hike back to my van."

"And then?"

"And then maybe I'll just pick up and head for where I came from."

"L.A.?"

"Before that. Cincinnati. I'm starting to think that if I have to resort to plagiarism"—he paused when he said the word, as if it made a bad taste in his mouth—"then maybe I'd better reassess my talents as a writer." He paused again. "My brother's always wanted me to go into his insurance business with him. Maybe I'll do it. But he isn't going to like the tattoo." He turned his head and touched the spot behind his ear again. It still looked like a vulture to me.

"If you let your hair grow out, it'll probably cover the tattoo," Abilene offered.

He smiled, the first time he'd done so. It made a nice change in his face. "Yeah, I guess it will. Thanks. And if I ever need a booby trap designer, I'll look you up. It's been a

. . . unique experience meeting you ladies," he added. "Not one I'll soon forget."

I decided not to investigate whether that was compliment or complaint. He shook hands with both of us. He headed into the woods, but a few feet away he stopped and turned.

"You know, if I were you, I wouldn't muddle around in this murder thing too far."

I started to protest the word *muddle*, but the somber tone of his voice stopped me. "What do you mean?"

"If what happened here wasn't suicide, then there's one very clever, very ruthless, very cold-blooded killer on the loose. A killer who might kill again to protect himself. So just . . . be careful."

29

I was glad Ute had turned out to be a different person than we'd thought. Glad, too, that he seemed to have had a change of heart and direction. But at the same time I found myself feeling mildly let down. He'd been our primary suspect, and now he wasn't.

So where did that leave us?

In spite of the ever-present problem of the note, Ute himself obviously had suspicions that Jock and Jessie had been murdered. He'd made that plain with his warning to us to be careful. He'd also offered his own long list of suspects.

So?

So drop it, I decided resolutely. That list of suspects was shaky as a six-foot tower of Jell-O.

We went back to the house for breakfast. Koop met us at the door. Some cats might have been indignant about being locked in all that time, but Koop, laid-back gentleman that he was, merely offered us an inquiring meow. *Everything okay now?* After hotcakes and bacon, Abilene went out to repair a loose board on the deck. I worked on the filing system.

Mac called at about 11:00. The doctor wanted him to see a physical therapist for his wrist for at least a couple of weeks, maybe longer, so it would be a while before he could come back up here. I was disappointed, and, I was gratified to realize, he was too, although neither of us went into effusive detail about it. I went on to tell him about our adventures capturing Ute and that the emu egg was doing fine, but we hadn't found a safe or any more gold coins.

"You're an interesting woman," Mac said. He sounded reflective. "I talk to ladies here in the RV park. They tell me about a game show on TV or a two-for-one coupon for a restaurant or invite me to play pinochle. You tell me about murder and mayhem and hidden treasure. And green eggs."

"Is that good or bad?"

"Hmmm." He sounded undecided, and I didn't press for a judgment. Probably because I was afraid it would not be a favorable one. Although I felt better when he said, "I miss you."

"I miss you too."

"If you could get away, maybe you could drive down just for the day? There's a Thai restaurant here that makes a great dish called Tom Yum Po Tak."

"What's Tom Yum Po Tak?"

"You'll just have to come see."

"Maybe I'll do that."

The following morning Abilene and I decided to drive into Dulcy. Without our resident skulker to worry about, I figured leaving the place untended for a few hours would be okay, although I did lock the gate securely when we went out.

In Dulcy, I went to the window at the post office, but no more mail had arrived. As if it were a spur-of-the-moment idea, I suggested to Abilene that we stop at the somewhat

259

pretentious-sounding Hair by Elsie next door to Gus's Groceries, and I was pleasantly surprised when she readily agreed. Frank had given us an advance on our caretaking salaries, so she had a few dollars.

The shop was not jammed with customers on this weekday morning, and Abilene got right into a chair. The woman couldn't work miracles with her short hair, but she evened up the most ragged spikes and gave it a little style with a curling iron. With her bruises almost faded away by now, Abilene came out looking very attractive.

A fact instantly noted by Deputy Hamilton when we stepped out of the salon and ran into him getting a Dr Pepper from the machine in front of the grocery store.

"Mrs. Malone. And Ms. Morrison. How nice to see you again." He was still working with the name that had been on the Social Security card Abilene had used as identification that day we'd found the bodies. I gave her a sideways glance, wondering if she'd correct it to Tyler, but she didn't.

"Would you like something to drink?" He motioned toward the machine. "Not the most elegant ambiance here, but the drinks are cold." He popped the lid on the can he was holding.

I looked at Abilene. She shook her head, and I said, "Thanks, no. We have some shopping to do."

"You're still working out at the Northcutt place?"

"Mrs." Abilene said suddenly.

"Mrs.?" Deputy Hamilton repeated.

"Mrs. Morrison. I'm married."

"Oh." He looked quite taken aback by the information. "I didn't know that."

An awkward time was had by all, I thought as the three of us just stood there. Abilene offered no further information, and I was trying to think what to say next when Deputy Hamilton took charge with a brisk change of subject.

"You've heard the news about Eddie Howell, I suppose?"

"Actually, no. Has something happened? We don't get a newspaper, and we haven't had the TV on the last couple days."

"Case closed. We got the killer. Of course, the DA still has to convict the guy, but it looks like a solid case. We have an eyewitness, and the gun that killed Eddie was found in the guy's possession."

"A drug involvement, as you suspected?"

"And how. Eddie was in it up to his ears, but he'd decided he wanted out. His 'buddies' felt he was too big a risk, knowing as much he did, so they made sure he couldn't blow the whistle on them."

"There are other local people involved, then?" I asked.

"Unfortunately, yes. But a friend of the guy who pulled the trigger on Eddie spouted names, trying to save his own neck. We made a clean sweep."

I hesitated about bringing this up but decided I'd always wonder if I didn't. "I've wondered if Jock and Jessie Northcutt could have been involved in drugs."

Deputy Hamilton looked surprised. "Oh? Well, I can't say about personal use, of course, but they weren't involved with the local drug scene. The drugs were coming out of Oklahoma City, and the police there have rounded up the ringleaders. This won't solve the local drug problem totally, but it puts a nice dent in it."

I was relieved to hear Jock and Jessie hadn't been involved. It was also one more reason to accept their deaths as homicide/suicide, not some clever murder.

"Their former employee, Ute, wasn't involved with the drugs either?"

"No. Much to my surprise," Deputy Hamilton admitted. He also sounded a bit disappointed.

"And that young man who was killed in the rollover accident?"

"Not involved in either the drugs or Eddie's death. Doesn't bring him back, of course, but I think it's a relief for the parents to know that."

"I'm glad to hear it too."

Deputy Hamilton gave Abilene a sideways glance, as if he'd like to know more about this sudden announcement of her married status. His gaze dropped to her left hand. No wedding ring. But he was too polite to pry, of course, about something that wasn't a police matter.

Abilene was jiggling on her toes, looking decidedly uncomfortable even if he wasn't prying, so I said, "We'd better get our shopping done so we can get back to the house and the emus. Thanks for bringing us up to date."

"You haven't found any more stray bullets out there, I take it?" He sounded serious enough on the surface, but I heard an unexpected undertone of tease.

No, no more stray bullets. Although we did capture one imitation survivalist. But I decided Deputy Hamilton didn't need to know that and went along with the tease. "No. Although Abilene did find a mysterious green object."

"Green object? Something suspicious looking, you mean?"

"Oh, definitely."

"Don't move it, whatever you do," he commanded. "It could be explosive. Are there wires or anything attached? Any writing on it?"

"No wires," I said solemnly. "No writing. And we've already moved it. But we definitely think it may be explosive."

He grabbed a deputy's ever-present notebook out of his pocket. "How did it arrive?"

"By emu express."

A blank look, and then Deputy Hamilton leaned back

against the Coke machine and grinned. "You're putting me on, aren't you, Mrs. Malone? You really had me going there for a minute. Strange green object," he scoffed. He tucked the notebook back in his pocket. "So what was it? Fur ball coughed up by that cat of yours? Or maybe feather ball belched up by one of those emus?"

"Actually, it's an emu egg. Which may explode into a real live emu any day now. We're trying to hatch it. Not personally, of course. With a heating pad."

"And it's actually green? You're not still putting me on?" he added suspiciously.

"Green . . . well, bluish-green to be more accurate . . . is the honest truth. And big."

"That's interesting. I wouldn't mind—" He broke off with a sudden glance at Abilene. I was almost certain he'd started to say something about coming out to see the egg and then changed his mind because of the information Abilene had dropped on him. "Well, good luck with your hatching, then." He lifted the can in a small salute, and we watched until he drove off.

Abilene's face had an uncharacteristic woebegone look, but she made no comment as he disappeared around the bend.

"Nice guy," I said.

"Nosy cop," she muttered.

We bought fresh milk and eggs and headed back out to Dead Mule Road. A bank of dark clouds loomed off to the southwest, and my skin prickled with that feel of a coming storm. I waited for Abilene to say something about her "Mrs." proclamation, but, as usual, she wasn't big on explanations. Finally I brought up the subject myself.

"I was surprised when you told Deputy Hamilton that you were Mrs. Morrison. I thought you intended to use your Tyler name now."

"Yeah, I do. But . . ." Her smooth brow, beneath the slight

curl of blond from curling iron, furrowed, as if this were a problem she didn't know how to handle. "Legally, no matter what name I use, I'm still married."

True. Escaping abuse in the middle of the night in a Porsche did not constitute divorce.

"Deputy Hamilton isn't really a . . . a nosy cop. I shouldn't have said that. It wasn't fair. He's nice, and I think I could . . . really like him. But, however awful my marriage to Boone was, I'm still married to him. And it wouldn't be right, to . . . get involved." She sounded troubled but resolute.

I was surprised. This was not the attitude many people had in this era of now-you-see-'em-now-you-don't marriages. I was also impressed by her admirable sense of right and wrong. However troubling and inconvenient and, given Boone's abuse, even unfair the situation might be, she was still married to him.

"Do you . . . understand?" She peered across the center console of the motor home at me, as if she wasn't certain she understood herself.

"Yes, I think I do."

"Do you think I'm being silly? I don't love Boone. I never did. I never wanted to marry him. And I know he had a girlfriend in town. It didn't matter to *him* that he was married. But . . ." Her voice trailed off uncertainly.

"No, I don't think you're being silly. We shouldn't base our actions on someone else's sins, no matter how tempting it might be to justify what we do that way. I think you're taking the high road here, being strong and wise and moral. I'm proud of—"

I broke off when Abilene gave a kind of snort. I glanced over and saw her lower lip wobbling. She blinked rapidly, and I realized both snort and blinks were an effort to hold back tears. I suddenly felt tearful too. Abilene's young life hadn't been a picnic. She'd never received enough hugs or praise or reassurances of her value as a person. The knowledge gave me an ache inside.

Yet Abilene, who'd managed to survive being shoved into an unwanted marriage, the responsibility of three children, and a husband who deliberately broke her arm, was not about to succumb to the weakness of tears now. She lifted her head. "You're not going to get all sloppy and sentimental, are you?" she muttered.

"Not if you don't want me to."

"Good."

"But I am going to tell you, whether you want to hear it or not, that I'm proud of you. I'm proud of your strength of character and your standards. And if I had a granddaughter, I'd want her to be much like you."

Another wobble of lip told me I might not be the only one about to go sloppy and sentimental here. I knew Abilene wouldn't want that display of emotions in herself.

"You're also one humdinger of a booby-trap builder. But if you build another one without including me, I may take another pair of horse clippers to your hair. And this time you'll wind up with a hairdo that will make you look like ol' Ute's twin."

Abilene's mouth dropped open as she took in my praise/threat. Then she nodded solemnly. "Okay, it's a promise. No more solo booby traps. I'll write it in blood if you want."

"A simple notarized statement will be sufficient."

Abilene grinned, tears safely under control now. "If I'd ever known either of my grandmas, which I didn't, I guess I'd want them to be just like you. Kind of grumpy sometimes but . . . nice."

So then it was my turn to snort and do the blinking routine as we stopped at the gate and Abilene got out to unlock it.

We had lunch, tuna sandwiches, and then decided we had time to haul the somewhat worse-for-wear capture net over to the burn pile before the coming storm arrived. I didn't see any lightning, but thunder rumbled in the distance. First we demolished the brush enclosure, so no other camper/skulkers might be tempted to spy on us. Then Abilene grabbed hold of one side of the net and I got the other, and we dragged it between us.

"How'd you ever get this thing out there and up in the tree all by yourself?" I panted as we slogged our way through the tall weeds. The net seemed to catch on every stick and rock.

"I just kept imagining it was Boone, and then I'd give it another yank or kick. Worked great."

We reached the burn pile and draped the bedraggled net over the coffee table. We could have a fine bonfire later this fall, although, given the contents, it wasn't going to be one that invited hot dogs and marshmallows.

Just a few days in the bright sunlight had faded the brown fabric on the sofa to a lighter shade. Wild animals had gnawed on the clotted blood, shredding the fabric and exposing tufts of stuffing. The smell was gone now, and the sofa could have passed for any discarded old piece of furniture rather than a site of death.

But even if the physical remnants of death were gone, I still had a Technicolor image of Jock and Jessie on the sofa. I stepped around behind the sofa so I wouldn't have to look at where they'd once sat in death, intending to rest a minute before we went back for the fallen branches in the brush enclosure.

And spotted something.

30

I stepped closer to the back side of the sofa. Still squeamish about touching it, I kept my hands clasped behind my back as I leaned forward. A gust of wind whipped my hair in my eyes, and I shook it away.

Abilene glanced up from where she was pulling burrs and cheat grass seeds out of her socks. "What're you looking at?"

I was looking at long hairs. One was tangled in the faded brown fabric, the other, about to blow away, fluttered in the wind.

Nothing surprising about that. A hair or two caught in the fabric of some piece of furniture is hardly unusual. Over time, I've probably vacuumed enough of my possum-gray out of various pieces of furniture to knit myself a bikini. If I were into bikinis.

But these were two long *blond* hairs. Who in the Northcutt household had long blond hair? Certainly not Jock or Jesse. An image of a Dolly-Parton-sized blond immediately came to mind, but these blond hairs couldn't have come from her. We'd moved the bloody sofa out to the burn pile before she arrived.

Unless these blond hairs had already been there, caught on the sofa during some earlier visit. When she was doing . . . what?

Mikki had never been on my list of suspects. Greedy, yes. She liked expensive things, and she'd snatched up anything valuable in the house like some kid set free in a toy store. She wasn't on good terms with Jock and Jessie. She resented their favoritism toward the first wife. She also hated penny-pinching to provide for Frank's kids.

Could she have assumed that if Jock and Jessie were dead, their assets would flow easily to Frank and thus to her greedy fingers? Was she willing to kill to make that happen? She'd been both surprised and resentful that there was no will, which was keeping the big assets out of her reach.

But could all that add up to the clever, ruthless, cold-blooded killer Ute had warned us about?

"Ivy, what *are* you looking at?"

"Come see for yourself."

Abilene circled the sofa. She confirmed my identification, which didn't take some high-tech expertise in forensic science. "A couple of blond hairs." Unspoken was *So what?*

"Don't you think that's odd? Blond hairs? And don't you think it's odd that they're on the back side of the sofa? That's not where a person's head would rest if he or she were sitting on the sofa. How did they get there?"

The sofa had stood perhaps six or seven feet away from the back wall in the great room. The space behind it was part of the walkway between front door and dining room. But a person would have had to be *crawling* behind the back side of the sofa in order for hair to catch on it at that height.

I had a quick vision of shapely Mikki on hands and knees

268

behind the sofa, gun tucked into her belt. Mikki rising up, her greed and hostility exploding in—

The vision collapsed right there. Jessie had been shot from in front of the sofa, not by someone creeping up from behind.

"Maybe the Northcutts entertained a group of very short, blond survivalists who chased each other around the room," Abilene said. I wrinkled my nose at that facetious suggestion, and, sighing at my lack of imagination, she added, "Or maybe they came from one of Frank Northcutt's kids. Either of them could have long blond hair. And they've visited here several times."

True. And kids could leave traces of themselves in the strangest places. I'd once noted an odd blotch on my grand-niece Sandy's bedroom ceiling. Turned out, agile and gymnastically inclined Sandy had tried a unique method to eliminate a spider and left a footprint up there.

"Does it look bleached or natural blond to you?" I asked.

Abilene leaned closer. "I don't see dark roots, but it would probably take lab tests to tell for sure. Or DNA tests could identify who the hairs came from, couldn't they?"

"I think the hair root has to be attached." I leaned closer. Yes, root was attached on at least one of these hairs. "And they could do an identification only if there were DNA samples from the other person to compare with."

I couldn't see us dashing around, snatching hairs from the heads of possible suspects for comparison. Nor could I see Deputy Hamilton excitedly ordering expensive and time-consuming DNA tests if we did come up with comparison hairs. It was a big stretch to think these two anonymous blond hairs might be connected to Jock and Jessie's deaths. And yet . . .

"I wonder why we didn't notice them earlier? The blond stands out against the brown fabric."

Abilene grimaced. "Maybe because we were too busy looking at dead bodies and blood."

Right. And swatting at flies. Neither had we done an in-depth examination of the bloody sofa when we helped Frank wrestle it off the deck. We were just anxious to get the unpleasant task done.

Abilene turned her back to the rising wind and folded her arms. The darkening clouds had moved closer. The wind lifted a spiral of leaves around her. "Okay, what possible connection do you think two blond hairs could have with Jock and Jessie's deaths, since you apparently do think it?"

Put so bluntly, I couldn't come up with anything specific. "It just seems odd, that's all," I said finally. "Like the bullet in the deer head over the fireplace. Very odd."

"The only blond we've actually seen around here is Frank Northcutt's wife, Mikki. Do you suspect her?"

"I guess I don't really *suspect* her . . ."

"But you don't really *not* suspect her."

"She was on Ute's list of suspects," I pointed out.

"But she was at a cosmetologist convention in Austin at the time of the deaths."

"Supposedly."

Abilene didn't reject my "supposedly" as I thought she might. She nodded slowly, acknowledging that even though Mikki had told Frank she was going to the convention, that didn't necessarily mean she'd gone there. "But even if these hairs are hers, they could be from a long time back. She was here at least once with Frank when Jock and Jessie were alive."

"But how long would a couple of stray hairs cling to a sofa?"

"Jessie wasn't the greatest housekeeper. Our first night

here, Koop came out from under my bed looking like a giant dust ball with legs. That sofa might not have been vacuumed since Jock and Jessie moved into the house."

"*You* aren't suspicious of Mikki, then?" I asked.

"I wouldn't say that," Abilene admitted. "But I'm trying to keep the fact that I don't like her from influencing my thinking."

Was dislike influencing *my* thinking? Because Mikki wasn't one of my favorite people, either.

"But . . ." she started, then trailed off as if she were reluctant to bring up what she was thinking.

"But?" I prodded.

"One time when I was alone with her she wanted to know if the police had asked any questions that sounded as if they thought the deaths might be something other than suicide."

"Could be simple curiosity."

"Could be her wondering if she'd pulled off a successful murder, or if she still had to worry the police might investigate further."

I remembered a few things about Mikki, minor tidbits that hadn't stirred my suspicions at the time but now looked more meaningful.

Her familiarity with the house. She'd been here, supposedly, only once, and yet she seemed quite knowledgeable about both house and contents. Because she'd searched the place after murdering them?

Her vehemence at claiming she was not surprised that Jock and Jessie had committed suicide. Was she being careful not to raise even minor suspicion that the deaths were not what they looked like?

And then how she'd suddenly become alert when I suggested suicide seemed out of character for Jock and Jessie.

271

Was she afraid I'd interest the authorities in that aspect of the deaths?

Plus her surprising knowledge about guns.

A flash of inspiration occurred to me. Maybe we couldn't snatch comparison hairs off her head, but there might be another source. I turned and headed full speed for the house, then stopped abruptly after about three steps.

"Now what?"

"I want to check on something, but one of those hairs is about to blow away. It could be gone any minute."

"But if we remove them from the sofa, there's no way to prove that's where they came from," Abilene pointed out. She lifted a finger to indicate a solution. "Wait here."

She raced off to the house. I didn't know what she had in mind, but I went back to the sofa and used my body to shelter the hairs from the gusting wind. The loosest hair was about to let go, and I could almost see the second hair unraveling from the fabric too. The weather vane atop the barn spun crazily as the wind shifted directions.

A minute later Abilene returned with the same butcher knife that had freed Ute from the net. She whacked a six-inch square of fabric out of the back side of the sofa, blond hairs safely attached. Clever girl!

Back at the house I carefully placed the section of upholstery in a large plastic freezer bag, sealed the top, and labeled and dated the bag.

"Very professional looking," Abilene said. "Just like the detective in a mystery book would do it."

Which was where I'd gleaned my technique, of course. But was what I had here important evidence in a crime? Or evidence of one LOL's overheated imagination?

"So now what?" Abilene asked.

I also raised a finger. "Follow me."

She did, yet with my hand on the knob of the bedroom

272

door, I stopped short. Out at the sofa, this had seemed like a clever idea, but now it felt both sleazy and far-fetched, a feeling enhanced when Abilene said in a horrified gasp, "We're going to look in their bed for Mikki's hair?"

"The linen hasn't been changed since Frank and Mikki were here. We can just take a peek at the pillows."

After a moment's consideration, Abilene apparently readjusted her thinking and nodded. "Good idea."

Actually, we didn't have to look far. The bed hadn't been made, and three hairs lay tangled right there on the left-side pillow. I wondered if that was normal loss or if Mikki should think about letting up on the bleach before all her hair wound up on a pillow or down the drain.

I draped the hairs over a tissue from a box on the nightstand, and, back in the kitchen, we compared them to the two sealed in the freezer bag. They looked alike, but then Abilene yanked out one of her own hairs and laid it beside the others. Except that Abilene's was shorter, I couldn't see any real difference among the hair samples.

Which was where microscopic examination and DNA came in, of course.

"Now what?" Abilene asked, as she had a habit of doing.

Yes, now what? I repeated to myself as I sealed the three hairs that we knew were Mikki's in another plastic freezer bag, labeled and dated also.

Mikki had jumped way up on my list of suspects, but I doubted what we had here would make Deputy Hamilton quick to order laboratory tests. He'd point out, as Abilene and I had already discussed, that even if both hair samples belonged to Mikki, the ones on the sofa could have been there long before the Northcutts' deaths.

Yet, in my opinion, it was still peculiar that the hairs were there at all. What logical, and innocent, reason would she, or anyone else, have for rubbing her head up against the

273

back side of the sofa? Although, to be honest, I also couldn't see any reason she'd have done it while committing murder either.

"I wonder if there's any way to find out if Mikki really was at that cosmetologist convention?" Abilene asked as I tucked the two freezer bags into the bottom drawer of a kitchen cabinet for safekeeping.

I considered how Kinsey Millhone, Jetta Diamond, or various other of my favorite clever private investigators might do it. I nodded slowly. "There might be."

Abilene went to make certain nothing was left outside that could be damaged by the coming storm. She moved the stepladder off the deck and brought the paintball gun and ice cream freezer that had been left out there inside, and I got on the phone.

I called Elsie at the beauty salon in Dulcy first. No, she didn't know anything about a cosmetologist convention in Austin. She never went to them. I put in a long-distance call to the Chamber of Commerce in Austin. They had information about various future conventions coming to the city, but the woman didn't know anything about a recent cosmetologist convention. "But there might be some state or national organization that would know," she added helpfully.

I eyed the computer. The Internet would undoubtedly be the place to look for such information. But not only could I not access the Internet from the computer, I couldn't even get past the opening screen that demanded a password. I tried Elsie again to ask about national or regional cosmetology organizations. She thought there might be some, but she didn't belong.

Obviously my sleuthing skills fell short of Kinsey Millhone's and Jetta Diamond's—by now both women would no doubt have a list complete with phone numbers, addresses, and hair color of people who'd been to a convention in Austin.

A harsh gust of wind rattled the fireplace chimney, and I peered out the window. The storm had definitely arrived. A flash of lightning silhouetted the barn and made it look like the cover of an old Gothic novel. I jumped back when thunder rattled the window. Dust whooshed up from the emus' well-trampled pen. I was glad we'd gotten those hairs off the sofa. They wouldn't have survived this.

Abilene came in a few minutes later, hair whipped like tangled straw. More wind blasted through the open door as she fought to close it.

She wiped windblown dust out of her eyes. "A big branch just blew down on the far end of the emus' pen," she reported. "It hit the fence and knocked a section of it down."

"What are the emus doing?"

"They're all crowded into the shed. But I think they could get out. They're really nervous. We should go see what we can do with the fence—"

"Not during the storm."

Another bolt of lightning and blast of thunder emphasized the wisdom of that opinion.

"Yeah, I suppose you're right," Abilene agreed reluctantly.

She paced from window to window, worrying about her emus. Wind-driven leaves whacked the glass. I watched the motor home, wondering if they ever blew over. Rain joined the wind and pounded the ground and deck like attacking bullets. I didn't see what danger the egg could be in, but Abilene went upstairs to check on it.

"If the electricity goes out and the heating pad goes off, one of us will have to take it to bed to keep it warm," she said. When I didn't jump in with an offer, she smiled wryly "I guess that'd be me, right?"

"Right."

The electricity didn't go out, and we stayed up until almost midnight. By then the wind had passed, and the rain slackened to a gentle drizzle. I knew Abilene wanted to take a flashlight and go look at the fence, but I said it could wait until morning.

"I don't think the emus are as stupid as everyone thinks. They're smart enough to stay inside the shed for the night," I added.

I heard Abilene get up and go out before dawn the next morning. She had breakfast ready by the time I got up an hour later. The storm had passed, but a layer of clouds still blotted morning sunlight.

"Emus okay?"

"They're fine. I propped the fence up, but the branch tore the wire in several places. It's going to have to be fixed or replaced, but I can't find any more fence wire in the sheds."

"I'll call Frank and see if it's okay to charge some wire at the farm supply store. You think you and I can fix the fence?"

"Oh, sure," she said confidently.

I called Frank right after breakfast, hoping to catch him before he left for work, which I did. I described the storm and the damage to the fence.

I got a not-surprising response. "Stupid birds," as if the downed fence were their fault. "I don't know who you can get to come out and fix it."

I repeated Abilene's assurance that we could do it. "If buying the wire is okay."

"Sure. Whatever the birds need." He sounded resigned, in a disgusted sort of way. "Oh, I was going to call you anyway. Some people down here may be interested in buying the place later on, and I told them it was okay if they want to come up and look around."

I was disappointed to hear that, because it would undoubtedly mean we'd have to move on. I suspected Abilene would be even more disappointed than I was. But, given the slow-moving process of estates, especially those without a will, the property might not be sold for a long time yet. I was about to hang up when I remembered there was something I wanted to ask Frank. I took a circuitous approach.

"Your kids . . . I remember you saying your boy's name is Jeff? And your daughter . . . ?"

"Courtney. She's fourteen, and he's twelve."

"What color hair do they have?"

"They're both dark brown."

"How tall are they?"

"Courtney's shot up like a weed. She must be five-seven already. Jeff's shorter. Five-three or so, I guess. Why? What's this all about?"

This eliminated the kids as source of the hairs. They were both too tall to casually brush the back side of the sofa while walking by, and the hairs were the wrong color anyway.

I hesitated, wondering how to answer what was certainly a logical question from Frank. I didn't really want to tell him I suspected his wife may have murdered his parents, especially with no more to go on than two blond hairs. But untruths stick in my throat like old fish bones, so I just told it the way it was, without making any incriminating connections.

"We found some stray hairs on the sofa where your parents' bodies were found. I thought maybe they came from one of your children, from when they visited here. But the hairs are blond."

"Oh, well, Mikki's blond." He sounded dismissive and a little impatient that I was wandering around in such trivialities.

"Yes, she is," I agreed.

That ended the conversation, obviously raising no questions

with him, but I found it meaningful that he simply assumed the hairs were Mikki's.

She now sat at the top of my suspect list like a vulture on a telephone pole. Although an annoying little voice inside me nagged, *Are you sure you should even* have *a suspect list?*

The police had no list of suspects. The Northcutts' deaths were settled with them.

And there were definitely problems with my suspicions of murder. Gunshot residue on Jock Northcutt's hand. Plus the biggie: the note with Jock and Jessie's signatures.

So why not just give it up, accept the easy conclusion, and concentrate on emu-egg hatching and fence building?

Because I had that ever-vigilant mutant curiosity gene, to which there appeared to be attached a hard-working suspicion gene. To say nothing about being plain ol' stubborn.

Dulcy Farm Supply sold fencing only in big rolls. Stuffing one into the motor home was rather like trying to cram a zucchini in a keyhole. Crawling over it to get to the driver's and passenger's seats up front was also a problem. The next dilemma, of course, would be unloading it when we got home.

A problem we both realized was secondary when we drove up to the locked gate at the driveway. A pair of emus stood on the other side, looking at us with those big, inquisitive eyes.

"They got out!" Abilene gasped.

She jumped out of the motor home and unlocked the gate. The emus took off down the road. They couldn't fly, but these two moved those scrawny legs as if they were trying out for the Emu Olympics. Which struck me as unappreciative, considering all Abilene had done for them.

I drove through the open gate, then got out to close and lock it behind the motor home so stray emus couldn't wander out. Which wouldn't keep them from wandering miles through the woods, of course, because the fence only ran along this front side of the property. The emu pen was empty when I drove into the yard, not an emu in sight anywhere. No Abilene either.

I was, I decided, rapidly advancing toward joining the "stupid birds" contingent of opinion.

"Abilene!" I shouted. "Where are you?"

She came out of the shed, carrying a bucket. "I'm going out to look for them," she yelled back. "I'll try to coax them back with feed."

She had a rope in the other hand, apparently for use if feed-inducement didn't work. We'd never tried leading the emus anywhere. I wondered how a rope around one of those long necks would work. About as well as lassoing a snake and trying to take it for a walk, I suspected.

But we had to do something. I looked down at my feet. I'd worn sandals and my toe ring to town, hardly suitable emu-hunting attire. "I'll go change my shoes and come help," I yelled.

I ran to the back kitchen door, which we always used as a main entrance, digging out the key as I ran. But when I stuck it in the keyhole I was surprised to find I didn't need it. Apparently we hadn't locked the door when we left. I chided myself for the laxity. I hadn't been worrying much about Braxtons lately, but I doubted they'd given up their vow of vengeance, and carelessness could have dangerous consequences.

I hesitated with my hand on the knob, half-afraid some member of the mini-Mafia might lunge out to meet me. Unlikely, but . . .

I thrust open the door and stepped aside at the same time, just in case. No Braxtons burst out. I waited a minute, then cautiously poked my head inside. The kitchen looked exactly as we'd left it, coffee cups on the counter, frying pan on the stove. A scent of the sausage we'd had for breakfast still lingered. The folders I was working with were still piled at the far end of the dining room table, dark screen of the computer as inscrutable as always. The paintball gun looked out of place just inside the door, but Abilene had set it there last night before the storm.

Okay, nothing out of the usual here. I briskly stepped inside.

Then stopped. No particular reason. Nothing was "off" in the way of sight, sound, or smell. Yet something didn't feel quite right. I strained, listening. A faint rustle.

I wasn't alone!

I looked frantically for some weapon, anything.

Koop scuffled through some fallen papers as he wandered out from under the dining room table, stretched luxuriously, and, with his one good eye, looked at me curiously as I stood there with hand to my pounding heart. I put the paintball gun I'd grabbed back on the floor, not too gently.

"Never mind," I muttered, annoyed that I'd let jitters make me mistake Koop for a threat. He wandered out the open door to the deck. "Make yourself useful," I called after him. "Go find some lost emus."

I went upstairs and changed to old jeans and solid shoes, but as I headed for the door again I noticed something I hadn't before. The basement door was ajar. Odd. I didn't recall being down there in the last day or two. But maybe Abilene had. I started to ignore it, then hesitated again and finally walked over and cautiously eased the door open.

The basement light was on. Neither of us would have left the light on, would we? Abilene was as thrifty as I was. She'd stoop to pick up a penny in the parking lot in town, same as I would. And then I heard a slight scraping noise . . .

Not Koop this time. He was outside.

I put a hand on the handrail and cautiously leaned way over to peer into the big basement room. Then I saw her. The bottom half of a woman in dark pants and sandals standing on the same stool I'd stood on down there. She was on tiptoe, apparently reaching up to do something in that section of shelves where I'd found the odd empty space, the space in which we suspected the Northcutts may have hidden gold coins.

Who was she? How had she gotten here? We hadn't seen a car. Had she gotten inside the house because we'd left the door unlocked, or did she have a key? Was this the murderer/thief, come back to search for more gold?

And what happened if she spotted me? I straightened up, hoping my bones wouldn't make a giveaway creak. First a prudent retreat, I decided, then I'd figure out what to do.

Another thought brought me to a halt: could this be the potential buyer Frank had mentioned, nosily but innocently inspecting the premises when she hadn't found anyone home?

Then the woman moved, stepping backward off the stool, and I recognized the blond hair when I saw her upper half. Mikki!

I almost said her name. *Mikki, what in the world are you doing down there?*

I stopped before I made that mistake, because it was not a trivial question. What *was* she doing down there? Not something a grieving daughter-in-law and loving wife should be doing, I suspected. She was wearing gloves, I now saw.

What now? The basement door was lockable, but it was a dead-bolt lock that had to be locked with a key, and we hadn't yet run across one that fit. But I could quietly close the door, shove a chair under the knob to keep her from getting out, call the police—

Big pothole in that plan. With this unexpected develop-

282

ment, I was more certain than ever that Mikki had killed Jock and Jessie. Never mind the problem of that note with signatures; she'd figured out some way to finagle it. She'd then stolen their hoarded Kruggerands and was now back hunting for more gold she suspected or knew was hidden here. And no doubt in my mind now but that those blond hairs on the sofa were hers.

But when the police arrived, would Mikki tearfully admit she'd done it and helpfully explain how? No way. Not with the ruthless cleverness and lack of conscience she'd shown in murdering her in-laws.

I pictured the scene when deputies arrived: she'd openly identify herself as Mikki Northcutt, Frank's wife, of course. She'd say . . . what? Probably that she'd come to take some of this oversupply of food stored in the basement down to the family in Texas. She'd be flabbergasted that I'd called the police, but she'd also be sympathetic and understanding about this elderly error. And they'd all exchange looks over my head, officials exasperated at being called all the way out here by this addled little old lady imagining boogeymen in the basement, Mikki pretending embarrassment about the misunderstanding. The gloves I saw as incriminating, a means to hide her fingerprints, they'd see as a practical guard against injuring her hands while loading supplies.

I needed something stronger to convince them she was not the innocent daughter-in-law gathering cans of powdered eggs and dried applesauce that she pretended to be. I leaned over again, to get a better look. She wasn't, in fact, gathering anything. By now she'd knelt and started digging around on a bottom shelf, definitely looking for something as she shoved cans around.

But while I stood there thinking what to do the woman apparently sensed she was not alone. She turned her head, and I saw her face. She stood up slowly, wiping her hands on the dark pants. We stared at each other.

Not Mikki.

"Who are you?" I said. I could see now that blond hair was the only physical characteristic she shared with Mikki. This woman's body was streamlined and fit, with none of Mikki's lush softness, her cheekbones sharp, her jaw angular, her eyes large and dark. Pretty, in a feline sort of way.

"Who are you?" she demanded without answering my question.

"I'm the caretaker, Ivy Malone."

"Oh. I'm . . ." She hesitated, as if she were momentarily reluctant to identify herself, but then added briskly, "Natalie, Frank's former wife. The children's mother. Frank told me I might as well take some of these supplies home to use. I was looking for boxes to put things in. I didn't realize Frank had someone staying here."

It seemed odd, if he'd okayed her taking things from the house, that he hadn't mentioned to her that he had caretakers here. Odd, too, that she'd actually drive all the way up here to pick up a load of survival-type supplies I'd almost guarantee her kids wouldn't eat. A trip also not exactly in character with the ambitious, high-powered real estate person Mikki had described.

Then I reminded myself that that was Mikki's view of the ex-wife, probably not an unbiased view. "I believe we talked on the phone once," I suggested.

"Oh?" Then she smiled with unexpected warmth. She stepped forward to get a better look at me. "Yes, we did, didn't we? I remember now. You were so nice. I just didn't realize you were staying on here."

"Are the children with you?"

"They're in school. I just decided to run up for the day."

All the way from Dallas for powdered cheese and paper

towels and maybe a few cans of foot fungus powder? I was skeptical. But this had definitely thrown a wrench into my Mikki-as-Murderer scenario. "Where's your car?"

"I don't have a key to the gate, so I hid it behind some brush off to the side of the road. You never know what kind of weirdos may be prowling around an isolated place like this. You're brave for staying here alone, you know."

I ignored the compliment and wondered, *Does "prowling weirdos" include odd-acting ex-wives?* I also noted she was assuming I was here alone.

"But you have a key to the house?"

"Jock and Jessie gave me a house key one time. We were on very friendly terms, you know? I always liked them. Just because I divorced Frank didn't mean I divorced *them*. The kids and I visited several times. I didn't mean to alarm you," she added. "I just didn't realize anyone was around."

All very plausible and normal sounding, and yet she was obviously nervous. She tucked a loose tail of her red blouse into the dark pants, slid a stray strand of blond hair behind an ear, and glanced at her watch.

Then I spotted something on the bottom step. A small, khaki-colored bag of a heavy, canvas-like material. I'd never seen it before, certainly had not set it there on the step myself. It was not, I could see by the shape, filled with bulky cans of survival food. In fact, if I were a betting woman, I'd take odds that it was filled with gold Kruggerands.

She saw me spot the bag.

"I-I found that," she stammered, now sounding not quite so sure of herself. "I think Jock and Jessie must have hidden it down here. They did things like that, you know. Wonderful people, but a little . . . odd sometimes."

"Did you look in it?"

She hesitated as if she might be going to deny peeking but apparently decided that wouldn't ring true. "I think it's full of gold coins." She managed to sound both surprised and appalled by the discovery. "Can you imagine, hiding something that valuable down here?"

How come Abilene and I hadn't run into this bag? I was certain there hadn't been anything left in that empty space I'd found. Had the Northcutts scattered gold-filled bags in various hiding places, like Easter eggs?

There were a dozen questions I wanted to ask. *Did you kill Jock and Jessie? Why? Did you preplan it just to get their hoard of gold or was it a spur-of-the-moment thing? How did you manage the signed note?*

This did not seem a prudent time to ask any of those questions. Best to let her think I was taking all this at face value and had no suspicions of her. Because if she'd killed once already—

At the same time a jab of guilt jerked me up short. Five minutes ago I'd been convinced Mikki was a murderer. Wasn't so quickly shifting my suspicions to ex-wife Natalie a little like some old game of eeny-meeny-miney-mo, I choose *you* as the murderer?

"Well, just leave the bag there, then," I said, "and I'll tell Frank about it. You should probably get your supplies loaded up now, if you're going to get back to Dallas tonight. The powdered cheese isn't bad."

"Yes, uh, that's a good idea. I think I saw some boxes on a shelf back here somewhere."

She grabbed the stool and disappeared farther back in the basement, out of my sight. My first instinct was to run. But if I did, it would tell her I was suspicious or perhaps even knew something incriminating, and she'd come after me.

Given the fact that she ran marathons, I didn't doubt but what she could run this LOL to the ground. But neither was I going to try to outfox her with some clever game of wits

286

down there in the basement. So far, if she *was* a killer, she'd pretty much managed to outwit everyone.

A crash, a screech, and a yelped oath, followed by a muffled thunder like an avalanche of tumbling marshmallows. Then just whispery rustles as something rolled into view.

I got down on my knees and tried to see what was happen-
ing in the basement without taking a chance down there.
What I saw were packages of toilet tissue, dozens of them,
maybe even hundreds, gleefully rolling and bouncing across
the basement floor as if they'd just been freed from hostage.
Several of them landed at the foot of the stairs.

"What happened?" I called cautiously.

"The stool slipped when I climbed on it. I fell."

"Are you okay?"

"I hurt my knee."

I hesitated. Was that a ploy to get me down there so she
could knock me in the head with a can of dehydrated bacon
bits?

A brief self-consultation told me she probably didn't yet
realize I suspected her. Maybe she'd decided to sacrifice the
bag of gold coins, and we'd play this out as if she really were
here to get a carload of survival supplies. I'd help her load

them, and she'd head for home, waving good-bye as if we were good buddies.

It was remotely possible, I conceded, that stocking up on toilet tissue and cans of powdered cheese was actually the reason she was here.

Cautiously I edged down the stairs.

Natalie was sitting on the concrete floor, one leg stretched out in front of her, the other bent, grimace of pain on her face as she rubbed the knee. Packages of toilet tissue surrounded her.

But my gaze riveted on something that had been exposed when she crashed into the mountain of toilet tissue, something she hadn't yet seen because her back was to that corner of the room. I looked away quickly, but not soon enough. She turned her head, her gaze targeting where mine had been.

"The safe!" she gasped. "I looked all over for that thing—" She broke off, her gaze darting back to me.

I tried not to look as if she'd said something that could be interpreted as incriminating. "Well, isn't that just like Jock and Jessie?" I declared. "Hiding something valuable under a mountain of toilet tissue."

I shook my head in a gesture of "can you believe that?" The safe was small, maybe fifteen inches square. Not large enough to hold any great amount of gold. The lock was a combination-style dial. I couldn't remember the numbers, but I knew where to find them. "Frank will be pleased. He's never been able to find any of Jock and Jessie's important papers."

"Just what I always wanted to do. Help ol' Frank," Natalie said, her tone disgruntled. She got a leg under her but couldn't reach anything solid to grab onto so she could stand up. "Now do you suppose you could come over here and help me stand up so I can get away from this miserable monument to Jock and Jessie's paranoia about the world running out of toilet tissue?"

Her pants had actually ripped where she'd hit the concrete floor with her knee. She hadn't faked the fall, and she didn't appear to be in good shape for running now. I kicked my way through the avalanche of toilet tissue—they'd favored Charmin—and gave her a hand. She got to her feet. I helped her stand while she took a couple of limping steps, her back bent as if it hurt to stand.

But then, like a snake uncoiling, she suddenly straightened, and her hand slid up to grip my upper arm, fingers closing around it like a rawhide handcuff.

"Wh-what are you doing?" I asked.

"Do you know what's in that safe?"

"Some papers. Maybe wills and a deed."

"There's at least a half million dollars worth of diamonds in there."

Her hand squeezed tighter, and her back was ramrod straight now. It felt as if the woman could bend steel with her fingers. And it suddenly occurred to me that knowing about the diamonds might not be good for my health. I was right.

"And I'm not going to let one old woman stand between me and those diamonds. Not after—"

She broke off, but I got the gist. Not after what she'd already done.

"Well, uh, hey now . . ." I mumbled irrelevantly while a whole lot of thoughts clattered around in my head.

At the top of the clatter was the unpleasant knowledge that if she was going to steal the diamonds, she couldn't leave me alive to identify her. Next was the thought that it really *was* murder, not homicide/suicide, and Natalie had done it. I started to wonder how she'd done it, but self-preservation kicked in, overriding even curiosity.

I did the first thing any self-respecting sleuth would do. I kicked her in the shins. On the bad leg, of course. This was no time for fair play.

She grunted in pain, and the leg gave way, dragging us both down, but the other leg held firm, and the vise-grip never faltered. Her teeth gritted as she straightened up again, and then she shoved me toward the stairs.

"Don't try that again," she warned.

"Wh-what are you going to do?"

No answer, just another vicious shove.

"How did you know about the diamonds and gold?"

Again no answer. Apparently we were not going to play Twenty Questions. We reached the foot of the stairs. I pretended to stumble over toilet tissue. I figured if she wanted me upstairs I was better off downstairs.

I didn't have any choice, however. She efficiently yanked my arm behind me, gave it an expert twist, and up the stairs we went. I remembered Mikki saying Natalie had studied karate. Perhaps there had also been a session on arm twisting. My bones felt breakable as toothpicks under her grip. She marched me through the kitchen and down the hallway to the master bedroom, my arm screeching every time she gave it a wrench. She was gimpy on the leg, but it slowed her only fractionally. Still keeping my arm behind my back with one hand, she opened the bedroom door with her other hand, still gloved. No fingerprints.

Inside, we marched straight to the gun cabinet, where I knew she expected to find an arsenal of artillery. She gave a grunt of unhappy surprise when she opened the door and found only empty hooks on the green felt.

"Mikki took all the guns," I said.

"Figures. Greedy pig." Then, as if it were automatic to make some negative remark about her ex-husband, she added, "She ought to use one of them on Frank, the jerk."

"Frank never said anything derogatory about you," I chided reproachfully. An irrelevant statement, of course, but anything to try to distract her. "Though Mikki isn't a big fan."

"The feeling is mutual. You'd think a woman in the hair business could get a better bleach job than she has."

I didn't tell her I'd mistaken her own bleach job for Mikki's.

She was still staring at the empty cabinet. I knew where the Saturday night specials Mikki had rejected were, but I wasn't about to point that out to Natalie.

Opportunistic Natalie could probably manage without a gun anyway. The kitchen held an ample supply of knives and various other sharp objects. And most anything can become a murder weapon if you're creative. One of Jock's old ties, or laces from Jessie's shoes, would do nicely for strangling. A pillow for smothering. And hands! What better weapon than a pair of rawhide-strong hands? I jumped away from those thoughts before they could make some mental gazelle leap into Natalie's head.

I tried to think of something to persuade her to give up this idea of killing me, something to her advantage, but nothing came to mind. From her point of view, letting me live was not an option.

A hopeful thought suddenly occurred to me. Abilene! She'd surely come back to the house soon. Tall, strong, toss-sacks-of-emu-feed-around Abilene was a match for Natalie any day! Natalie thought I was alone here, and if I could just stall, keep her talking long enough for Abilene to return to the house . . .

"You've handled this very cleverly," I said conversationally. "The authorities and Frank are all convinced Jock and Jessie's deaths were a double suicide."

She didn't deny my oblique allegation. "You're curious about how I did it, aren't you?"

"You certainly fooled everyone."

"Yeah, I did, didn't I?" She laughed with a delight that gave me shivers.

She wanted to tell me, I realized. She'd pulled off this fantastic feat but had no one to whom she could boast about her accomplishment. Who safer to tell than one soon-to-be-deceased LOL? And, as far as I was concerned, the longer it took to tell, the better.

"The note was the really clever part, of course. How did you manage that?"

"It wasn't part of my original plan. I just intended to get them out of the way and make it look like a home invasion thing. But it occurred to me the police would then be looking for a killer. Much better if it looked as if one of them killed the other, then took his—or her—own life. Then there wouldn't be some big manhunt for a killer."

I nodded. The grip holding my arm behind me had relaxed slightly, but I knew it could clamp down again fast as a rattrap if I tried to jerk away. "Good thinking. But how did you do it?"

I looked over my shoulder and saw her smile with satisfaction at her own cleverness. "Jock and Jessie needed their signatures notarized on a bunch of papers about selling rights on some books they did years ago. They were going to go into Dulcy or Horton to have it done, but I reminded them that I'm a notary public because I need to be for the real estate business, and I could do it. They could just sign the papers, and then I'd add the notary seal when I got back to Texas and mail the papers from there for them."

"Is that a legal way to do it?" Then I realized the irrelevancy of that question. A minor matter about illegally notarized papers hardly mattered when you were planning murder. Natalie didn't even seem to hear me anyway.

"I got the papers lined up for them to sign, one on top the

other there on the dining table, so all they could see were the signature lines. But what they didn't know was that I had an extra page stuck in the middle, one that was blank except for signature lines. Worked like a dream. They signed everything."

"And then you typed in the message about leaving this world in loving togetherness."

"Exactly. I thought the wording was a nice touch."

Oh yes. Very sensitive. "But I still don't see how you actually killed them. I mean, from everything I've heard they really liked you. They even gave you money. But surely they didn't just sit quietly on the sofa and let you shoot them?"

I wasn't positive about the money, since the information came from Mikki, but Natalie agreed with it, her tone scornful. "Oh, well, yeah. As long as it was some piddling little amount for the kids. But then I had this chance, this chance of a lifetime, to get in with a group putting up a fantastic new shopping mall. It'll be the showplace of Dallas. We'd borrow the money to finance it, of course, but I needed to come up with $250,000 right away to get in on the deal. That's why I came up here. But when I asked to borrow that much, Jock and Jessie turned me down flat. Even when I offered to pay much higher than the going interest rate, which would make it an excellent investment for them, they weren't interested. Jessie said the only investments they made these days were in the hard stuff, gold and diamonds. That paper money and shopping malls and everything else would soon be worthless. Stubborn, pigheaded old fools!" she suddenly added angrily.

"So you killed them and found the gold coins they'd invested in?"

"No, of course not." She sounded impatient with that foggy line of thinking. "There wouldn't have been any point in killing them if I didn't already know about the gold. I found

294

it an earlier time when the kids and I were visiting and I was poking around down in the basement. And I overheard them talking about investing this huge amount in diamonds and storing them in a home safe. *Then* I decided to kill them. If they wouldn't loan me the money."

"Ah."

"But I gave them a last chance, even after I had their signatures on that blank sheet of paper." She sounded defensive, as if this "last chance" justified everything that came afterward. "Jessie was sitting there on the sofa when I asked again to borrow the money. This time she laughed, as if I'd told some big joke."

"So you ran and got a gun?"

"I'd already gotten the gun from the cabinet in the bedroom."

"Because you figured they were going to turn you down."

I felt a movement behind me that might have been a shrug. "Whatever. I like to think ahead. So I just pulled the gun out of my pocket and shot her. Jessie was surprised, I think."

No doubt. "And Jock?"

"He heard the shot and came running from outside. I saw him crossing the deck. I ran and hid behind the sofa. The end table and big lamp blocked him from seeing me."

The source of those blond hairs, I realized. Natalie pressing her head hard against the back of the sofa while she hid and waited to kill again.

"He rushed over to the sofa. He didn't scream. He sat down beside her, and he was just making these . . . awful little blubbering noises. I think he couldn't believe what he was seeing." She swallowed hard, as if that had somehow affected her. But not enough to change what came next. "I didn't want him to have time to do anything. So I reached over the sofa and shot him in the head."

She spoke matter-of-factly, as if what she'd done was inevitable. I shivered. In reaction, she jerked my arm again, and pain slammed through my shoulder and across my back.

"Jock had gunshot residue on his hand." I had to keep her talking until Abilene showed up. "How did he get that?"

"I thought of that. His fingerprints had to be on the gun, and his hand had to show that he'd shot it. I . . ." For the first time her voice wobbled, as if the memory was getting a little gory even for her. She was speaking now almost as if in a trance, as if she were watching the memory unroll on some movie screen inside her head. "I wiped my prints off the gun and put it in his hand. I put my hand over his and shot toward the far end of the room."

Leaving gunshot residue on Jock's hand and a bullet in an already dead deer head.

"Then I put one more bullet in the gun so there wouldn't be an unexplained one missing and set it on the sofa beside his hand. I got the paper with the signatures on it and typed the message and set it on the coffee table. But there was . . . blood everywhere. I realized it would look strange if the note wasn't blood-spattered too. That some smart cop might figure out it was put there after they were dead. So I-I took a tissue and dipped it in Jessie's blood and spattered the note."

Not the most cold-blooded thing she'd done, of course. But somehow so . . . personal. And very thorough. As if she committed murders and set them up to look like suicides every day.

I looked over my shoulder at her. "Then you arranged it so they were holding hands."

"It seemed appropriate." Her gaze suddenly focused on me, as if she'd come out of the trance. "So now you know."

"Then you loaded up the gold coins." Dropping one out in the parking area, although I didn't mention that.

"But I couldn't find the safe with the diamonds."

Which was the reason for this return trip, and my potential demise. My legs felt as if my bones had melted. I sagged under Natalie's grip, but she didn't seem to notice.

Now what? What else could I do to keep her talking? Was Abilene close enough that if I screamed bloody murder she'd come running?

I didn't have a chance to talk or scream. Natalie suddenly yanked me around so she could lean over and use her free hand to open the shallow drawer below the main part of the gun cabinet. Not good, because I already knew what was in the drawer. The Saturday night specials lay there like two toys. Two dark, evil toys. She picked up one of the small guns.

Now my thoughts about Abilene jerked into reverse. *Keep her away, Lord. Don't let her come to the house, or Natalie will kill her too!* Then a hopeful possibility occurred to me.

"Jock and Jessie wouldn't leave a loaded gun lying around," I pointed out.

She smiled. "Wouldn't they?"

True. I tried again. "Mikki took all the ammunition along with the guns." That fact I was certain about, because Abilene and I had looked for bullets when she was thinking about taking a gun out in the woods with her.

Natalie nudged the drawer shut with her good knee and opened the second one below it. The left side of the drawer, where the ammunition had been stacked, was empty. The right side held a jumble of equipment for cleaning guns, several gun manuals, and some small paper targets. And I was wrong about Mikki taking all the ammunition. I don't know how Abilene and I had missed seeing the small green box when we were looking for bullets, but when Natalie swept a gloved hand through the drawer, there it was.

Mikki, couldn't you have been more thorough?

I had no idea if the carton held the type of bullets these

small guns used, but Mikki probably wouldn't have left it if the bullets fit any of the guns she'd taken. The carton of bullets might even be irrelevant, I realized bleakly, because it would also be just like the paranoid Northcutts to keep fully loaded guns in the cabinet.

Now, however, Natalie had a dilemma. She needed two hands to check if the gun was loaded. If it wasn't, she'd definitely need two hands to stuff ammunition into it. Which meant she had to let go of me.

Wrong. Natalie figured out another option.

She shifted her grip from twisting my arm behind me to returning to that rawhide-handcuff grip on my upper arm and stuck the barrel of the gun in my ribs.

"Want to take a chance on whether it's loaded?" she asked with chilling playfulness.

Well, no.

"Are-are you going to shoot me right here?"

She was still eying the carton of bullets as if she'd like to grow a third hand to grab it. But then she said briskly, "No, I think you'll suffer an unfortunate accident out in the woods. Unknown hunter, transient wandering through, something like that."

"In that case, the authorities will be looking for a killer."

"With a little luck, your body won't even be discovered for weeks." With her hand on my upper arm, she turned me toward the door.

"What if we get out there, and *then* you discover the gun isn't loaded?"

This was obviously a very real possibility. She yanked me to a halt, eyebrows scrunched in a frown.

An interesting situation here. Natalie threatening me that the gun might be loaded. Me threatening her that it might not be loaded.

Natalie again chose an alternative that hadn't occurred to

me. She kept the rawhide grip on my arm but took the gun out of my ribs and aimed it at the open closet.

Click.

No bang. No bullet. The gun wasn't loaded.

Hallelujah, Lord, thank you!

Kicking her in the shins hadn't worked before, but it was the only weapon I had. I picked up my foot and whammed it against the side of her leg. Fortunately the bad leg was closest, and this time the distraction of the unloaded gun apparently helped.

She *oofed* and her hand loosened. I ran.

I tore down the hallway, around the corner, across the kitchen. My hands trembled so badly that it took several seconds of fumbling with the knob to get the door open. I hesitated a moment. I needed something for protection.

I grabbed the only item available. The paintball gun sitting there by the door.

I didn't know how long it would take Natalie to get the Saturday night special loaded. Or maybe she'd run me down first and then load the gun.

But for the moment I was free . . . and running!

I thundered across the deck and parking area. I dodged around the motor home, putting it between the house and me for protection as I raced for the shelter of the sheds and then into the woods.

A hundred feet into the trees and brush I paused to catch my breath and listen. No pounding feet behind me. Nothing at all from the direction of the house. Which didn't mean she wouldn't be coming in a few more seconds.

Keep Abilene away, I prayed breathlessly. Because Natalie would kill her too. I had no doubt about that. *Send her far, far away on her emu hunt!*

Then a rustle and crunch . . . I whirled. Had Natalie already sneaked into the woods without my seeing her?

A long neck and inquisitive eyes poked through the brush. An emu. Great. Just what I needed.

Was there any way to use an emu to my advantage? I couldn't think of any. I waved an arm. "Go away. Go back to your pen." The emu regarded me with interested curiosity.

Okay, the thing to do was put as many miles as possible, as fast as possible, between me and Natalie and the gun.

Except if I did that, Abilene might come back and walk right into a bullet. Somehow I first had to find Abilene, and then we'd both run.

Except the stupid bird apparently had had enough of liberty and now wanted human companionship. It shoved its thick body through the brush toward me, wings lifted as if in greeting. I raised both arms and waved the paintball gun at it. What I did not need was a big bird making noise in the brush, Natalie thinking it was me, and the bird noises leading her straight to me.

"Shoo! Go away!" I whispered with as much force as you can put into a whisper.

I may as well have been whispering endearments. The bird kept coming. Okay, drastic measures were called for. I raised the paintball gun, took general aim, and fired. Whoosh! A pink blob appeared on the emu's chest. The bird reared its head up to full height, a surprised expression in those big eyes.

"Sorry," I muttered, feeling guilty for shooting at it even though I knew the paintball couldn't really have hurt the creature through that thick barrier of feathers.

Then, through the brush, I spotted a streak of red crossing the clearing, headed this way. Natalie's red blouse! The knee didn't seem to be slowing her down now. I forgot the emu and headed deeper into the brush. But after fifty feet I stopped. I must be making as much noise as a whole herd of emus crashing around in the woods. Would I be better off if I just made myself small and invisible in one spot? Yes. That way, Natalie would find me only if she accidentally blundered onto me.

But where? I looked around frantically. Brush that seemed so thick and impenetrable when I was trying to claw through it now looked dangerously skimpy and open-aired. Maybe back by the swampy area, I decided. The vegetation was even thicker there.

Carefully, as quietly as possible, I worked my way toward the swamp. Only to realize the emu was following. And it was making no effort to be quiet.

I didn't make it to the swamp. I edged out from behind an old rotten stump, and there we were, Natalie and me, practically face to face. She didn't waste time with small talk. I ducked back behind the stump just as she shot.

The gun was definitely loaded now. The shot slogged into the edge of the stump, rotten splinters flying.

Okay, she'd missed this first time. But she had *bullets* to shoot with. And what did I have? I looked at my gun. I had pink paintballs.

My chances of splattering her into surrender looked considerably more doubtful than her chance of blasting me into *dead*.

I heard her feet crunching on dry leaves as she moved forward. She wasn't bothering to be quiet. I didn't dare peek around the stump to see how close she was getting. I crouched and zigzagged for the protection of a thick tree trunk off to the side. Many times in my life I've felt invisible. This was not one of them. Two shots, close enough to *zing*, chased me.

I kept running, but I didn't reach the tree. A tangle of roots flipped me like the gymnast I wasn't. I landed face down in the dirt and curled there. Waiting, every muscle rigid. What did a bullet feel like? Or would I even know I'd been hit before—

"Hey, get away from me!"

Puzzled, I lifted my head. Me? Get away from her?

No, not me. The emu was buddying up to her now. Curious as always, it pecked at the gun in her hand. It jabbed at the watch on her wrist.

"Stop it! Get away!" She slapped at the emu with one hand, then lifted the gun. Hey, she was going to shoot it!

I grabbed the paintball gun that had fallen beside me and from a sitting position got off three quick shots. One added a second blob to the emu's feathers, another pink-blobbed the front of Natalie's red shirt. This diverted her attention from shooting the emu, and she shot at me again. The bullet kicked up dirt a foot away from my feet. But my third shot at her . . .

Natalie screamed, dropped the gun, and grabbed her face. "I can't see!" She dipped her head, frantically shaking it and swiping at her face.

The emu, apparently deciding this was not a friendly environment after all, took off through the brush.

"I can't see!" Natalie shrieked again. "You've blinded me!"

I'd hit her in the *eye*? The only spot on the body really vulnerable to a paintball, the only place it could do real damage?

Pink goo covered her face now. All *that* in one little paintball? She jumped around, hands covering both eyes, repeating her one line. "I can't see!" The dripping pink stuff had gotten into her mouth too, and she gagged and spit.

My first horrified instinct, because I didn't want to blind anyone, not even Natalie, was to run to her and wipe the pink stuff out of her eye.

Which I did.

But not before I grabbed the little Saturday night special where it had fallen on the ground. I kept the gun in one hand while I dabbed a tissue at her eye with the other. It was not an easy target, the way she was hopping around.

When she finally lifted her head, squinting and blinking, I stepped back, but I kept the gun targeted squarely midcenter on her.

"Are you okay?"

She was still blinking, and the eye did not look good. It was puffy and reddened from all the rubbing, and teary streaks ran past her nose through the pink goo. She was going to have one big, bad black eye, if not worse. She wiped her mouth, grimacing and spitting again.

"The stuff isn't poisonous or anything. I think Frank said you could even eat it, and it wouldn't hurt you." Although I hadn't seen any recipes that began, "Take two cups of paintballs . . ."

Frank also hadn't specified what a paintball might do when shot directly into an eye, which I'd apparently hit dead on. Could the impact of the paintball hitting her eye actually blind her? Or that pink stuff inside the outer shell do permanent damage?

She gave up trying to keep the eye open and covered it with her hand again. Her nose was now running too. Her other eye regarded me balefully. She could apparently see the gun in my hand clearly enough, but I could also see her measuring me. Calculating if I'd actually shoot, or if she could overpower me before I did.

We regarded each other warily. I had a finger on the trigger, but I didn't know if you had to do something else to actually shoot. Cock it or something? So I wasn't too sure of my status here.

But I *was* the one in possession of the gun now, and she

obviously wasn't certain I wouldn't just plug her broadside. She suddenly took a new tactic so unexpected that my mouth dropped open.

"We could split the diamonds. There's plenty for both of us."

She wanted to play *Let's Make a Deal*? I was so astonished that the barrel of the gun actually dipped off target. She took a step toward me, apparently ready to call off the deal if she could slam me to the ground. I lifted the barrel of the little gun back to direct aim on her midsection.

She stopped. "It could be a good deal for both of us," she coaxed.

I suddenly became aware of a noise farther back in the woods. A voice screaming.

"Ivy! Ivy, what's going on? Where are you?"

Natalie jumped, startled. "Who's that?"

"Over here!" I yelled back to Abilene.

"I thought you were alone." Natalie looked at me accusingly, as if I hadn't played fair.

"So sue me," I muttered.

Abilene burst through the brush a minute later, rope still coiled around her arm. "What's going on? I heard shots." She spotted the gun in my hand. "You're shooting at someone?" she asked in astonishment. Then she saw Natalie, with her eye injured and her blouse pink-blobbed, and her astonishment expanded. "Who's she?"

I gave Natalie an identity. Natalie just stood there glowering, injured eye continuing to drip tears through her fingers and down her cheek. "I wasn't shooting at her. She was shooting at me. And then I shot at her with the paintball gun." I motioned to the bigger gun on the ground. "I hit her in the eye."

"I see," said Abilene, although the situation was apparently as clear as swamp water to her.

I gave her a quick update on murder, blond hairs on the sofa, bullet in the deer head, gold and diamonds. "Natalie suggested we split the diamonds," I added.

Natalie wasn't one to give up easily. "Three ways," she bargained quickly, looking at Abilene. "All we have to do is find the combination to the safe."

"Why should we divide anything with you?" I challenged. "I've got the gun. And now we both know it's loaded."

Natalie's good eye widened, as if she believed the threat. Probably because it's what she would do if she were in my position. She took a faltering step backward, her eye on the gun in my hand. "You . . . you wouldn't—"

"No," I agreed, albeit a bit regretfully. "I wouldn't."

Abilene tossed a loop around Natalie's body and efficiently bound her wrists behind her. We took her to the house, kept her tied, me offering a helpful (although not particularly appreciated) dab with a tissue on her eye or nose now and then until Sgt. Dole and Deputy Hamilton arrived some forty-five minutes later. I told them what I knew, while Natalie continually protested that she knew nothing about murder or gold or diamonds, that I'd tricked her into coming out to the woods and then shot her in the eye with some strange weapon, bottom line being that I was stark raving crazy, a major menace to society. Her eye continued to swell and water, some bruising obvious now.

I showed the officers the safe in the basement, with its

accompanying landscape of toilet tissue. In all honesty, I'd have liked to open the safe right then and there, but that isn't the way the law works, of course.

I wasn't certain Sgt. Dole and Deputy Hamilton weren't giving serious consideration to Natalie's accusations about my sanity level, but it was Natalie, not me, whom they marched off to the police car. Along with the safe, the Saturday night special, the paintball gun, the bullet I'd saved from the deer head, the bag of gold coins and the gold coin Mac had found, two freezer bags of blond hairs, and the gloves off Natalie's hands. They also assured Natalie a doctor would examine her eye and issued stern instructions that Abilene and I must come in for official statements the following day.

Sgt. Dole never admitted that their earlier conclusion about homicide/suicide may have been mistaken, but he made one final thoughtful observation. "She'd probably have gotten away with it, wouldn't she, if she hadn't been so greedy and come back for the diamonds?"

I wanted to bring Frank up to date, but he wasn't home when I called. After a short consideration, I told Mikki what had happened. I expected restrained glee on her part that the ex-wife was in trouble up to her eyeballs, but I was both surprised and gratified when her first question was a concerned sounding, "What about the kids?"

"I don't think Natalie is going to be home tonight." Maybe not for a long, long time, if ever.

"We'll go up to Dallas and get them right away," she said instantly.

It seemed anticlimactic now, after all that had happened, but the emus were still on the loose and we had to do something about them. I was feeling rather kindly toward them now, considering that one of them had basically saved my life. Natalie would surely have gunned me down, if not for the distraction of a pecking emu.

I figured we'd be out hunting emus the rest of the day, maybe the next several days. But when we went out, all but two of them were gathered around the outside of the pen, apparently willing to exchange freedom for easy food. The other two came in the next day, one of them missing a considerable number of feathers, although we never did know what happened to it.

Frank and Mikki came two days later. By then there was news. A judge had issued a search warrant for Natalie's house, and the police had found several hundred gold coins hidden there. She had no legitimate way to account for them, and the authorities were now trying to find out when and where the Northcutts had purchased the coins. Frank also said Natalie's eye had not been permanently damaged.

"You're some shot with that paintball gun," he added admiringly.

"Purely accidental," I had to admit. Except for considerable help from the Lord, who has control of paintballs as well as everything else in this universe.

And the safe? Abilene and I weren't allowed to be present for the grand opening, but Frank was. The papers he needed were inside. Properly executed wills, leaving everything to him, with the provision that he see to the care and education of the children. The children were living with Frank and Mikki now. I suspected all would not be smooth sailing there, but Frank seemed hopeful, and Mikki wasn't grumbling. I knew they'd all be in my prayers for a long time to come.

As for diamonds, it turned out that Natalie wouldn't have been any better off even if she'd found the safe the first time she searched. Nor would there have been some treasure in gems to divide if we'd gone along with her illicit scheme.

Because there was, to be exact, one diamond in the safe. Set in Jessie's engagement ring from long ago. Had the Northcutts never actually invested in diamonds? Or were they hidden somewhere else?

A mystery as yet unsolved by the time we put Koop in the motor home a few days later, climbed in ourselves, and headed down the road. The people interested in buying the ranch had showed up, liked it, and made a deal with Frank to rent and live there until the legalities were straightened out and they could buy the property.

"I'm really sorry," Frank had said apologetically when he told us. "I know you expected to be here for a while, but it's just too good a deal for us to turn down."

"That's okay," I assured him. "We don't mind."

Especially when he gave us an exceedingly generous bonus for our short-term employment, and Mikki actually offered hugs. Abilene was teary about leaving the emus behind, but the future owners, the Andersons, seemed as captivated by the birds as she was. They assured her the green emu egg would stay right in the bedroom until it hatched.

The day we left, when Abilene went out to give a personal good-bye to each bird, she made another discovery that had both her and the Andersons twittering with excitement. An emu was protectively sitting on *something* far back in the pen, huffy about anyone investigating what, although presumably it was another egg or two. "Send us an address, and we'll mail you a photo of whatever hatches!" Mrs. Anderson said.

But the best part for me was that I'd called Mac to tell him our job was over, and he'd enthusiastically said, "Come on down here!"

So that's where we were headed on this crisp and lovely fall morning as we drove down Dead Mule Road for the last time. I'd called Margaret Rau to say good-bye, and she told us to be sure and stop to see her if we got back this way. Her dog Lucy had given us a good-bye bark into the phone too.

Now Koop was purring, the radio was on, and Abilene

was tapping her toe and thumping her thigh in time to the bouncy rhythm of a new Alan Jackson song.

And me, I was feeling an exuberant sense of freedom. The Braxtons hadn't found me. Maybe they'd given up and were out of my life for good! I'd be seeing Mac again by evening, I had a good traveling companion, and all was well.

Abilene stopped tapping her toe when a pickup passed us going the opposite direction. She leaned forward and peered intently at the pickup in the rearview mirror, but I could see in the mirror on my side that a cloud of road dust obscured the truck.

"Someone we know?" I asked.

She hesitated, still watching. "Maybe those people with the birdhouses on the island. They have half a dozen old pickups."

"Or the Andersons mentioned some relatives coming."

"I hope they take good care of the emus."

"I think those birds are going to be treated like the kings and queens of the emu world."

We decided to stop in Dulcy to pick up a few groceries before heading down to Hugo. Frank had loaded our small freezer and cupboards with everything from steaks and roasts to cans of corned beef and jars of marinated artichokes. Plus enough toilet tissue to carry us on a round-the-world excursion. But we still needed some fresh items.

A school bus was parked in the grocery parking lot, and the store was unexpectedly busy with the busload of kids loading up on chips and other snacks for a field trip, so it was a good twenty minutes before we headed out to the motor home with our plastic sacks of eggs and milk and lettuce.

Halfway there, Abilene stopped short. Two men were walking across the parking lot. One was short and wiry, the other big-bellied and burly. Abilene's head swiveled as she

311

frantically looked for some route of escape, but it was too late. Both guys looked up and spotted her.

I didn't need to be told who the wiry guy with the visored cap and nasty smile on his face was. Abilene's expression said it all as the two men changed direction and headed toward us. Our ploy with the Texas postmark apparently hadn't worked to detour Boone, because here he was.

"Well, well, if it isn't my loving wife," Boone Morrison said in a mocking tone. "The one who walked out on me, stole my car, and totaled it."

Not a word about concern for her, I noted. No inquiry about whether she'd been hurt in the accident. Not even a question about what had driven her to leave him. Only the Porsche mattered.

"I'm sorry I wrecked the car," Abilene said. She could have mentioned that this wouldn't have happened if he had been a decent husband so she wouldn't have felt she had to run for her life, but she didn't do so. Instead, though her voice wobbled a little, she pointed out what we'd already discussed. "But you can buy yourself another one with the insurance money."

"Insurance money? That's a laugh. The insurance was expired. I didn't find the notice until after you were gone. Because you'd hidden it."

"You always picked up the mail." Abilene sounded panicky. "I didn't know anything about insurance—"

"The Porsche is totaled, it wasn't insured, and all thanks to you," he interrupted flatly, making the pronouncement like some lofty judge rendering an unchallengeable decision of guilt.

I wanted to kick him in the shins. Blaming someone else for his own laxity with the insurance! Yet at the same time I knew how guilty Abilene felt because she *had* wrecked the vehicle.

312

Then Boone proclaimed sentence in addition to judgment. "And you're not gonna get away with it." He took a menacing step toward her. "You're gonna pay—"

"Not here," the other man warned with a glance at the parking lot swarming with kids. "Not now."

Boone looked around as if only then becoming aware that he and Abilene weren't alone here. "Yeah, right." He clenched his fists. "But I will get you, Abilene. Don't ever doubt it for a minute. I will get you. And you're gonna be mincemeat when I do."

Then his face moved in the mechanics of a smile. He lifted a hand in mocking salute. "So, see you on down the road." He gave me an odd look that made me feel as if fishhooks were ripping through my skin. "You too."

The two men stalked off toward an old blue pickup. We stood there watching them go. So, I'd made it onto Boone's hit list too. For a reasonably pleasant, inconspicuous LOL, I do seem to rack up an unusual number of murderous enemies.

"Who's the other one?" I asked finally.

"Boone's cousin."

"The sheriff?"

She nodded.

"You recognized the pickup back there on Dead Mule Road?"

"I thought it might be Boone's cousin's pickup. But then I figured I was probably just being . . . overly jumpy."

Boone hadn't mentioned catching up with us in Hugo, but he obviously knew our plans. How? With a Titanic-sized sinking in the pit of my stomach, I knew. Because of the Braxtons, I'd been careful for months not to tell anyone where I was headed, but Frank had been so concerned about us, and feeling so guilty about cutting off our jobs, that I'd assured him we'd be fine, that we were going to take a leisurely drive down to Hugo and just relax for a while.

I hadn't warned him not to tell anyone. He and Mikki were supposed to leave the ranch only a couple of hours after we did. But apparently Boone had gotten to them first with one of his wily stories about needing to find Abilene because of her parents' sudden deaths. Or maybe he'd used a nonexistent brother or sister's death this time. Whatever, it had worked. Boone knew we were headed for Hugo, and he had mincemeat on his agenda.

Abilene was still staring after the now-disappeared pickup. I nudged her with a carton of milk.

"Let's get going before they come back."

"To Hugo?"

"To any place but Hugo."

Abilene looked alarmed. "Oh, you can't do that. You want to see Mac again, and I don't want you in danger if Boone finds me. I'll just catch a ride—"

"Remember what you told me once? That alone you'd survived Boone, and alone I'd survived the Braxtons, and together we could survive anyone and anything?"

"Yeah, but—"

"But nothing. *Together* still holds." Along with some help from the Lord, of course. "Get in the motor home and let's go."

Abilene still hesitated.

"You get in the motor home or I'm going to pick you up and dump you in there," I threatened.

She looked at me. "You couldn't—" she began, scoffing at my LOL stature. But apparently she also took a second look at my determination. "And then . . . maybe you could."

We headed out of Dulcy in the opposite direction from Hugo. A dozen miles up the road a sign showed a town named Piggett off to the west. We took the road. Beyond Piggett I

314

whipped down another gravel road, and at the next town we angled off in a different direction.

Where were we going? I didn't know. Neither did I know if Boone knew what we were driving, or what resources his sheriff cousin could use to find us. But I had no intention of leaving an easy trail for them to follow, and we zigged here and zagged there.

I drove until I was too tired to keep going. Abilene kept apologizing for not being able to do her share of the driving, and I assured her that one of our first priorities after we got settled somewhere would be getting her a driver's license.

I wasn't sure where we were when we finally stopped at a rest area for the night, but it was brightly lit and several RVs were already parked there. A couple of people standing by a travel trailer gave us friendly waves. As safe a place as we were apt to find.

After a quick supper I went looking for a phone to call Mac and explain our change of plans, but when I found the phone it wasn't working. I wondered what to do now. Mac would be really worried because we hadn't showed up. It was at least 30 miles since we'd passed through a town, and I didn't relish the idea of driving all that way back.

A woman about my age was just dumping a plastic sack of trash into a can by the restrooms.

"Do you by any chance know how far it is to the next town?" I asked. "I need to find a phone. One that works."

"I have no idea. But you're welcome to use our cell phone."

"Oh, I couldn't—"

"We have one of those plans with more minutes than we can possibly use. C'mon over to the motor home and I'll get it."

I was gratified by her generosity, but not totally surprised. RVers are a helpful lot.

Her husband had the generator running and was watching TV in the motor home. The woman handed me the phone and told me to take it somewhere quiet.

I got under one of the rest area lights and punched in the numbers. Mac picked up immediately, confirming that he was worried.

"Hi, it's me," I said. "We aren't going to—"

"I can't . . . you. You're breaking—"

I spoke more loudly. "This is Ivy. We're—"

Speaking louder, I realized, does not help much when a call is breaking up with patches of static, because Mac said, "Ivy? That . . . where . . . you?"

We struggled for a couple more minutes, but only garbled, scattered words came through. Once I did hear Mac say something about *not coming?* so I was relieved that that much had apparently gotten through to him.

But finally it was all just static, and I pushed the off button. *Sorry, Mac,* I thought regretfully. Regretful that he was undoubtedly still worried about why we hadn't shown up, regretful that once more our plans for time together had gone awry. No Tom Yum Po Tak.

I returned the cell phone to the helpful couple and wandered over to a little railed-in viewpoint a few feet above the rough landscape of arroyos and sagebrush surrounding the rest area. *This is disappointing, Lord. But you know that, don't you? And it's okay. You know what you're doing. You're with us wherever we go. If it's in your will, Mac and I will meet again, won't we?*

I went on talking to him, and I wasn't aware that Abilene was leaning against the rail beside me until I opened my eyes.

"Praying?" She sounded curious.

"I like to keep in touch."

"You can pray just . . . anywhere?"

316

"Any place, any time."

She was silent for a long moment before finally saying, as if she knew she'd had a starring role in my prayers, "I'm a problem, aren't I? Things would be a lot less complicated for you if I'd never knocked on your door that night."

"I think the Lord led you there, and he put me and my door in that exact spot, at that exact time, purposely for you to knock on. A blessing for both of us."

"*Both* of us?" She peered at me. "I can see how you've been a . . . a blessing to me—" She stumbled over the word as if it were alien to her. "But me, a blessing to *you*?"

"Oh yes," I said, not a doubt in my mind. "A regular, old-fashioned, sent-straight-from-heaven, let's-all-say-hallelujah blessing!"

Abilene laughed. "I've never said hallelujah in my life. I've never even known anyone who said hallelujah."

"It means Praise the Lord. It doesn't seem to be used as much these days, but it's a good word. Try it."

"Hallelujah," Abilene murmured, her tone wondering.

"Praise the Lord," I echoed. Then I leaned over to pat her hand under a sky full of God's stars. "And don't you ever forget, not ever, that you *are* a blessing."

Contact the author:

Lorena McCourtney
P.O. Box 773
Merlin, OR 97532
email: lorena2@earthlink.net

She's One Spunky Sleuth

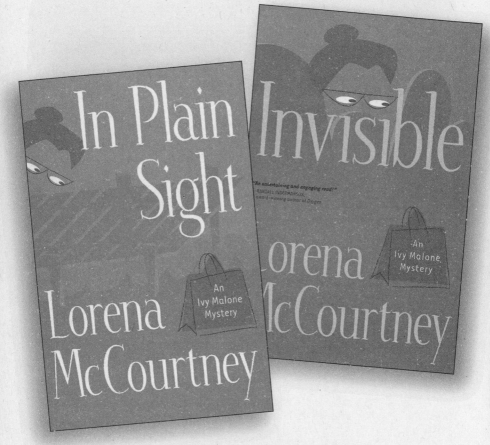

In Plain Sight

An Ivy Malone Mystery

Lorena McCourtney

Invisible

"An entertaining and engaging read!"
RANDALL INGERMANSON,
award-winning author of *Oxygen*

An Ivy Malone Mystery

Lorena McCourtney

Don't miss books 1 & 2 in the Ivy Malone Mystery series!